# ACKNOWLEDGEMENT

Thanks to my sailing and fishing mates who put me right on certain bits, to a friend in the police (he knows it's him) for his help, Ben, again, for help on Hanoi, to Singapore Airlines for peacefully transporting me to the East and, of course to Mary, Hugo, Justin, Laura, Carol and John for their interest, continual encouragement and candid advice; and finally to The Sowetan for a few helpful e-mails and to Barbara Slaughter from the World Socialist Web Site, wsws.org, for the use of one of her articles. Thanks again, bunch.

www.nickwastnage.com

# No Snowdrops in July

To Ian

## Nick Wastnage

*Nick Wastnage*

PublishAmerica
Baltimore

ISBN: 1-4241-1966-9
PUBLISHED BY PUBLISHAMERICA, LLLP
www.publishamerica.com
Baltimore

Printed in the United States of America

Much of this book is set in Vietnam. I was lucky to visit the country, to meet up with my son, Ben, who was spending his gap year there. Ben and his housemate, Dan, provided me with much inspiration. I would like to thank them both, and dedicate the book to them. Good luck.

# 1

Monroe Lidlington watched the dark, muddy coloured stain of the coffee run down the wall in a perfect vertical line until it hit the skirting board, dribble, not so neatly, down its surface and start to form a puddle close to where the remains of a smashed cup lay in pieces on the floor boards. The old wooden chair creaked as he shifted his position from one side to the other before remaining quite still with one leg outstretched, the other slightly bent at the knee while his eyes focused on the visual manifestation of a marriage just shattered. Wearily, he brought his legs together, sat up and joined his hands behind his head, just touching the top of his shirt. He knew, hidden behind the large murky splodge, where the full velocity of the cup had met the grey washed wall, would be a sizeable hole in the plaster; but he wasn't in the least inclined to look. He sighed, dropped one hand onto his left thigh, while with his right he drained the remains of his own, now cold, coffee.

'You've surpassed yourself, my dear. This time you've really screwed up,' he said out loud as he heard the clatter of his wife's feet, backwards and forwards over the floorboards upstairs. He was angry.

He stood up, kicked the bits of broken crockery into a semi-organised pile and took three paces to the sink. Standing with his hands against the edge of the old porcelain basin he gazed out into the dark night and started to cast his mind back to what had brought the evening to such a dramatic climax.

*Not that rows with Juliet were unusual*, he thought, if anything it would out of the ordinary if a weekend passed without one. But he was in no doubt that this was the big one. She'd come in, moody as usual, after a long journey from London down to Cornwall. He'd been too pre-occupied with checking the tides and weather for his fishing trip the next day to realise that she had something on her mind and wanted to offload it. When she entered the kitchen she'd started to talk. Instead of listening, he'd made a cursory wave and then taken a call from Les about the next day's details. As soon as the call was over Juliet flew at him, accusing him of ignoring her, particularly when she had something important she wanted to tell him. He had apologised, poured them both a drink and tried to listen as she had started to describe a horrific mining disaster in South Africa, involving her company. It had all gone over his head. Fuel for the engine, time to depart to catch a good tide, the state of the nets and other minor but important details had filled his mind.

'You're not interested in the slightest, are you?' Juliet had said with a raised voice, an angry look of resignation on her face.

He had said he was sorry, but she ignored him. Instead, troubled, she'd gone off to do some work on her laptop while he decided to prepare a quick supper. It took him about fifteen minutes. He put on a saucepan of penne pasta to boil, chopped up some anchovies and a handful of sun dried tomatoes and assembled an avocado and rocket salad. He poured the drained pasta into an earthenware serving dish, threw over the chopped fish and tomatoes, seasoned it all with some freshly ground black pepper and a drizzle of Cretan olive oil, tossed the lot together and carried the large steaming bowl to the old farmhouse table. He called Juliet, cut some bread and pulled out some cutlery. He repeated his call as he sat down.

'I'm not hungry,' she had shouted down the hall, tersely.

Monroe put his fork down. He tried to ignore his annoyance and picked up Juliet's meal and, together with a slice of bread and some salad, took it to her.

'I don't want anything,' she said furiously, without looking at him. She was sitting by her laptop, looking stressed, with her notebook open next to her and typing intently.

Somehow he held back. He remembered clearly wanting to throw everything all over her head. Instead he had said, 'What do you want me to do…'

'Monroe, don't be so fucking lame,' she'd said with a raised voice. 'I told you, I'm not hungry. Leave me alone. This is important.'

About an hour and a half passed before Juliet reappeared in the kitchen. Monroe had just made a small cafetière of freshly ground Colombian coffee. It was a new one he was trying from the recently opened Starbucks in the town. Juliet's face looked pale and drained. She stood looking at Monroe, pulling a cigarette to her lips from a packet she'd left earlier on the worktop. She looked away for a moment to light it.

'Coffee,' he had asked. She carried on walking towards one of the big carver chairs.

'Thanks,' she said, sitting down.

'So what's your problem,' Monroe asked, trying a little appeasement, as he carried her cup over from the other side of the room to the table. He sat down at the opposite end.

'Nothing.' She didn't look at Monroe. Her face was transfixed.

He slowly poured some sugar from a dispenser onto his spoon and gradually tipped it into his cup. He stirred it around, looked up again at Juliet and said, 'I'm going on a fishing trip with Johnny and Les tomorrow.'

Juliet didn't seem to hear what he had said. She turned away, blowing smoke into the air.

'I said, I'm going…'

'I heard you the first time. I'm not interested, Monroe. Right now I couldn't care if you were flying to the moon.' She still hadn't looked at him.

'Why do you bloody well sit here if...'

'I can, can't I? It's my house as much as yours. You offered me a cup of coffee.'

'But you're ignoring me.'

'Grow up, Monroe.' Juliet flicked the ash from her cigarette into her saucer and turned to face him.

'Look. When I wanted to off load earlier you weren't interested,' she added.

'OK. I said I was sorry. I was just a little pre-occupied.'

Juliet stood up and started pacing around the room, puffing away as she moved. Anger and hate showed in her eyes.

'You're always bloody pre-occupied. You're never around when I want you. Just this once I thought I'd be able to talk to you. But no.' Juliet stopped, let her hand with the half-smoked cigarette drop to her side and looked at her husband of twenty-one years straight in the eyes.

'Monroe, I want out. I've had enough of you. I'm going.' She started to go towards the door.

'Fine,' he replied, trying to stay calm. 'What do want me to tell Greg?'

'Monroe,' she said, almost spitting out the word. 'Tell him the bloody truth. We're fucked.' She grabbed her coffee cup and flung it with all her strength against the wall.

'Like that fucking cup.'

\* \* \*

Monroe straightened up from the sink and turned around. He put his thumbs inside his belt and hoisted his loose fitting jeans up around a trim waist for his fifty-five years. Leaving his thumbs tucked behind his belt and his fingers flat against his jeans he looked at Juliet. She was standing in the doorway to the kitchen with a holdall in one hand. So this is it, he thought.

'Where're you going?' He couldn't think of anything else to say.

'That's my business. From now on I don't have to tell you anything.' Juliet was standing quite still. Her anger seemed to have subsided somewhat. She looked for a moment at the mess on the wall and then back at Monroe. A small wry smile spread over her face.

'That'll give you something to do,' she said looking back at the wall. She turned and started to walk down the hall.

Monroe looked at her. *Tidy figure, practical clothes, hair in a bob—so bloody perfect*, he thought. He felt no emotion.

'No way,' he yelled back at her. 'I'm going to leave it just as it is. A monument to your sweet temper.'

'I hate you, Monroe,' she said, turning back before she reached the front door, her face flushed with anger.

Monroe put both his hands in his pockets, rocked back on the sink and shouted, 'Feelings mutual, dear.'

The door slammed shut and Juliet was gone.

Monroe stood still for a couple of seconds and then walked over to where the bits of broken cup lay scattered on the floor. He bent down and carefully gathered them in his hands, wiping a few sticky drops of cold coffee from the polished boards with his fingers. Standing up, he looked at the broken porcelain for a minute. How ironic, he thought. She'd broken a cup from the set he hated most and she liked. He dumped the pieces on the worktop and made for the cupboard in the corner. Pulling up his jeans again and straightening his long sleeved t-shirt, he opened the door and reached for the bottle of Ardbeg malt whisky.

*How do I feel?* he asked himself, watching the light straw coloured liquid rise in his favourite tumbler. I don't know, he answered. I don't feel upset. Maybe angry, maybe relieved; but not sad or anything like that. Outside the dusk had given way to the black of the night, making the light that was shed from under the kitchen worktop insufficient.

The middle of the room was a pool of darkness. Monroe could just about make out the brass ship's clock on the wall, telling him it was nearly 10 o'clock—time to catch the news. In the half-light he looked around the room, stopping for a second or two to gaze at mundane appliances—the kettle, the unwashed utensils from supper, the half-eaten loaf of bread. He turned back to his glass, took a good slurp and, whisky in hand, wandered off to the sitting room.

Juliet and Monroe's house could be found halfway up one of the narrow, windswept hills that led off the road running round the harbour in Padstow. Two of their bedroom windows had a view of the Camel Estuary with the tiny picturesque village of Rock over on the far side. It was a comfortable four-bedroom terraced house constructed in local grey stone with a slate roof and built around the turn of the last century. Over the years Juliet and Monroe, with some help from their son Greg, had carefully improved and maintained it. Except for a few replacements, the original floorboards were intact and ran uncovered through all the rooms of the house. In the kitchen the boards were sanded and varnished, elsewhere they'd been bleached and limed. Interesting and original rugs, adding warmth and colour, were scattered throughout. At the back of the house, a small, intimate walled garden led off from the kitchen's dark green wooden units and scrubbed pine worktops.

Monroe found the news boring. He turned off the TV and reached for his chunky tumbler from the large Indian style wooden coffee table that sat between the two deep-seated couches. Sitting back, he began to feel what he believed were the first symptoms of shock—uneasiness, slight confusion, indecision. He let his eyes float around the room, roaming the peachy coloured walls until one of the paintings or drawings that Juliet and he had collected from all sorts of places around the world would catch his eye and bring back a memory. Each of the knick-knacks and ornaments described in its own way a trip or a visit together; and the animated and happy photographs of the three of them told a unique and different tale. He didn't know what to make of it all. Should he just take a big black bin bag and chuck the lot away? Except, of course, the pictures of Greg.

*What am I going to do about Greg?* I can't just ring him up in Vietnam, all those miles away, and say, Hey, Greg. Your mum and I have just split. Sorry. How you're doing. But Juliet's not going to do anything about it. Bad news was never her sort of thing. When my mum called to say my dad died she didn't tell me. She just left it. The first time I knew the poor old boy had gone was when my brother called to talk about all the arrangements. So I guess it's down to me to tell Greg. He'll be devastated.

Monroe pulled himself up and went to refill his glass. The taste of the whisky brought memories of the time when Greg and he had last gone to a football match together—just before he'd started his prison sentence. They'd managed to get tickets for Manchester United against Arsenal at Old Trafford. After eighty-seven minutes, when United were 2-1 up, Greg and he had finalised the plans for the evening's celebrations. A swift drive down the M5, dump the car at home and then off to the pricey Indian—they couldn't really afford—followed by a few drinks at the pub next door. Then calamity struck. In extra time Arsenal scored from some sloppy United defending followed by a penalty. 2-1 to United had quickly become 3-2 to Arsenal. Greg and he had got so drunk in Manchester, that they had to stay over in a seedy hotel and return the next day. Monroe laughed when he remembered how cross Juliet had been.

With his glass full again he slowly sauntered back into the sitting room and dropped into the big leather chair that he called his own. Holding his drink in his right hand he let his arms rest on the thick padded sides of the chair and leant back into the deeply absorbing upholstery. He sipped on his drink, closed his eyes and for a brief moment he felt at peace with the world, like he imagined a seagull, as it glided high in the sky on a summer's day. After a minute or two he came back. His eyes caught site of the picture of Greg and all his school mates on the day they all received their A level results. Their were ten of them; six guys and four girls, dressed in an assorted mixtures of jeans, shorts, t-shirts and trainers, and in a line, with their arms around the person or persons adjacent and all grinning from ear to ear. They had achieved.

Greg obtained three A grades against a predicted two Bs and a C. Monroe smiled as he remembered how he'd leapt for joy in the garden when Greg called him on his mobile. At first Greg's phone had kept breaking up. For the first three conversations, all he'd heard was Greg saying 'Dad, I got…can you hear me? Can you hear me? Dad I got…'

That night, Greg, Juliet and Monroe had gone out to celebrate. It was then that Greg broke the news about taking a gap year to travel to South East Asia. Monroe recalled the kick he'd felt in his stomach as he had tried so hard to say something positive. Waves of irrational fear had flooded his mind. Would he ever see his son again? Greg might catch some ghastly disease or be seriously injured and have to go to a poorly equipped hospital. Or he could be caught up in a terrorist atrocity of some sort.

Monroe raised his glass to his lips and took a large sip. He savoured the familiar peaty taste of the whisky, letting his mind move on. He stood up from the leather chair, pulled up his jeans and took a few aimless paces around the room before stopping by the nearest couch. He rubbed his chin and sat down again. Within his reach was the newspaper he'd discarded earlier. He picked it up, flipping inattentively from page to page until he closed it, smoothing out the creases and kinks in an attempt to make it resemble the paper that had been put through their door that morning. He was uneasy. He went over to the cupboard that housed his music system and put on a new Madeleine Peyroux album that Greg had given him before he went away.

There was no reason for Monroe choosing the particular album that was playing. It had been on the top of the pile, making the necessity of him having to make a choice redundant. The music, he hoped, would act as a sort of anaesthetic to the complex and uncontrolled thoughts that were bombarding his mind. But it wasn't long before the soft and warm melodies had achieved the reverse effect and turned his thoughts back to Greg. *I'm really proud of that guy*, he thought. In Greg, Monroe saw a person achieving many of the things he'd wanted to do himself and didn't—either because it hadn't been available or he didn't have the talent.

'How I love him,' he said aloud as a track started that they'd both admired. He fretted again about how he would tell Greg the news about Juliet and himself. He picked up his scotch and drained the glass. Holding it at arms length in front of him, he twisted it around several times before putting it down with a decisive clunk.

'I'll have to go out there and tell him,' he said aloud and stood up. *He'll take it badly*, he told himself as he walked back to the kitchen with his empty glass.

Monroe picked up the half-full whisky bottle and studied it. He managed a contorted smile as he reluctantly came to the view that he'd probably drunk far too much. He routed around the work surface looking for the familiar cork that only Ardbeg and a handful of other good malt distilleries use as their bottle closure. He picked it up and gently fondled it a few times in his hand before pushing it down the bottle's neck. *Enough*, he told himself, and then gave the cork an extra push with his right thumb before kissing the bottle and starting to push and shove it to the back of all the other bottles in the cupboard. It didn't occur to him to make things easier by taking one or two of the others out first. The gin bottle at the front was the first to move. To begin with it looked as though it was gently shaking. Then it started to slowly tip forward. The slow motion film that Monroe was watching started to speed up. Instinctively he put out his hand to catch the bottle and saw two smaller bottles at the front topple as well. His other hand reached up to halt their fall as a large bottle of Pimm's, on the right, fell straight out with a huge clunk onto the work surface and rolled towards him.

'Oh my God,' he yelled out. 'I've scored a strike,' and then burst out laughing as one by one each of the bottles toppled out of the cupboard. With his hands working overtime he managed to either catch or break the fall of most. He found the whole experience hilariously funny. Doubled up with fits of laughter, he tried to stop several bottles rolling off the work surface while simultaneously catching a falling quart bottle of Drambuie. He ended up lying sideways on the floor with the contents of a broken beer bottle dripping over his face. He was overtaken by a fit of hysterics, made even funnier by the thought of how much Juliet would have disapproved.

Later, he felt quite sober. He'd cleared up the bottles and disposed of the broken ones; he had even taken a cloth to the coffee stain on the kitchen wall and done his best to remove it. By midnight he was ready to turn in, but he thought he should check the late weather forecast. Strong onshore winds and a flood tide told him they wouldn't be able to venture that far from the harbour. He knew they'd made a mistake in planning the trip for tomorrow. But it was too late now to cancel, and anyway he wanted to go. It would be the first time he'd been out with the boys, as he called them—Les was 68 and Johnny 78—since he came out of prison. They had asked him to go as part of his rehabilitation process.

Les and Johnny had regularly visited him in prison. They seemed to have the knack of timing their visits to coincide with his feelings of self-pity and the dumps. Johnny used to stroll in with a couple of magazines and a new book. He'd sit down, pass the gifts over, ask Monroe briefly how he was and then, in response to Monroe's moans, he'd tell jokes non-stop until it was time to leave, by which time Monroe had forgotten all about his own problems. Les was different. He'd be more sympathetic and listen a bit. Then he'd change the subject and talk about current affairs and sport.

Before Greg went away he visited Monroe as many times as he was allowed. The two of them, despite the age difference, always had much to talk about. With shared interests in football, music, films and books, Monroe looked forward to Greg's visits. They always left him mentally stimulated. Greg believed his father was innocent, beyond doubt, and tried to persuade him to appeal: but Monroe had explained that as he was only in for two years, it wasn't worth it. An appeal could take at least a year to be heard. If he behaved himself he could be out on parole in less time. As it happened, he was free in ten months. Greg's loyalty and concern touched Monroe. He knew that it wasn't just blind love or unstinting duty that lay behind his son's open-hearted behaviour. It was simply his generous nature.

For the last half-hour, while Monroe had been churning everything around in his mind, he'd been sitting in the kitchen on the same chair that Juliet had sat on earlier, oblivious to the dense and humid atmosphere, the stench of cigarettes still hanging in the air. Eventually the stifled conditions got to him. He leapt up and flung back the kitchen door to let a cool draught of night air enter the room; with it a noticeable drop in temperature and some relief from the stuffiness of the room. His tiredness suggested sleep but he knew he couldn't attempt it. Too big an emotion was fermenting inside him. It was anger, and inducing it was his memory of Juliet's ambivalent attitude to his time in prison. Greg, Johnny and Les visited him as often as they could, whereas Juliet came just once, and right at the beginning of his sentence. He knew it was because she had never accepted his innocence. Greg had told him that. But it didn't make it any better.

His animosity and hatred towards her started burning inside him. Like the fanning of a small flicker on a wood fire it started to grow into a roaring flame. He looked at his watch, kicked closed the kitchen door, locked it and made off down the hall in the direction of his front door. Ten minutes later he'd reached the corner of his road and the harbour perimeter road. Being high season there were still a few holidaymakers having a stroll in the warm night air, enjoying the intoxicating whiff of the sea drifting up from the harbour. Monroe stopped. The noise from moored boats, their ropes and steel halyards slapping against the wooden masts and rigging as they rocked to and fro in the choppy sea, had caused him to look into the harbour. A dark watery mass, sparkling, twinkling in places as the light from the moon glistened on the black surface.

*It's high tide,* Monroe noticed, *soon it will start to ebb.*

# 2

Johnny Edwards leaned back against the varnished wooden trim that edged the small cockpit of the fishing boat. He rested his backside onto the narrow width of decking and looked up at his friend, Les Saunders.

'He'll be here in a minute,' he said without a hint of irritation and in his perfect Oxbridge accent. 'Monroe's not one for being late.'

Johnny stood up and reached out for the salt encrusted handrail that led up to the canopy housing the wheel and pulled himself up. With a proficiency that comes with doing a task many times he slowly started to unpick the lashing that held the wheel in position whenever the boat was moored. For someone of 78, although a little frail, Johnny cut a memorable figure, gained no doubt through years of distinguished diplomatic service. One metre eighty-two tall, and lean, he was wearing a pair of old faded navy jeans, well frayed at the bottom and hanging about eight centimetres above his ankles, a pair of worn navy canvas deck shoes and a pressed light blue polo shirt, its seams in places parting, bearing a faded Ralph Lauren logo on the breast pocket.

'My guess he's gone to the baker's and there's a queue. He told me he'd bring some breakfast,' Les replied, without taking his eyes off the nets and equipment he was busily checking.

Both men carried on with all the routine tasks in preparation for their trip. The small fishing trawler was tied up alongside the quay, close to where local traders had sheds and small shops selling fish and related products to the general public. Monroe had originally owned the boat, using it regularly with his two friends for forays up and down the northern Cornish coast. He sold it to Johnny and Les when he went into prison. The trips were solely recreational, but on each occasion they endeavoured to catch enough fish to provide them and friends, who'd made a request, with a good supper and some for their freezers. They'd catch an array of species. Mainly mackerel, stone bass, small dabs, occasional Torbay soles that had sneaked past Lands End, and a type of grey mullet with a little golden flash on the gill cover unique to the waters off Padstow, made up their haul. The boat was six metres long and one metre ten broad at its widest, with no cabin. The cockpit, running about one and a half metres in from the stern, had slatted bench type seats around the edge and led on to a raised canopy that gave shelter to the wheel. For'ard of the canopy was a large empty space, three and a half metres long, for the nets and storing the catch. Each winter, when the boat came out of the water, the three of them would painstakingly maintain and repair any part of the vessel that needed attention.

'He's late now,' Les said looking at his watch. 'It's nine.'

'He'll be here. You know he will,' Johnny replied. He was standing near the boat's bow and helping Les with the nets. The strong onshore wind had caught his fluffy white hair, making it stand on end. He fed a piece of net to Les who was neatly folding it backwards and forwards so it would run free when they decided to cast it.

'I know,' Les replied, continuing with his tasks as he spoke. 'But he's got the petrol.'

'I see.' Johnny looked up as a sailing boat cast off in front of them. 'Not much we can do about it, then,' he added as he watched the yacht slowly slip out of the narrow dock towards the larger part of the harbour. Under motor power, a woman steered while a younger man and woman stood on the cabin roof and started to uncover the mainsail.

'I supposed you want to warm up the engine,' he said as the wind caught the yacht's sail, causing it to heel over a few degrees to its leeward side.

'Would have saved a bit of time, Johnny,' Les replied, sounding unconcerned.

'But we're not in any hurry.'

He shrugged his shoulders and went to the opposite side of the boat, nearest to the quay, and looked as far as he could see. He was younger by ten years than Johnny and the more streetwise of the two. He'd run his own garden design business for many years before retiring. His worldly savvy complemented Johnny's occasional vague moments. Shorter by 15 centimetres and more rounded than Johnny and dressed in baggy cotton navy chinos, a faded red shirt and a red and white scarf tied around his neck, he looked the least notable of the two of them.

'There he is,' he said suddenly, pointing up the quay. Monroe was swinging a carrier bag in one hand, holding a petrol can in the other, and walking quickly towards the boat. He broke into a run as he approached.

'I'm sorry,' he said, apologetically, as he climbed aboard, dumping the carrier bag and going immediately over to the hatch where Les had opened the doors that housed the engine. Monroe hastily started to empty the contents of the can into the fuel compartment.

'My sincere apologies,' he added, looking up at his two friends as the petrol glugged away into the reservoir.

'I didn't sleep that well.' He threw apart his hands and grimaced, seemingly to emphasis his ill luck.

'I overslept, and then, this morning, bumped into a gigantic queue at the baker's.' He glanced at the flags and ensigns of the nearby boats fluttering in the strong wind and shook his head.

'It's gonna be a bit bumpy. And we've got a flood tide,' he said.

'No problem,' barked Les. 'Won't trouble us. Let's get going.'

'Doesn't worry me,' Monroe replied, as the engine kicked into life and he bent down to adjust the throttle. 'Just take us a bit longer.'

He stood up and positioned himself behind the wheel as the other two started to release the bow and stern lines.

'And all I ask is a windy day with the white clouds flying,' Johnny said with his right arm pointing to the sky as the boat juddered into motion

'Let her go, Les,' Monroe yelled.

Les coiled his line, placed it neatly over a large cleat and climbed back into the cockpit. He reached for cold box.

'Beers?' he yelled, taking out three cans of Becks, flipping the ring pulls and passing them round, the foam oozing through the holes.

'That's good,' Monroe sighed, as he took a swig.

A look of satisfaction started to spread across his face. He leant to one side of the canopy housing and let the sea air fill his nostrils. The noise of seagulls yelling as they swooped across the bow, checking for food, dulled the erratic sound of the boat's engine as it settled into a more continual rhythm. Monroe looked down on his friends and smiled.

'Thanks for asking me.'

'To you, my honourable friend,' Johnny replied holding his can up in the air to make a toast. 'Back where you belong.'

'Yeah, mate. Good to have you with us again.' Les raised his can and touched, in turn, the cans of the other two.

'Thanks, guys,' Monroe replied, nodding his appreciation and touching the peak of his baseball cap. He put his beer on the ledge above the wheel, increased the engine's speed and headed out of the harbour in a north-westerly direction into the Irish Sea.

Their first plan had been to make for a spot about ten miles from land, where they'd been before and the fish were plentiful. But the sea conditions made that impossible. Instead they trawled up and down the coast, within five hundred metres of the harbour entrance. For most of the time they stood together in the cockpit, joking, telling stories and drinking beer; the sun's warmth dulling the chill of the strong breeze.

'What's up, Johnny,' Monroe asked, after about a couple of hours. He rose to join Johnny in the cockpit.

'I don't know,' Johnny answered, looking slightly perplexed. 'I've had to put on some more power. We seem to be drifting a bit, as though something's pulling us out to sea.'

'Do you want me to take over?' Monroe asked, putting his hand on the wheel.

'No thanks. I'm fine,' Johnny replied gripping the wheel, adjusting it to every tug that pulled them in the opposite direction.

'By the way, how's Juliet? I forgot to ask.'

'Fine, thanks,' Monroe replied quickly, shooting Johnny a quick glance as he moved back to where he'd been sitting.

'What about Greg?' Les added as he leant over the side of the boat and examined the net.

'Have you heard from him?'

Monroe turned to look at the net.

'He's fine, also, I think,' he replied and paused. 'I'll be going out to see him soon.'

'What, to Vietnam?' Les looked at Munroe. 'I was there in the early sixties, before the war. Be interested to see what it's like now. Where do you think you'll go? Hanoi or Saigon?'

'Oh, Hanoi,' Monroe replied, still intently looking at the trawl net. 'That's where he is.'

'I…think,' Les said slowly and seriously. Like Monroe, his gaze was fixed on the net.

'We've something big in that net.' He looked at Monroe, who'd met his gaze. 'I guess it's a dolphin or something similar. What do you think?'

Monroe looked back at the net.

'Yep. There's certainly a big one there. I saw something solid turn over a minute ago, but it's gone again.' He looked up at Johnny.

Johnny slowed the engine.

'I guess we should pull it in then,' he said, climbing down from the wheel to take a look.

Monroe wound in the large winch, situated in the centre of the for'ard area, while Les stood over the bow, watching the net carefully as it closed on the boat. Johnny stayed at the helm, keeping the vessel steady and with just enough forward momentum to stop the tide pushing the boat out to sea. The warm sun of the morning had disappeared behind some large grey clouds. Each of them, within minutes of each other, had pulled on a sweatshirt or jumper. It seemed strangely eerie.

Monroe slowed up the winding under Les's direction. The net was close to the boat and required two of them to pull it onboard. Les let it float until it was alongside. Each time a wave washed the net against the boat a slow, deep thudding sound broke the silence. Les and Monroe exchanged sombre glances.

Monroe stared down at the squirming fishes and into the net. He could just about make out the outline of a long black object about one and a half metres in length. It didn't seem to be moving. Les and he pulled hard to bring the laden net onboard. It was so heavy they could hardly lift it. They called Johnny for his help.

'I was looking down from up there,' Johnny said, motioning with his head to the canopy as he joined the other two.

'Looks a bit thin for a dolphin,' he added, meeting the worried, inquisitive looks from his colleagues.

'What is it?' asked Les.

'I don't know,' Johnny replied, frowning.

'A shark?' he added. He didn't sound convinced.

'Look,' yelled Monroe. 'Over there. That dark patch.'

The three sets of eyes all turned to where Monroe was pointing.

'That's blood,' Monroe said, breaking the silence. 'No mistaking it.'

'Come on,' Johnny said, assertively. 'Let's get this over with. I'll call one, two, three, and then all pull together.' Each of them took a firm hold on the net.

'Ready…'

The net rose up slowly out of the water. An awful and shocking site met their eyes. Monroe let out a large moan and vomited several times into the sea. He let go of the net and slipped down to the deck. He rolled over and vomited again.

'Get the long hook,' Les shouted to Johnny. 'I'll try and hold it here.'

While Johnny ran off, Les clung desperately to the net with both his hands, not wanting to drop it back in the water. He glanced once or twice at Monroe, lying in a heap on the deck. Timidly, he looked again over the side. He shuddered. Many fish darted back and forward, entangling themselves amongst the swirling blood and the unmistakable strands of human hair attached to a lifeless head, bobbing below the surface. He, too, was sick.

Les grabbed the woman's leg that was sticking out of the water and Johnny took hold of one of her arms and they pulled. As the body broke the surface and drew level with the boat's side, sea water poured off the remains of the black clothing cladding her bloated body, sluicing away most of the eels and fish that had surfaced with her. With one heave the two men wrenched her over the side to fall prostrate with a great squelch and thud on the cockpit bench; water and blood oozing from all her orifices. At the back of her head was a large, gaping bloody hole. Gingerly Johnny took hold off her hair and started to turn her head over.

'No,' Monroe croaked. 'Please don't. Let her stay like that.'

Johnny and Les turned to where Monroe had been lying. His right elbow was on the ground supporting his head. His fingers covered his mouth. He raised his left hand and waved in a negative gesture.

'No, no,' he mumbled. He looked ghastly.

'That's Juliet, I saw her face in the water.'

# 3

Only the continuous chugging of the small engine broke the silence as the boat headed solely towards the harbour. The smoky fumes from the diesel had masked the usually prevalent salty tang from the sea and the smell of wet rope and wood varnish. Earlier, by his own volition, Johnny had jettisoned the nets and set an immediate course for harbour. He stood a sad and solitary figure at the wheel, expressionless, with his gaze fixed on the boat's direction. Ahead, he could see many other vessels. But at that particular moment Monroe, Les and himself accompanied Juliet's distorted corpse alone through the sparkling sea; a symbolic trail of white foam in their wake. Monroe was sitting alone, as he'd asked, with a rug around his shoulders and starring at the dirty grey tarpaulin that shrouded Juliet's body on the aft bench. Les, who had made tea for all soon after they'd rigged up the temporary cover, sat on the opposite bench to Monroe and starred out at the empty seascape. Often he'd turn and look at his friend, presumably prepared to go to him and offer counsel if it was needed. Johnny, at the helm, would occasionally throw a one liner at Les about the weather, the sea conditions, their speed and other details about their passage, and Les would give a straightforward reply. Neither would talk for long. They were in shock.

Monroe raised his head; his body bent forward and looked slowly from Johnny to Les. He caught neither pair of eyes; both were in their own worlds. And then Les turned around and met his gaze.

'How you're doing, old mate?' Les said immediately.

Johnny looked down at the two of them for a minute and then returned his attention to the sea ahead.

'I can't think what this is all about,' Monroe stuttered with his eyes closed. His trembling hands were clasped in front of his mouth. He was chewing the edges of both his thumbnails. 'That was a bullet wound, wasn't it, Johnny?'

Johnny focused on Monroe.

'I think you're right,' he answered in a sombre tone. 'Do you want another tea?'

Monroe shook his head from side to side. He then started to stroke his forehead with his left hand by opening and closing the tips of his thumb and fingers in the opposite direction. His eyes remained closed.

'Have some of this.' Les got up, sat next to Monroe and pushed his brandy flask close to Monroe's face.

Monroe slowly sat up. With his eyes open he leant against the bench's back support and starred at Les. A slight smile spread across his face.

'Thanks, mate.' He stretched out his arm and took the flask.

Les's left hand reached up to straighten his scarf while he wriggled around to allow his right hand to pull out a pack of cards from his pocket. Without a word he shuffled the cards a few times and then dealt one face down in front of Monroe and one for himself. Monroe, who'd been watching him, looked down at the card on the slatted bench. He raised his head and looked at Les with a questioning expression.

'Pontoon?' he gingerly asked.

'If you're up to it,' Les replied.

'OK,' Monroe answered, picking up and examining his card. He reached into his pocket and pulled out a 50p piece. He placed it down by his card. Les dealt again. Monroe picked it up and studied it with a dead-pan expression.

'I'll stick,' he said, placing his card face down on top of the first one and looking straight into Les's eyes. Les gazed at Monroe for a few seconds and then picked up his two cards.

'Pay 21s,' Les said, turning over two tens.

'Cost yer 50,' Monroe said, turning up a ten and an ace. He had a slight smile on his face.

After about 15 minutes, Johnny, who'd been silent while the other two had been playing pontoon, said, 'I think we should alert the police in Padstow.' He turned to look at Monroe.

Monroe closed up the three cards in his hand and held them together while he looked back at Johnny. *Of course*, he thought.

'Yeh, go ahead, Johnny,' he said and placed his cards down on the bench and stood up. He looked sideways to the stern of the boat to where Juliet lay dead, hidden under a makeshift shroud. For a moment, he gazed transfixed. *Is this all some cruel nightmare?* he asked himself. Tentatively he took a couple of paces forward and stood still for a little while, looking down at the tarpaulin. Les and Johnny watched him, exchanging glances several times. It must have seen like ages to them before he reached down and took hold of a corner of the tatty cover. He gasped as he looked down on his wife's disordered body. An engulfing wave of disbelief washed over him.

*It can't be*, he said to himself.

'No, no,' he yelled out, and felt his head start to gently shake. Tears welled up and he wiped them away against his bare arm; the dried salt, from when he'd been pulling in the net earlier, stung his eyes.

*This was not how it should have ended.*

'She shouldn't have been murdered,' he said aloud, slowly. 'That's unjust.' And then he shouted, 'The bastard.'

Watched by his two friends he stood for a little longer, looking down, and then simply released the end of the cover to let it flap back over Juliet's face. He sauntered over to the bow of the boat and stared out to sea.

* * *

Johnny pushed the brass handle of the throttle forward to slow the engine as the fishing boat passed alongside the Padstow light and turned into the harbour entrance. For the last part of their return passage Monroe had sat quietly watching as the coastline became closer and closer. Les and Johnny had gone about the business of tidying up and making the boat ready for its mooring, leaving Monroe content to sit alone with his thoughts. The closer they drew to the quay the more Monroe became tense and worried. What he had previously thought was an illusion, a trick on his eyes, was becoming a reality. The side of the quay was lined with people looking in their direction. A man and a woman with large professional cameras were running along the quay's edge to keep level with the boat while snapping away.

'My God,' Monroe said and turned away. He looked at Johnny and Les. They either hadn't seen the gaping crowds or were ignoring them.

'Look,' Monroe said, pointing at the quay.

Les stopped scrubbing the small deck and looked up. His eyes swept back and forwards and then panned to the left.

'It's because of that,' he said, pointing further up, to where they were heading.

A large area of the car park, stretching down to where they usually alighted from the boat, had been cordoned off from the public. Two large white tents had been erected and an ambulance and a couple of police cars were parked adjacent. Police manned the cordon, stopping any onlookers who might try to dodge under the ropes. All the berths, normally full with only one or two vacant spots, were empty. A policeman signalled with his hand to Johnny, indicating where they were expected to tie up. Johnny put the engine in neutral and let the boat's momentum gradually take it towards where, what seemed like, a reception committee was waiting. Monroe dreaded what was to come. He stood and watched the final moments as Johnny skilfully brought them alongside until Les was able to jump off and make the boat secure. Immediately a smart young woman, slim with brunette hair tied in a ponytail, came aboard accompanied by a younger man. She took one look at Monroe and came straight up to him.

'Mr Lidlington, I'm so sorry. I'm Detective Inspector Symes.' She held her hand out to shake Monroe's.

'This is my colleague, Detective Sergeant Wilson.'

'Hi.' Monroe shook the two detectives' hands. He looked beyond their heads to the quay and saw a group of people, some dressed in white overhauls, waiting to come onboard. He felt weak and sick. He turned back to Inspector Symes. She seemed impatient for something.

'What is it you want, detective?' he said, weakly.

Inspector Symes looked serious. She kept her eyes firmly on Monroe.

'Is there somewhere we can go, Mr Lidlington?' she asked.

'You can go where you like, Inspector,' he said, trembling. 'That's my wife lying dead over there,' he looked in the direction of Juliet's body.

'And I want to go home. Excuse me.' Monroe started to walk around the policewoman and her assistant.

'I'm sorry, Mr Lidlington. I know it's difficult for you but there are some formalities we have to go through.' Inspector Symes had moved slightly to her left to block Monroe's departure. Monroe stopped. In the corner of his eye he caught site of Johnny's long legs announcing his presence as he stepped into the cockpit to join them.

'My name's Edwards. I'm a friend of Mr Lidlington. Can I be of some assistance,' he said, looking down at Inspector Symes.

'I'll need to talk to you as well, Mr Edwards. But right now I'm trying to get a statement from Mr Lidlington. If you would like…'

'I don't know your name, madam. But you are creating a bit of a fuss here.' Johnny looked up at the quay to the assembled team waiting patiently and watching the events unfold.

'Are you insensitive?' he added sharply. 'Can't you see that Mr Lidlington is in deep shock?'

Inspector Symes didn't bat an eyelid. She turned back to Monroe.

'If you will formally identify the corpse.' She looked across to where Juliet's body was lying, still covered in the same tarpaulin. 'As that of your wife, Mr Lidlington. Then you may go.'

'I told you it's my wife,' Monroe snapped quickly in a raised voice. 'I'm going right now. Thanks Johnny.' He put his right foot on the bench and heaved himself up onto the deck. He turned his head to have a last look at where Juliet was lying. Les had joined the two police and Johnny in the cockpit.

'Let me come with you, Monroe,' Les said, jumping up.

'No.' Inspector Symes put up her hand. 'I need to talk to you.'

'I'm OK, Les. But thanks anyway. I'll be in touch.' Monroe put up one hand and made a quick wave and then turned and started to walk away from the boat. Sergeant Wilson looked at Inspector Symes and started to follow Monroe.

'Let him go. We'll talk to him later.' Inspector Symes looked at the waiting pathologists, policemen and administration staff.

'Get going,' she yelled before turning back to Johnny and Les.

'I need to talk to both of you—now.'

* * *

Monroe put the key in his front door and turned it. He pushed it open, went inside and took a few steps down the hall to the kitchen. *Everything's as I left it,* he thought, as he looked around. His half-drunk cup of coffee, an empty orange juice glass, a plate with the crumbs from a piece of toast. It was all exactly as it had been that morning. But why should it be any different? he asked himself as he poured a glass of water and drunk it down in one. Inside his head he felt detached and light headed, a swirling tipsy feeling he normally associated with an excess of alcohol. He stumbled over to the work surface and put out his hands to support himself. A throbbing pain, increasing in its intensity, started in his head, his shoulders felt as though a lead weight was resting on them and his legs were turning to jelly. Swaying from wall to wall, reaching out to them for support and occasionally sliding to the floor, he managed to stumble to his sitting room and sprawl full length on one of the couches.

It was dark when he woke. The pain in his head had subsided but he felt drained and desperately thirsty. He rolled off the couch onto the floor and lay there for a moment before trying to haul himself up. Propped up and with his legs stretched out, resting on a rug, he found the unbelievable events of the last twenty-four hours were fighting for some recognition in the hazy reaches of his mind.

Almost without warning he found he was crying. The tears poured in torrents down his cheeks. He let his head drop forward and sobbed for several minutes.

'Oh Greg, how am I going to tell you?'

Drops from his tears had formed into a small pool on the wooden floor between his legs. He wiped them with his hands and then tried to dry his fingers on his jeans.

'How the hell am I going to tell him?' he said, standing up to fetch a drink. He shivered and decided to find another sweatshirt to pull over the top of the dirty, tear-stained one he'd put on earlier.

The piercing ring of the doorbell came at 6 p.m. Monroe had been trying to book a flight to Hanoi to meet up with Greg. *I don't want to see anyone*, he said to himself as he ignored the bell and dialled again the number of the travel company he'd been calling before the interruption. While he waited for an answer he fiddled with his half-drunk mug of cold coffee and tried to scoop a handful of nuts from the packet that lay torn open on his worktop. The ring came again, more insistent than before.

'Oh shit,' he yelled as he plonked the phone back in its cradle and started to walk down his hall.

'Can we come in?' Inspector Symes said, making it obvious that she wasn't going away in a hurry. She was wearing the same knee length skirt and short-sleeve blouse that she had been wearing earlier. Monroe didn't answer. He'd just nodded and turned to lead them to the living room.

'Sit where you like,' he said without facing the two detectives as he'd made for the leather chair. He watched them both take an opposite couch and then look at each other. Inspector Symes turned towards Monroe. She had a taut, angular face and large piercing eyes that seemed to Monroe to bore right into him. He looked away for a second to see what Detective Wilson was doing. Monroe guessed he was at least ten years younger that Symes, probably in his early thirties. He wore a well-cut pair of greyish trousers, a short-sleeved light blue denim shirt and a pair of loafers. His black hair was cropped short and he had a rounded face.

'Get on with it,' Monroe snapped, looking back at Inspector Symes.

'Mr Lidlington,' Inspector Symes said with the same expressionless look that Monroe remembered from their earlier encounter. 'You're wife died from a single gunshot wound to her head. Forensics tell us that she was dumped in the sea after she had been killed.'

Monroe drew in a large breath of air and closed his eyes. He put his hand over his mouth, dropped his head and sat still for a few moments. When, eventually, he sat up he found two sets of eyes starring at him.

Sergeant Wilson straightened up in his seat so he was sitting upright.

'Mr Lidlington,' he said, sounding like an announcement and with a broad Cornish accent. 'Can I ask you when you last saw your wife?'

Monroe looked across to Inspector Symes. He met a pair of cold eyes focused intently on him.

'When, Mr Lidlington?' she asked.

Monroe rested his chin on his left hand, returning Inspector Symes's stare. 'Last night.'

'What time last night?' retorted Wilson, scribbling away with a freshly sharpened pencil that he'd just taken from the breast pocket of his shirt after the lead of his last one had broken on him.

'I don't know, I can't remember exactly.' Monroe switched his gaze back and forth between the two detectives. He felt he was being interrogated.

'Is this some sort of inquisition?'

Inspector Symes rose up and straightened her skirt. She took a couple of paces around the room, looking at the photographs. She picked up one of Greg.

'Is this your son?'

Monroe looked at her as she turned to face him. She was standing about two metres away. He guessed, judging by her trim figure, that she was a member of a gym and exercised often. His eyes moved up to her face. *Hard but attractive*, he thought.

'Yep,' he answered, curtly.

'When and how are you planning to tell him about his mother?' she asked, looking at the framed photograph she still held in her hand.

Monroe could feel himself becoming annoyed. He didn't care much for this woman's attitude and she was asking questions he considered unnecessary.

'That's my business,' he snapped back at her.

'I'm sorry,' Symes said, sounding apologetic. 'I just thought it would difficult for you.'

'It will. But that's my problem.' Monroe shifted in his seat and watched Symes replace the photograph and sit down.

'Look,' he said angrily. 'Can't this wait? My wife died today. Surely I'm entitled to some time on my own?' He stood up, pulled up his jeans and started walking towards the door.

'Now if you don't mind.'

Neither of the two detectives moved. Symes looked across to Wilson.

'Your enquiry Sergeant Wilson. I just came along for the ride.'

Monroe stood looking at her. *You bloody lying, cynical bitch*, he said to himself.

Sergeant Wilson coughed and brushed the tops of his trousers as though he needed to remove crumbs or something similar.

'Emm, just a couple more questions please.' He looked down at his notebook. 'You said the last time you saw your wife was last night, Mr Lidlington.' Sergeant Wilson, red in the face, looked up to Monroe, still standing.

'Did you not see her this morning?'

'No, she wasn't here. She didn't sleep here.'

'Where was she? Mr Lidlington,' the policeman retorted quickly.

Monroe saw the two sets of eyes starring at him, waiting for his answer.

'I don't know. She walked out at about nine, I think.'

'You didn't ask where she was going?'

'No, we had a row and she stormed out.'

Nobody spoke for a bit. Symes and Wilson looked at each other and nodded their heads. Monroe watched them.

Inspector Symes rose again and walked over to the fireplace. She leaned against the large wooden beam that doubled as a mantelpiece and turned to look at Monroe standing next to her.

'One more question please, Mr Lidlington.'

Monroe was confused. His earlier anger had subsided and seemed to be replaced by a slight feeling of nervousness and insecurity. *Why is she being so persistent and insensitive?*

'Go on,' he timidly replied.

'Do you know of anyone who would have wanted to kill your wife?'

*Kill her. Who'd want to kill her?* Monroe asked himself. He became rather disorientated. The dizziness he'd felt earlier had returned, this time accompanied by nausea. He reached up to the mantelpiece for support and with one hand on it, turned to face Symes.

'We're waiting, Mr Lidlington.'

'For what?' Monroe asked, thinking that if he looked anything like he felt he must have appeared quite ghostly.

'Who might have wanted your wife dead?' Symes asked without flinching.

'I've no idea. Now, please will you both leave. I…'

'Where were you at 1.30 this morning? Mr Lidlington?'

Monroe looked in front of him to where he thought he'd heard some words. *The room seems cloudy, full of a dense fog*, he thought. In the haze, he saw Juliet and Greg standing side by side.

'Where were you at 1.30 this morning? Mr Lidlington?'

'I don't know. In bed I suppose, asleep. Ask my wife.'

# 4

Bishopsgate, London, EC2 is contiguous with the monetary seriousness of Threadneedle Street and its Old Lady and the commercial bustle of Shoreditch. It also housed the impressive headquarters of The Miax Corporation UK. Or so the regularly polished brass plaque that sat adjacent to the doorway stated. The building rose ten floors, twinkled and sparkled on a sunny day, and had a huge glass revolving door as its entrance. Large sheets of smoked glass, joined to each other by the division of each floor, clad the outside. Inside, marble covered the floors and walls of the vast, open ground floor reception area where a large, round central desk dominated the otherwise empty space. The few staff who managed the welcome counter were dressed in light grey, well tailored suits, white shirts and silk grey ties for the men and silk blouses and silk scarves for the women. Each wore a discreet silver label badge, the worldwide symbol of The Miax Corporation. Once visitors had been courteously received they were directed to the spectacular bank of glass lifts, against the back wall, that would take them to their respective floors. Each floor was called first by the colour of one the three woods used for furnishing the entire building—beech, cherry or maple—and then a number. Hence BEECH 1 (for ground), BEECH 2, and BEECH 3; CHERRY 4, 5, and 6; MAPLE 7, 8 and 9. Joe Walters, chief executive of Miax UK and the creator of this—for many—irritating scheme, made an exception on his floor. He called it simply ASH.

The Miax Corporation operated in all parts of the world, but predominantly third world countries. Construction was its business. It built shopping centres, schools, car parks, official buildings and the like; it owned gold and diamond mines; excavated and formed roads, dams and all types of man made open space projects; and more recently built and managed hotels. Miax's name would be on the bidding list for all major projects and more often than not be it would be awarded the contract.

Created by Frederick de Boer in South Africa at the beginning of the twentieth century, the business stood alone from the many other ventures of the time by setting standards of efficiency, excellence, staff welfare and involvement that, at the time, were unheard of. Surviving both the First and Second World Wars, Miax became a world leader, respected and well known as an international corporation until Frederick's death in 1982 at the age of 95.

Van de Boer, Frederick's son by his second marriage, who took over the business from his father, although well versed in the company's procedures, lacked the drive and dynamism to continue to grow the business in the face of growing competition. While Van was able to keep the business safe financially, hungry competitors saw the opportunity to gradually chip away at Miax's world dominance. In 1992 Van, suffering from the early stages of cancer and worried about Miax's declining revenue, was so impressed by a young twenty-eight-year old man called Joe Walters, who had chosen to write a thesis on Miax for his MBA, that he hired him to set up a London office and to source new customers.

Joe, at the age of 39, had reason to be proud of his achievements. In ten years he'd grown Miax UK to be the most important constituent of the Miax Corporation. All projects worldwide were managed through London, leaving the Johannesburg office to deal only with global finance and future development. Van, distracted by his declining health, had been more than happy to let Joe continually extend his supposed geographical boundaries. By the time of Van's premature death the London office had tentacles in every continent of the world.

Jan de Boer, 30 and Van's second son and more used to a life travelling the world in search of mind enhancing experiences than running a multi-national corporation, unexpectedly took over the reins from his father after his elder brother, the long-prepared heir, had tragically been paralysed by a polo accident. So when Joe, shortly after Jan's succession, suggested that Miax UK became the centre of all global operations, Jan readily agreed, leaving him in Johannesburg to assume the nominal title of Chairman and Chief Executive.

\* \* \*

Juliet Lidlington joined as head of public relations at Miax two years before her death. Joe had wanted a competent and high-flying executive to spin the company's image to be seen as a transparent and caring organisation in today's world of corporate misdemeanours. 'My grandfather, Frederick de Boer set up a straight, paternal company and that's how I want the world to see us,' Joe had said to Juliet at the interview. She'd been attracted by the proposition for two reasons. Having just experienced a bruising departure from the government's spin machine, an opportunity to rehabilitate herself in the real world of commerce was welcome. Secondly, Joe had made it quite clear to her that she could do most of her work from her home in Padstow, only travelling to London to meet with him once a week. Occasionally, he'd said, a second day might be required. For a while all went well. She found the job everything she had wanted and expected, and Joe would frequently express his satisfaction for her work. But when Monroe's business was forced into liquidation, he investigated by the fraud squad, she'd found it inconceivable that her husband hadn't spoken to her about his problems. Later he was charged with continuing to trade the company when he knew it was insolvent. From then onwards a rift between them developed, made worse by his time spent in prison. The one or two days a week in London soon stretched to three or four and sometimes a whole week. There wasn't another man, just her work.

\* \* \*

At 8 a.m. a silver BMW 7 series turned left just after the entrance to Miax UK and stopped. Out of the door sprung Joe Walters dressed in a neat, dark grey suit, a blue shirt and wearing a navy silk tie with small grey oval shapes embossed on it. His shoes were black and highly polished. He carried a soft leather case.

'Thanks, Jim. Pick me up at seven, please.' Joe smiled quickly at his driver and pushed the door closed. As the revolving glass entrance door slowly rotated he looked up and down, backwards and forwards at the large panes of glass until the movement had ceased and he was able to exit into the lobby.

'Good morning, John,' he said to the receptionist he was approaching. The man looked up. 'Could you please call the window cleaners and tell them that they need to come back and clean the glass in the revolving door again. It's dirty.'

'Yes, Mr Walters. I'll call them immediately.' John picked up the phone and started to dial.

'Thanks.' Joe returned the morning's greetings from the other receptionists, turned and strode off to the nearest lift. He had the lift to himself. As it rose to the tenth floor he caught sight of himself in the mirrored walls. He wasn't good looking, but not ugly either, just quite ordinary with a trim and well exercised figure, a head of hair and no need for glasses.

Down in the lobby as the lift ascended John held the receiver in one hand, waiting for an answer from the window cleaning company, and looked around at his fellow receptionists. He shook his head and shrugged with resignation.

'That's Mr Walter's for you,' said a colleague, busy with a visitor's pass.

Every article within Miax UK offices had been agreed by Joe. He meticulously spent hours of his free time authorising the purchase and placement of all items, whether they were furniture, IT equipment or things aesthetic, like pictures. Nothing would be allowed to go on the walls—posters, notices, directional signs—without his approval. He had planned the building with the architects down to the minuteness of detail. His mark was on it and that was how it would stay. Without fail, every morning he would find some sort of fault with what, to all other employees, was an immaculate, clean building.

Joe walked through the door to his outer office at 8.35 and stopped. A young girl, her long black hair tied back in a pony-tail to show her strong Italian features, looked up from her paper and greeted him while he fumbled around inside his case, holding it open on his left knee. He returned her greeting and pulled out a narrow cloth ribbon with a small brass key attached to it. He took a couple of paces to the solid ash door that divided his office from the outer one. Once inside he closed the door behind him and after placing his case on his desk made for the far corner where all that was needed for making a cafetière of fresh coffee had been prepared. As he drunk his coffee he stood still for a moment looking at the view right up and down Bishopsgate.

His office, like the rest of the floor, had been furnished in ash wood. Within a few feet of the main door sat a large wrap around desk, to which the far end had been appropriated to his laptop and a small TV screen. On the opposite end a black and a green telephone had been arranged side by side. The middle of the desk was empty—void of papers, files or any desk accessories. Behind it stood a high-backed, padded grey leather chair, eerily turned in the direction of where he'd walked away from it the previous evening. The walls were covered in a fine grey felt, divided by matt metal uprights, the floor laid with limed ash. Against most of the walls stood custom made low-level wooden cabinets, neatly but sparsely filled with books, files, DVDs, documents and the odd ornament. A solid ash oval table, three metres in diameter and no more than a metre wide, matching wooden chairs and grey upholstered seats occupied the area to one side of the window. The other end was taken up by four armchairs, arranged in groups of two, either side of a wooden low-level table, under which a light coloured rug lay. There were no pictures on the walls or framed photos on any surface.

Joe refilled his cup and carried it to his desk. He undid two buttons of his jacket and sat down, reaching out for his coffee. He opened the flap of his case and pulled out a small leather pouch and a notebook, placing them neatly side by side on his desk. Taking a sip from the coffee, he swung his chair round to his laptop. Within seconds he was looking at his latest e-mails. He turned to take a sharpened pencil from the pouch, flipped open the notebook and swung back to face the screen. Referring to a list in his notebook, he deleted several e-mails, each time ticking the entry in his notes. When he'd finished he stood up, fastened the two buttons of his jacket and walked with his cup towards where the cafetière was standing. His phone rang.

'Not yet, I'll call you,' he answered and drained his cup.

With his notebook open on a second page and using another sharp pencil from his pouch he started to wade through the contents of three hanging files he'd removed from his filing cabinet. He ran his eyes over each document in every file, removing several and placing them in a pile on his desk. Finally, he struck out again entries in his notebook and then tore out the two pages he'd been referring to and put them with the documents he'd withdrawn from the files. He picked up the pile of papers, took them to his shredding machine and destroyed them.

Thirty seconds after he'd rung to say he was ready his PA, Anna, knocked on the door. She was wearing a neat dark green blouse with occasional black flecks, a small black and yellow silk scarf, a knee length tailored grey skirt and carrying in both her hands all the paraphernalia for planning and managing Joe's day.

'Good morning,' she said with a smile as she placed her pile of stuff on Joe's desk, leant across to receive his gentle kiss on the cheek and went to pour herself a coffee.

Anna, of a similar age to Joe, had been with him ever since he set up the UK office. He'd interviewed almost 100 people for the job and was beginning to doubt if he'd ever find what he wanted—a first class, highly efficient and reliable PA who could be left to plan and organise his busy schedule with little or no recourse to him. She hadn't applied to his advert, but was recommended by a friend of Van de Boer who knew that her previous company was going to make half its workforce redundant. A tidy, trim figure and an appropriately stylish, but understated, way of dressing compensated for her ordinary looks.

Ten minutes after Joe and Anna had been ensconced, his black phone rang. (The green one was a direct and secure line to Jan de Boer.) Joe and Anna looked at each other with disapproving looks. Anna reached across and simply turned the phone off. As she returned her attention to the pile of papers in front of her, an insistent knock sounded on the door. Apologising to Joe for such a breakdown in the laid down procedure, she got up and strode purposefully to the door. With a stern look, she opened it.

'Oh, Anna,' sobbed the young girl who had greeted Joe earlier, her hand covering her tear stained face. She lurched forward and flung both her arms around Anna's neck and wept. Anna stepped back in an attempt to bring her into Joe's office. The young girl looked up, took a few short sniffs and followed Anna.

'She was murdered,' she snivelled and then broke into more deep gasps as Anna, her arm around the girl's shoulder, guided her towards the four easy chairs.

Joe rose from his desk, did up the two buttons of his jacket, pushed the door to his office shut and walked over to where Anna was on her knees trying to comfort the deeply traumatised young woman. He appeared shocked. Anna glanced quickly up at him.

'Could you arrange for some tea,' she said, clearly disturbed by the girl's state of mind. Anna gently clasped each of her hands on the sides of the girl's head and raised it so their faces met.

'Sarah, I know it's difficult, but please try and tell us what you're talking about.'

'I can't, I can't,' the girl rasped as she buried her head in her hands.

Joe opened the door to the waiter and took the tray in his hands. 'Thanks,' he said and turned to take the tea to his desk.

'Milk, Sarah?' he yelled across the room.

The girl raised her head, looked at Joe and nodded, her face forlorn.

'I'm sorry, Mr Walters. It's all so awful. Why did they do it?' she sobbed.

'Do what, Sarah?' Joe asked as he walked towards the two women, carrying two cups of tea. He bent over and placed the two cups, black for Anna, on the table. He looked up to meet the young girl's gaze. She looked stunned.

'You don't know?' she said putting her hand up to cover her mouth.

'Oh, no. I can't. I can't go through all that again.' She started to whimper.

Anna reached forward and grabbed her hand.

'Please try, Sarah. We haven't a clue what's going on.'

Sarah turned her head and looked at Anna. The same stunned look still spread across her face. She took a deep breath and started to talk in a slow, quiet manner. Joe watched and listened for a few seconds, stood up and turned to walk to his desk. Seated, he busied himself by glancing through the mail and documents Anna had brought in earlier. A flicker of movement caught his eye. He looked up and saw Anna, holding a large wad of tissues, helping Sarah to her feet. With her arm around one of Sarah's shoulders, Anna walked her passed Joe's desk.

'I'm sorry, Mr Walters,' Sarah said, turning her head to face Joe as Anna escorted her through the door.

A few minutes later Anna re-appeared in Joe's office. All colour had drained from her face. She was visibly shaken and looked grave. She sat down opposite Joe.

He placed his hands on his thighs, leant forward and with a troubled look asked, 'Who is it then?'

'Juliet.' Anna immediately put her left hand up to her right eye to stifle a tear.

'What, murdered?' Joe looked aghast. He leant forward across his desk to peer into Anna's face.

'I'm afraid so, Joe,' Anna replied in a quiet and composed voice.

'I don't believe it. Are you sure about this?' Joe seemed indignant.

'Apparently her body was pulled out of the sea yesterday.'

'Drowned?' Joe had risen from his chair and was pacing around the room.

'No.' Anna turned to follow Joe's movements. She shook her head. 'She'd been shot in the head the previous night and dumped in the sea.'

Joe stopped in his tracks. He seemed to reel with shock and then dropped himself down in one of the chairs they had been sitting in earlier. He loosened his tie and flung his jacket over the opposite chair.

'That's awful,' he said, quietly.

'It gets worse, Joe.' Anna had joined him, sitting opposite.

Joe looked at her, seemingly alarmed.

'What do you mean?'

'Her husband, Monroe pulled her body out of the water when he was on a fishing trip with his pals yesterday.'

'That's terrible. How did we find out?'

'Monroe called in, himself, this morning.'

'He what?' Joe looked astonished.

'Let me finish, Joe. It's difficult enough. Apparently he's flying to Vietnam today to tell Greg. Juliet was so proud of Greg and always telling us about how well…' Anna stopped. Her voice was beginning to tremble and she was starting to loose her self-control.

'I'm sorry, Joe. It's all so horrible. That poor boy. All those miles away.' She sniffed and threw her head back.

'Joe…' she gasped and fled the room.

Joe sat upright in his chair. He placed both his elbows on his desk, his hands up to his mouth and formed an arch, his two index fingers touching his lips, his thumbs supporting his chin. He sat in the same position for a while, starring out of the window.

'Joe,' Anna said as she re-entered the room, having adjusted her make-up to hide any signs of her earlier discomposure. 'I think we should make an announcement.'

Joe, wearing his jacket and with his buttons done up, picked up a piece of crisp white paper, lying adjacent to his pen, and held it in his hand while Anna seated herself.

'Something along these lines?' he said as he pushed the paper towards her.

'I'm also going to write to Monroe.' He looked across to Anna. 'She was popular, wasn't she?'

'Yes, she was,' Anna replied, nodding her head as she read Joe's announcement. She looked up at Joe.

'Do you mean this about giving everyone the day off, today?'

'Yes. And make it known that anyone who wants to go to the funeral may do so.' Joe looked squarely at Anna. 'You're to have the day off as well. We'll close the office.'

Apart from Joe, Anna was the last to leave. He watched from his window until he saw her tiny figure appear at the front of the building in Bishopsgate and walk off to the nearest tube station. He went back to his desk and opened up his laptop.

> To Jan de Boer
> From Joe Walters
> Subject: Tragic news
> Dear Jan
>
> Today I heard the tragic news that Juliet Lidlington had died. It appeared that she had been murdered, apparently shot in the head and then dumped in the sea. Her poor husband, Monroe, found her body when on a fishing trip.

Everyone here, as I'm sure you can imagine, is devastated. I've taken the liberty of closing the office for the day. The funeral will be in about a week. I'll let you know all the details.

I'm writing to Monroe, who—poor chap—has to go to Vietnam to tell his son the terrible news.

Juliet will be sadly missed as a person and friend to many in the office, and it goes without saying that the loss of her skills in the business is incalculable.

Jan, I'm taking a couple of days off myself to get over the shock.

Regards<br>
Joe.

Jan de Boer wiped the perspiration from his forehead with a small grey sport's towel, the Miax emblem embossed in the bottom right corner. He removed his key from the punishing piece of gym equipment he'd been using and walked off to the men's locker room. Once showered and dressed he went to the brassiere and ordered orange juice, scrambled eggs, toast and marmalade for two and called up the office.

'Anything I need to come in for?' he asked his secretary as he flicked through the Johannesburg Globe. He listened for a while to her tearful response.

'How awful,' he said as he turned over the page to check the price on one of his investments.

'Please do a notice and emm…send a message to Joe asking for Juliet's husband's address. I'll write to him.' He took a sip from the orange juice that had just arrived with his breakfast.

'Anything else?' He waited.

'Good, well I think I'll take the day off as well. It's shaken me up. Do the same if you want to, my dear. Bye for now.' He put the phone down and looked up to meet the eyes of a beautiful young woman.

'Hi, honey. I've ordered you breakfast,' he said as he rose to greet her with a kiss.

# 5

Greg wiped the sweat from his hands onto a pair of faded shorts that had seen better days and sat back on his saddle, his left leg on the kerb, his right still touching the pedal, and pulled out a crumpled plastic water bottle from his back pocket, amazed that it hadn't fallen out during his short journey. He took a grateful swig of what remained of the lukewarm water and watched as the endless stream of bikes, scooters, motor bikes and motorised cycles and the odd car pour across the intersection of Hao Lo and Pho Hai.

Humanity, urgent and with clear intentions, teamed before his eyes. People on wheeled transport, men and woman walking—some dressed traditionally, many wearing western style clothing—were going about their business. Nobody ambled or idled. Whatever or wherever they were going was important and there was no time to waste. Greg had come to realise in the last six months that life and all its necessities was a serious matter to Asian culture, and what he witnessed before him was a testament to that.

An earth-shattering thunderclap broke his thoughts. Quickly, he pulled his bike off the road to join huddles of people dashing for shelter under the few awnings. Space was short and he knew that even if he found some refuge from what was to come he'd soon be pushed and elbowed out of it. That was Vietnam. Large drops of rain, heavy and full, fell rapidly on his bare hands, sticking out from under the awning to support his bike. A second later, a louder crash of thunder heralded spectacular flashes of lightning, after which torrents of water poured down from the heavens. He felt a determined push in his back and found himself standing in the road, flooded by warm mud coloured water, and soaked to the skin. He moved back up the street to where he saw a narrow alley and was able to manoeuvre himself and his bike under the cover of the large overhanging tiles of a house. Like the rest of the population of Hanoi he waited until the worst of the torrential downpour was over.

As he contemplated the length of time he'd have to remain in his temporary retreat he stretched and arched his back to provide some relief from the constant ache he always experienced when he cycled. Why, he didn't know. He was fit and lean and exercised more often and in many different ways than most people of his age. Every day he had to use his bike, and each time he experienced the same pains at the base of his spine. At first it had annoyed him, now he just tried to forget it, putting it down to the chronic state and age of the bicycle he'd been issued with by the department of education. Not much worried Greg. He tended to let life take its course, ignoring as much as possible the inconveniences and setbacks that many others would fret about. For someone who stood one metre eighty tall with tousled brown hair, blue eyes and a firm and interesting face, Greg showed no signs of vanity or conceit.

A woman dressed in black trousers, a white long sleeve tunic, tucked at the waist, and a large conical coolie hat, nudged passed him, telling him life was moving again. Stretched across her shoulders was a long bendy strip of wood, at one end of which wicker panniers of rich green vegetables counter balanced the wrapped parcels of goods at the other end, the wood dipping and flexing with the similar weights as the woman purposely went about her business. Greg felt the end of her carrying equipment touch his arm. He turned to apologise for blocking her path. She snarled at him. He could see pain in her eyes.

*How raw this city is,* he thought, as he prepared to cycle off toward Ho Hoan Kiem Lake before the next cloudburst. He cycled quickly to dry his clothes, darting all over the road to miss the streams of water gushing down from awnings and the splashes from large puddles. Every now and then a motorbike or cycle would come perilously close in an attempt to drench him with the spray from their wheels. But he was wise to it. He'd been in the city for nearly eight months.

Towards the bottom of Hao Lo he noticed a ripple of movement in the green leaves of the overhanging trees, so prevalent in this ancient and modern city. It indicated a refreshing breeze and some relief from the airless conditions. Greg slowed his pace and let his eyes wander over the dull, yellow old colonial French buildings, their ochre-tinted walls cushioning the heavy dark green shutters that hung by the large sash windows. On some, the stains of pollution and rain had run into the flaky and crumbling paint to make a mosaic of deeply atmospheric colour and texture.

*I'll miss all this,* he said to himself. *Despite its madness.* He dismounted and propped his bike up against one of the large trees with sprawling branches, like an octopus's tentacles, that surround the lake. The familiar stench of ammonia hit his nostrils. *I won't miss that,* he thought, quickly moving his bike away to another tree with a large white band painted around its trunk. Habitually, towards the end of an evening, old Vietnamese men would wander amongst the cool canopy of the many trees and choose one to urinate against, a custom the authorities were trying to discourage, hence the bands of white. He moved to a wooden bench and sat, while waiting for his friend to arrive, watching the scooters with their young lovers pull up and park around the lake's lengthy circumference. At the end of the day this was their favourite spot and like competitors at a speedway they'd line up, each owner hoping his model was better and more impressive to his girlfriend than the one that was parked next to him. Greg found this old fashioned form of flirtation rather quaint and worthy.

He was tired. He'd been up at seven to cycle ten miles across the city to where he was teaching young Vietnamese children English. He'd been teaching all the time during his stay, but this last assignment, lasting four weeks, was the most intensive. Organised privately, it supplemented the meagre wage he received from the education department and helped to fund his forthcoming trip down south to Ho Chi Minh City and then on to Cambodia and Thailand, before returning home. As much as he was excited about the trip, and completely absorbed in his spare time with all the planning and preparation, he found the thought of returning home and seeing his parents again similarly uplifting. Of course he missed them, he admitted. They were wonderful and he loved them dearly, although at first, when he arrived in The Far East, the freedom from the constant need to conform and seek their approval for his actions was so invigorating that he wondered if he'd ever return. But now he was ready to be re-united.

*I wonder how mum and dad have got on*, he thought. Maybe, now I'm away, they don't argue as much. He felt a tap on his shoulder.

Pungent, vibrant smells of street cooking, horns blasting, motor-cycle engines accelerating and the general bustle told Greg and his friend that the city was wrapping up for the day. They ambled casually through the old quarter to find a favourite street café. All around, men and woman were busy standing behind wooden tables, chopping and preparing the varied intensely coloured fresh ingredients used in all the local dishes. Great bunches of coriander hung on metal meat hooks; big bulbs of garlic, the size of a man's fist, lay waiting to be sliced; large tentacles of fresh ginger were grouped together with green, red and yellow coloured peppers, and small, red and green chillies, their modest size disguising the intensity of their fiery impact, were piled high in round wooden bowls. It was intoxicating.

The streets were still damp from the earlier deluges, awnings dripped and thunder rumbled away in the background, occasionally becoming louder with the odd flash of lighting; but the constant dust, thrown up by the many building sites, no longer clung to every item of clothing and exposed skin. The intense August humidity had given way to a lighter, cooler feel. A bunch of bedraggled children begged and tugged at Greg and Matt's shirts. At first they ignored them, both knowing that any money they gave would go straight back to whoever had sent them out and be used to buy drugs. Once they had reached a mobile food cart Greg bought the children some food and then moved on. Begging, and the atrocious poverty in Vietnam was a fact of life and one of many things that westerners found shocking and upsetting. Greg had, reluctantly, become accustomed to it, accepting that there was little he could do to change things. They stopped at one of the endless kiosks that sold pirated CDs for 10000 dongs, or 50p, just as the storm returned. Thirty or so people, wet and dripping and mainly westerners in search of a bargain, crowded into the shop, no more than ten square metres, and watched as the rain pounded the street outside for about half an hour. Giant flashes of lighting turned the night into day, while illuminated sheets of rain poured endlessly from the sky. When it eased Greg and Matt were the first to leave.

Later, in the flickering glow of candles and electric lights strung between the overhanging trees, occasionally dispersing large drops of water, they sat facing each other across a rickety scrubbed wooden table, sipping bowls of beef Pho. Piled up randomly in the tiny space between them were heaps of maps of Vietnam and South East Asia, open and folded back from where they'd left them and, in places, damp. In their earlier time in the country, exposed for the first time to such a variety of appetizing and colourful dishes, they'd eagerly devour all the different types of Vietnamese food. Now, in the latter weeks of their stay, with their funds diminishing, they found Pho, as did most Hanoi residents, to be a cheap and nourishing staple diet. Outside all the numerous street cafés, found in every road and on most corners, large steel pans would simmer away for days, boiling down shins of beef, garlic, fresh ginger, coriander, fresh chillies and small onions until an aromatic and nutritious broth was ready to be served. It came in a large bowl with noodles and strips of beef, prawn or chicken and cost about 50p.

Both of them were 19 and had volunteered for the assignment as part of their gap year before university. Although neither had met before, they bonded together on first meeting, finding in the other similar views on most things. They're musical taste, if not identical, became complementary; they both taught English to Vietnamese teenagers at the same school; each had a wicked sense of humour and, although different and unique personalities, they came together like a key in a lock, each character trait of one fitting into a niche or cranny in the other's make-up. Often, when one was down the other would be up, and vice versa. Consequently, serious bouts of depression and homesickness were almost a non-occurrence for either of them.

Once, after Greg's bike had to be repaired three times in one day on his way home, and then he found his wallet and camera had been stolen, Matt sat him down and said, 'Don't bloody move, mate,' before rushing out to buy as many of the local, 8p a pint, beers his money would allow. For hours they joked and played, building pyramids with the empty cans and watching them fall over to build up again until finally they'd drunk all the beer and then, sobering slightly over coffee, talked about their favourite topics—globalization, the world's poor, human rights, third world debt, how they could make a difference to the world. The next morning, nursing sore heads, they solved the problems caused by the loss of Greg's wallet with little trouble.

After they left the café, they cycled round the lake together and back to their house. They lived in a modern, brick built dwelling that rose three floors above the ground. Large wrought iron gates, partially solid in places, acted as the front door. Downstairs, leading in from the street, a tiled, lightly furnished sitting room was separated from a small but adequate kitchen by a circular staircase rising up to the other floors and the bedrooms. On each of the two lower floors was a front bedroom with a large balcony and a primitive shower. Nestled side by side on the top floor were two tiny bedrooms, their dimensions no larger than a prison cell, and a WC. Their house guest—a large hairy spider frequenting mainly the bathrooms—they left well alone.

Greg dumped his belongings on the couch and set about writing an email.

> *Hi Dad and Mum*
>
> *This is the last e-mail I'll send from this location. The day after tomorrow we leave on our trip. We're stopping first in Ho Chi Minh City, or Saigon, for a few days before exploring the south and then going on to Cambodia. I'll send you an e-mail when I can. Looking forward very much to seeing you both again in about six weeks. Hope you are both well—and mum, don't work too hard.*
>
> *Much love, Greg.*

Monroe swallowed hard to try to clear his ears from the effect of the change in pressurisation as the aeroplane started its descent. He pressed the wheel of his Ipod to stop Beethoven's Pastoral playing, unplugged his earphones and packed both items away in his bag. He brushed some crumbs and flecks of paper from his lap, zipped up the mini rucksack, placed it on his knees, folded his hands over the top and stared out of the window. He felt terrible. His heartbeat was beginning to race. Beads of perspiration were breaking out on his forehead. A nauseous sensation filled his stomach. He hoped, if he was going to be sick it would not be while he was still strapped in his seat and all over the person sitting next to him. For most of the long flight, the manner he'd break the terrible news to Greg had been out of his mind. With the onset of landing the awfulness of what was to come was inescapable and his only thought.

The plane bumped a couple of times as it touched down. Monroe felt each one. He rubbed his hands together and discovered that his palms were wet. He burped; apologised to his neighbour, who appeared disapproving, and looked around to see how he could ensure he was one of the first off the plane.

'Excuse me,' he said as the plane came to a halt and he started to push past his neighbour.

'Hold it, buddy,' the passenger said in a deep southern American accent, frowning at Monroe.

'We take our turn around here.' The man stood up, pulled down his bag from the overhead locker and turned his back on Monroe. Monroe belched, this time putting his hand up to his mouth.

Walking out of the plane onto the top rung of the steps to the tarmac was, for Monroe, like walking into a blast furnace. The heat and humidity hit him with a bang, taking his breath away. He didn't think he'd be able to manage the descent without falling over. Gingerly he put one foot in front of the other until he'd reached the bottom, all the while holding on to the handrail. He was a mess, he admitted as he looked at his perspiration sodden t-shirt and grey face in the mirror of the washroom. *I'm no help to Greg if I'm like this,* he told himself as he splashed some cold water over his face, cleaned his teeth and ran his fingers through his cropped grey hair. Finally he straightened up his t-shirt and pulled up his jeans.

Outside the airport he joined the queue for a taxi. He wondered if he should first go to his hotel to check-in and clean up before going to find Greg. *That's just putting it off,* he thought. Better to get on with it.

'Where you go?' a Vietnamese man asked him from the open window of a taxi drawn up alongside him. Monroe showed the driver the address from one of Greg's e-mails. The man looked at it, scratched his head and then said something in Vietnamese that Monroe didn't understand, but took to mean, get in.

Minutes later he was sitting on the broken back seat of an old, battered Honda Accord that bumped and swerved around the great swarms of people abreast of cycles or motor bikes, intent and serious in their various activities. Most of the riders carried goods of some form loosely attached to their vehicle. Some carried great rods of steel and long pipes on their shoulders, protruding dangerously well beyond the length of their conveyance. And then there was the livestock. Wooden crates of clucking chickens, open plastic containers of squirming fish and eels, a live pig in an old upturned bath, caged birds and boxed snakes, all attached in some way to the various types of transport.

Through the open window Monroe could make out the huge sprawling growth of new construction. Just about everywhere he looked houses, hotels, offices, warehouses and shopping centres were rising from every empty plot of land. To join up the mass of development into a coherent and liveable form, great roads were being cut through what was once jungle or scrubland. The air was still and dusty, leaving a fine residue on Monroe's clothing and bag. Different and contrasting smells hit his nostrils. Sewage and the dank odour of wet mud, diesel fumes, choking forceful cooking aromas, burning rubber and wood, all combined with the suffocating heat to bring about a creeping feeling of disorientation.

The taxi slowed and turned into a small narrow street lined with a mixture of multi-storey houses, buildings akin to western bungalows, shacks with corrugated metal roofs, shops, half-finished constructions supported by wooden poles, empty plots, trees everywhere and a tangle of power and telephone cables, intertwined with everything and seemingly holding the whole intriguing mishmash together. Monroe's heart started to beat mercilessly.

The slow crawl down the road as the driver checked the number on every building did nothing to relieve Monroe's unease. All the symptoms he'd experienced before at various times were bombarding him now in one frightening attack. He felt sick again. He was perspiring heavily and could see his hands shake as he leant forward and handed over Greg's e-mail, folded and crumpled from being in his back pocket, to show the address and number.

'I think it's there,' he managed to say, leaning on the scratched, torn upholstery of the back of the front passenger seat and pointing to a house that resembled the photo Greg had sent home. The taxi drew to a halt. Monroe picked up his small bag from the seat next to him, opened the door and got out. The driver remained in his seat, expressionless.

'How much,' Monroe asked holding out a great wad of Vietnamese money. The man said something sounding like 20. Monroe counted out what he thought was 22000 and passed it over. The driver looked at him with a sad, pathetic looking expression and then, in an unexpected bout of activity, flung his arms around, moving both his hands quickly backwards and forwards to his chest several times with great intensity. His earlier mournful face had changed to a pleading, almost begging one. Monroe took the man's behaviour to mean he wanted more. Vaguely he remembered being told the dong was pretty worthless and handed over his wad to the driver for him to take what was wanted. Monroe watched helplessly as the man, having tucked all the money in his top pocket, laughed, while simultaneously pulling hard down on the steering wheel and accelerating off up the street. Monroe ran up the road, shouting after him. The driver sped off in a large cloud of dust, disturbing wandering chickens, which clucked and flew off the ground the few centimetres they could manage. But it was all to no gain. In the dusty distance Monroe could just make out the taxi as it reached the main road, turned left and drove quickly away.

He shrugged his shoulders, giving the matter little thought, and turned to walk slowly back to where his case stood outside the house. He focused on the two grey iron gates, about three metres in height, partly solid, partly open with vertical bars. Adjacent to the top edge of the right hand gate was a small blue metal plaque screwed into the stone façade. There was no mistaking the number—P3—painted clearly in large white letters. For a moment Monroe was unable to move. He stood facing the building knowing full well that this was Greg's home. The number was correct and the house resembled exactly Greg's picture. With his legs feeling like leaden weights, an empty sensation in his stomach, he nervously ventured towards the front door, leaving his bag in the street where he'd dumped it. A large shiny padlock held the two gates firmly closed.

*What if he's not here? Has he gone?* he asked himself, suddenly remembering that the last time he spoke to Greg, he'd mentioned vaguely something about doing some travelling. He fiddled furiously with the padlock, hopelessly trying to release it, and conjured up in his mind the awful scenario of Greg missing Juliet's funeral and not being aware of the tragedy until his return to England in six weeks time.

With his emotional state worsening, his eyes raced wildly from one corner of the front of the building to another, searching for a bell or knocker. By now his shirt was drenched in his own sweat, his hands trembling, his whole self shaky. He stood on tiptoe, took hold of the bars and peered inside. In what looked like a sitting room, he could make out a small, black cloth-covered couch in front of which was a Formica topped coffee table.

'Greg, are you there. Greg, it's me, dad. Anyone in?' he yelled through the bars, several times.

\* \* \*

Greg's happy go lucky nature was at its height as he sauntered out of the back room of the shop where he'd had his hair cut short for the forthcoming trip. For the last 48 hours his life in Hanoi had been frantic. Most of the people he'd met, in one way or the other, had become a good friend; and he had to say goodbye. The Vietnamese teachers at the school, his karate tutor, neighbours, his pupils; all had made him welcome and helped to make his stay in Hanoi happy and enjoyable. He wasn't going to just bow out of their lives without a proper farewell. And then there was all the packing and cleaning that had to be completed. He had accumulated so much stuff in eight months; but it just didn't fit in his rucksack. Many things had to be either given away or disposed of. *But now I'm finished*, he thought, and soon he'd be off to the railway station and on route to the south.

For Van and Tam, owners of the shop that had provided Greg and Matt with almost all of their basic needs, he had a special farewell. They'd treated the premises as a true convenience store: buying from it all their essential groceries, having their haircut, picking up occasional English papers, receiving and sending e-mails, calling up taxis and generally relying on the shop and its willing and friendly family to provide them with any unforeseen need that they, as foreigners, inevitable came across.

'Mr Greg, you come back,' Van said, clasping Greg's hand tightly.

'Of course I will. When, I'm not sure,' Greg replied, feeling a wave of sadness come over him.

Tam put her hands around Greg's neck.

'When you come back? When? When?' she asked, pulling Greg towards her.

'Soon, I hope. But first I have to see my parents and then go to university.' Greg looked at them both. He realised again what he'd discovered many times in the last few weeks. He loved this country and its amiable, benevolent people.

'I've got to go now,' he said pulling away from their grasps, knowing that if he didn't leave at that moment it would become harder and harder.

'I promise I'll come back. Love you all.' With moisture in both eyes he turned and walked away.

At first his pace was slow. He turned a few times and had a last look at Van and Tam waving from their front door. He waved back, glad that they hadn't followed him down the street. After the third wave he resisted the pressure to turn again and, instead, started to think about the trip down south. His pace quickened until he was running and skipping, swinging his carrier bag of last-minute essentials and kicking the odd small stone in an attempt to emulate David Beckham and Ryan Giggs or some other player from his early-teen worship of Manchester United. Excitement had become his prevalent emotion, extinguishing and masking the sadness of his departure. He ran from side to side of the street, tossing his bag in the air, lunging at objects with his feet, returning a wave from the odd resident wishing him farewell.

Mixed emotions ranged in his mind. He was excited about the trip, wondering and anticipating what sights and pleasures were in store. He was intrigued about how different Ho Chi Minh City would be from Hanoi; and then Cambodia. *What will it be like?* he asked himself and then thought of his parents and seeing them again in about six weeks. It made him happy. Yes, he told himself, I'm ready now to move on.

\* \* \*

He stopped. In fact he froze on the spot. He could not believe his eyes. Outside his house, peering in through the iron bars was his father.

'What the hell,' he said out loud. 'What's he doing here?' He started to run, thinking only how wonderful it was to see his dad again, not concerned at all as to his motive for being here unannounced. He speeded up; closing the gap between them, the sounds from his father's voice, yelling his name, becoming louder and louder. And then, as though he was part of a film that was unexpectedly being slowed down, he lessened his pace until he was almost walking. Coming towards him slowly and looking terribly troubled was a man who resembled his father in every physical way, but looked as though his spirit had been broken.

*My God, he looks dreadful,* he thought as he came to a halt.

'Dad, what's wrong? What's happened?' Greg knew the answer would be bad. He looked into his father's eyes, leaden with huge, heavy bags under them.

'What is it, dad? Tell me quickly.'

For a split second father and son stood and looked at each other. Both were speechless. And then they surged forward and flung their arms around each other. Both of them burst into tears.

'It's mum,' Greg said pushing his father away and looking into his eyes.

'She's dead, Greg.'

Greg gave his father an incredulous look.

'What did you say? What do you mean?' He looked desperately for some gesture from his father that said he'd been mistaken in what he just heard. There wasn't one. Instead, he felt a massive surge of desolation sweep through him.

'No, no,' he sobbed, grabbing his father again. 'It can't be. How? Tell me it's not true, please, please.'

Monroe pushed Greg back a bit, held Greg's two arms in his hands and looked squarely into his son's tear stained face.

'I afraid so. She was murdered.'

* * *

Half an hour later Greg and his father were sitting side by side on the couch in Greg's house. Matt had returned just after Greg had opened up, finding the two of them clutching each other, propped up against the wall. Greg was sobbing loudly onto Monroe's shoulder. Once Monroe had quickly introduced himself and explained, Matt had made them both tea and left them alone.

After a while Greg, ashen, looked up at his father and asked in a trembling voice, 'What have the police said?'

'Nothing really. I haven't seen much of them. I came straight away.' Monroe looked better than he had done before. Some colour had returned to his face and the heat didn't seem to be bothering him so much.

'Didn't they come to see you?' Greg, with a look of consternation, had turned to look at his father face on.

'Oh yes. Some jumped up female detective came on Saturday night and almost accused me of doing it.'

Greg recoiled in his seat.

'That's ridiculous, dad. Why on earth would they think that?' He looked away for a moment and then back at his father. The expression on his face had changed.

'Dad?' he asked.

'Yes.'

'How were you and mum getting on?'

# 6

Greg placed the two mugs of steaming cappuccino on the uneven surface of the long narrow garden table; its old slate top already warm from the morning sun. In an apathetic manner he took a couple of steps from the patio to the small patch of uncut lawn and aimlessly kicked a discarded cigarette butt, thrown down by someone after the funeral, the previous day, until it reached the far flower bed. He stood still for a few moments, gazing down and seemingly lost in his own thoughts.

'You coming, dad?' he yelled through the open stable door to the kitchen. He sat down in one of the flaky, once green, wrought iron chairs and looked towards where he expected his dad to appear. Earlier, at eight, when he'd taken his father a cup of tea, Monroe had suggested that Greg took the first shower. He'd done that, and now waited for the first conversation alone with his father since the two of them had said their farewells to his mother the previous day. He cupped his hands around his coffee and slowly sipped the hot strong liquid, sucking it through the frothy surface that clung to his lips. He shifted his chair, its legs grating noisily on the hard York stone slabs, and made space for Monroe to sit next to him. All around them, terracotta tubs of red geraniums, blue and white lobelia, multi-coloured impatiens and mixed petunias wilted from a lack of water.

'I must give those plants a drink,' Monroe said as he pulled his chair close to the table and took a sip from his coffee. 'They haven't had any water for days.'

Greg looked at the pots and then back at his dad.

'I'll do that for you later, dad.'

Monroe, wearing a baggy pair of long khaki shorts, a white t-shirt and a pair of sandals, smiled at Greg.

'Thanks,' he said starring his son in the face. He noticed the great bags hanging loosely under Greg's eyes, his face pallid and grey.

'How did you sleep?' Monroe asked.

A thin weak smile came across Greg's face. He hadn't shaved for days and was wearing a dirty pair of jeans and a loose fitting sweatshirt with no shoes or socks.

'A bit. How about you?'

'Not much,' Monroe replied, bending down to suck the froth from the top of his coffee.

'At first I couldn't,' Greg continued. 'I just felt so desperate and sad. Then I woke up at about three, feeling cold and thirsty. So I guess I must have had about two hours. I came down to get some water. You were snoring soundly.' Greg smiled.

'After that I didn't get back to sleep, just tossing and turning, thinking about everything. I thought most about mum's friend, Lucy, and all that wonderful stuff she said about what mum and her got up at uni.' He looked up at his father.

'Had you met before?'

'Mum and I used to see a lot of her. But then she moved to America and only mum used to go over.' Monroe looked across to his son.

'What are you're going to do now?' he asked, watching Greg closely.

Greg's head was down.

'I don't know. Everything feels like shit. I never, ever, thought anything…' Greg stopped. His words were fading. He was finding it difficult to speak. He put his hand up to his mouth.

Monroe stretched over and put his arm around Greg's shoulder. Many times in the last week he'd done the same. As he expected, Greg had taken the death of his mother badly. On two occasions he'd broken down, completely desolate, and on the flight back from Hanoi, Monroe had to give him two strong sleeping tablets to knock him out.

After a terrible two days, with Greg distraught almost all the time, Monroe had decided to involve him in all the funeral arrangements and that had seemed to help. Somehow, Monroe knew, he had to find a way of instilling a new purpose in Greg, or he'd become consumed with his own sorrow. He stood up and put a hand on each of Greg's shoulders. Slowly Greg raised his head.

'Go back, Greg.'

Greg turned and looked at his father, a look of astonishment spread across his face.

'What do you mean, dad?'

'Go back to Vietnam and finish off. I'll pay.'

'Dad, I couldn't. I'd hate it. I don't have any wish to do that.' Greg paused for a bit.

'I'm not going to leave you,' he added, looking at his father with incredulity. 'You don't really think I'd do that, do you?' Greg had turned his chair right around now and was sitting looking straight at his father.

Monroe walked over to a nearby watering can. He picked it up. Holding it trailing in his left hand he moved towards the outside tap, just next to the door to the kitchen.

'You don't have to worry about me. I'll be OK. Thanks for your concern. But I think it'll be good for you.' He paused for a minute to consider carefully what he was going to say.

'Look, Greg. I know you loved your mum and will miss her for the rest of your life.' He stopped again to check if what he'd just said was causing any distress. He turned from the tap, still holding the empty can, its spout pointing towards the ground, and added, 'But she would have wanted you to get on with your life. Staying here will only make things worse. Why don't we check out some flights…' Monroe stopped. Greg had stood up and was leaning with one hand on a chair, looking at his father.

'Don't you want me to stay with you? I thought you might want some company.' Greg's blue eyes contacted with his dad's, and then he looked away.

Monroe sat down and looked up at Greg.

'That's bloody silly. You know I want you here. I couldn't want anyone more,' he paused, 'but you've got your life to lead.' Monroe reached up and gave Greg's arm a tug.

'Sit down and let's talk about it.' Monroe watched as Greg stood for a few moments clearly digesting what his father had said.

Greg looked bewildered. He sat down next to Monroe.

'Dad, even if I did want to go, I can't. They've all moved on. There's no one left in Vietnam. They're all somewhere in South East Asia.'

Monroe pushed back in his chair. His fingers drummed lightly on the table as he stared at Greg. He thought he noticed a slight change in his son's bearing. The signs of deep trauma in his face had eased somewhat. He seemed to be waiting for Monroe to come up with an answer.

'What about Matt? Where is he? You could join up with him, wherever he is. I'll pay to get you there.'

'What about you, dad?' Greg asked, looking forlorn and almost hopeful at the same time. 'What are you going to do?'

'Well,' Monroe replied, stopping himself to think. 'I've things to sort out. Then I'll start on my book.'

'What book?' Greg asked, standing up and clearly surprised. 'You've never written a book in your life.' He frowned and ambled away from his chair and sat in the one with the wobbly leg. Steadying it, he looked at his father with a questioning expression.

Monroe wiped his hand over the top of the table, brushing the flaky bits of slate to the edge, to gather in his other hand.

*I'm right. His attitude has changed,* he told himself.

'I know,' he replied. 'But I'm going to start.'

He stood up and walked towards an empty cracked flowerpot, in the corner of the patio, full of dirt and weeds, and deposited the pieces of slate he'd collected from the table. He turned and looked for Greg, who was walking towards him, purposefully with a positive look on his face.

Greg leant down and picked up a couple of slate flakes from the flagstones that had missed the flowerpot.

'What's the book about, dad?' he asked, looking his father in the face. He sounded interested. 'Are you serious?' he added.

'How I was stitched up.' Monroe put his arm around Greg's shoulder.

\* \* \*

The shadows shortened, the warmth of the day increased. Bees flew from one flowerpot to another and father and son talked enthusiastically about Monroe's plans over two more frothy cappuccinos and the remains of the granary loaf, French butter and chunky English marmalade. Together they watered the pots and tubs on the flagstone patio, removing the faded plants, pruning the thirsty clematis and honeysuckle that covered the old brick wall enclosing the garden. Their joint activity seemed to act as a stimulant, invigorating and refreshing the two of them. At midday, while they were moving a large pot from one side of the garden to the other, Monroe decided to try again.

'You should go back, you know,' he said as they lowered the pot into its new position. He twisted the container a little to line it up and waited for Greg's reply.

Greg stood up, wiped his hands down his jeans and looked away. He started to nod his head.

'I think I'll take you up on your offer, dad.'

* * *

Monroe hitched up his jeans, leant on the closed half of the kitchen door and listened. Drops of rain were falling. The sound of their plops and pitter-patter as they hit the leaves and trees gradually increased in intensity until it developed into a consistent shush, bringing with it a damp smell and an imaginary thankfulness from the drought struck plants. Monroe crossed his arms on the door's frame and watched, relieved that the sudden change in conditions had brought relief from the stifling humidity, and, in the process, negated the need for him to water his neglected garden. He turned, caste a quick glance at the shepherd's pie he'd placed in the oven a few minutes earlier and, leaving the top part of the door open, walked towards a small pile of CDs at the far end of the worktop. Just as the first bars of Pachelbel's Canon started up his doorbell rang.

'Told you, oh boy, I'd come to see how you were.'

Wearing navy chinos, a light denim shirt and a Panama hat, Johnny stood on the doorstep, looking every bit the old colonial diplomat. At the end of his long left arm a bottle of whisky dangled as though it was attached in some way to his body. He flipped it over, catching it squarely in the middle of the bottle before tossing to his right hand and thrusting it in Monroe's face.

'Thought we might do this a bit of damage. Sorry, old chap. Couldn't get your favourite.' He handed the bottle over. 'Hope this one's OK.'

'Come in, Johnny,' Monroe said at once, and laughed.

'You're incorrigibly generous. You don't need to do that.' He shook his head as he looked at the label on the bottle and said, 'Of course it's all right. You know that.' He clapped his arm around Johnny's shoulder and pushed him into the house.

'Let's try it,' he said, pulling Johnny inside.

Johnny followed Monroe through the hall and into the sitting room, where he'd left the french windows slightly ajar. A cooling draught kept the rain out. He switched off the CD player and pulled out a couple of chunky whisky tumblers. He poured two large slugs into each glass and gave one to Johnny, gazing through the narrow opening in the doors to the rain soaked patio.

'Need this bit of weather,' Johnny said as he took the glass and examined its amber liquid.

'Wonderful. Thanks' he added, lowering himself into the leather chair.

'Cheers, old man. Here's to you.' He raised his glass in the air.

'And to you,' Monroe responded. He was unsure how to kick off the conversation. Johnny hadn't been in touch since the funeral.

Johnny took another swig, clasped both his hands around his glass and leant forward, looking at Monroe. For the next ten minutes Johnny did most of the talking: non-specific chit-chat about the weather, too many tourists and the state of the local fishing industry. Monroe was content to let Johnny ramble on. It helped him relax.

'Thanks, old man,' Johnny said, as Monroe topped up his glass. He leant back in his seat, smiled calmly at Monroe and said, 'So how are you? Are you coping?'

'I'm OK, Johnny. I'm doing all right.' Monroe could see Johnny's deep, perceptive eyes staring hard. 'Thanks for asking.'

'What you going to do now?' Johnny stood up, his whisky in his hand, and peered into the garden. He turned to look at Monroe. 'I hear Greg's gone. You'll miss him.'

Johnny's question raised a slight whiff of suspicion in Monroe's mind. *Why's he here?* he wondered.

'You're right,' he replied, moments later. 'I will. But it's the best for him. I took him to the airport yesterday. He called just before you arrived to say he'd got there safely.' Johnny smiled and nodded his head.

'Want to stay for some supper?' Monroe asked as the smell of the shepherd's pie wafted in from the kitchen.

'I can't, old boy.' Johnny drained his glass and put it down on the coffee table. 'Smells wonderful. Got to go and make sure the wife's OK.'

He started to walk in the direction of the door, picking up his Panama from the end of the far couch.

Monroe rebuked himself. He'd forgotten Johnny's wife had MS. Johnny had to do all the shopping and cooking.

'How is Rose?' he asked as the two of them reached the front door.

'Not bad. Well as can be expected and thanks for asking.' Johnny turned and put his arm around Monroe's shoulder.

'Glad you're coping. If there's anything you want don't hesitate to call.'

* * *

Monroe awoke to the bright rays gradually turning his bedroom from darkness into light. When the first dart of brightness had poked through the bottom of his curtains he'd turned and tried to bury his head under the pillow. Now the whole room was awash with dazzling sunlight, and it felt warm. He scratched his head, looked at his watch and jumped out of bed. It was 5.30 in the morning. Wearing just a pair of shorts and another of his favourite white t-shirts he made for the kitchen. He pushed open the stable doors into the garden, filled a glass with orange juice from the fridge, dropped a couple of pieces of granary bread in the toaster and went to sit outside. He rested his elbows on the table, dragged his hands down the sides of his face.

*Should he start with the clothes, or her papers?* he asked himself as a bright yellow butterfly landed on the edge of the table; still and symbolic. He sat still and watched, awe-struck by the creature's beauty, a moment of perfect stillness. And then the toaster popped, its clunk breaking the morning silence and causing the butterfly to flit away.

With a vengeance Monroe attacked Juliet's clothes. One by one he took the hanging garments from their hangers and bundled them up in black bags, discarding the wire and plastic hangers in an untidy pile on the bedroom floor. Next he started on the drawers. Without stopping to think, he scooped up great handfuls of knickers, bras, tights, socks,

70

scarves and again stuffed them into plastic bags. Then he had to deal with her jumpers, sweatshirts and coats. There were shoes, boots and belts to discard. *I'll give her jewellery to one of her charities*, he thought.

Purging any sentimental thoughts, doubts, moments of vacillation from his mind he ploughed on and on until he had filled nearly 20 black bin liners with Juliet's clothes and shoes, leaving only her make-up, which he was going to give to young Jodi, the girl who came to clean and who'd just lost her husband in a fishing disaster. At midday he called the charity shop and asked them to pick up the bags at their convenience.

He lightly spread some Dijon mustard over two slices of granary bread, placed a couple of thin cuts of Wiltshire ham on one of the pieces, lightly sprinkled the meat with black pepper, and put the other piece of bread on top to make a sandwich. With a glass of water, an apple and a banana he carried it all outside, using a large plate as his tray. He sat under a weeping silver birch tree on the stone wall that bordered the large flower bed. The tree gave him some protection from the light drizzle that had just started to fall.

*I've packed all her stuff away, but don't feel sad. Surely I should feel something?* he asked himself. Have all my feelings for her dried up completely? Or is this my body's natural way of protecting me, only to have a bigger reaction later? I suppose the whole bloody trauma— fetching and telling Greg, the funeral, Greg's return and now all this— has frozen everything? *Or am I unnatural? Hated her so much, I'm pleased she's gone?*

Monroe kept on tormenting himself with question after question, repeating many times the same ones and getting no satisfactorily answer until he'd finished all that was on his plate. When he looked down he couldn't remember the taste of anything, only that he felt fuller. He picked up the empty plate and glass and carried them in to the kitchen. Inside, he switched on the kettle, shaking some granules from an instant coffee jar into a mug. With his back to the worktop he thought about what he had to do next. The prospect of going through

Juliet's papers bit by bit, her will, bank accounts, filled him with dread. I've done enough today, he thought. Maybe I can do it all tomorrow. He shook his head. No, that will only make it worse, he told himself. With the coffee left unmade, he set about gathering all her stuff together.

By 4 p.m. he had a huge pile on the dining room table. Gradually he went through each item, dividing them into three distinct piles. One was stuff to throw away—documents and things that he figured died with Juliet, one was current stuff he had to deal with including her will, money and some of her work stuff; the last pile were items that he thought Greg would want. Those he put in a big cardboard box, to go in the loft.

In the corner of the room the 17th century grandfather clock chimed nine times. Monroe sat up and pushed hard on the deep back of the leather chair, looking down on the floorboards at the few remaining papers of Juliet's scattered all around his bare feet. He was still wearing the same shorts and t-shirt that he'd pulled on hurriedly in the morning. He felt numb, both mentally and physically, enveloped in a great wave of tiredness. He imagined what he was experiencing was something similar to being suddenly immersed in an avalanche. It affected every part of his body. He couldn't move a single limb; even his smallest of fingers seemed to be locked by some force that had taken control of his body and mind. He gave in and gently closed his eyes.

He awoke on the tenth chime. Slowly, he rose from the chair, kicking the two or three letters and papers by his feet to one side and made for the kitchen. Holding his whisky bottle in one hand he reached up for a glass and plonked it down on the work surface next to the large larder type fridge. While he poured he grabbed a plate, pulled out the cheese and tried to unwrap it. Then he did three things in rapid succession. He gulped a large slug of whisky, cut a huge chunk of cheese and bit an inelegantly large portion from it. It wasn't enough, he cut another slab and put that in his mouth, washing it down as before. The warmth of the whisky flowed through his body. Its intoxicating effect started to liberate his brain, and a third piece of cheese abated the weakening pangs of hunger he'd felt a few seconds earlier. He started to feel sensations that he took to be the beginning of the return of normality to his body.

All day, without anything to eat, and with a great intensity he'd purged Juliet from his life. Nothing, apart from the few things he'd kept to sort out her estate and Greg's mementoes, were left. Bach's Branderburg Concerto blared loudly from every speaker in the house as he lay full length on the couch letting the power of the music complete the washing and cleansing process he'd physically executed all day. Without disturbing the tumbler balanced on his stomach he let his left arm flop to the floor. He touched a paper. Picking it up he stared at an airmail envelope addressed to Juliet.

'Shit,' he muttered. 'How did I miss this?' He pulled out the letter and started to read its contents.

'My God, what a bitch,' he yelled. He sat up, drained his glass and screwed the letter up in a ball and threw it right over to the french windows. He flopped back onto the couch and closed his eyes.

# 7

Monroe and Greg wandered down the narrow sloping road, bordered by small eighteenth and nineteenth century houses, all inhabited by students, that led from Palace Green into Owengate. Hungry and thirsty, they put their heads around the door of the first pub they found. A big log fire roared in an open fireplace, large oak beams stretched across the low ceilings, small dark wooden tables with rickety chairs sat in darkly lit corners; seemingly original floorboards, stained dark, covered the floor. It gave off a sort of cosy enticement, an intoxicating atmosphere. Groups of people, most young, sat and stood around talking and laughing. Some stood in twos or threes, apparently engaged in earnest conversation for a while until one of them cracked up and the others followed. Smoke and the smell of beer wafted through the air.

*If this is going to be Greg's regular,* Monroe thought, *he'd have to go far to better it.*

'What you having, dad?' Greg asked, smiling appreciatively. He looked around, both hands in the back pockets of his torn jeans, waiting for his father to reply. A new grey sweatshirt that Monroe had bought for him a couple of days earlier hung loosely of his shoulders.

Monroe fumbled in the pocket of his trousers and smiled. 'I guess we chose the right one,' he said as he looked around, trying to locate his wallet.

'A pint of whatever looks good. Here, take this.' He held out a twenty-pound note. 'Order some food, as well. Cumberland Sausage for me.'

'Thanks, dad. I'll pay you back one day.' Greg replied, smiling as he turned towards the bar.

'Yeah,' Monroe added, and huffed as he sat down to wait.

They'd just spent two hours unloading and setting up all Greg's belongings in his room for his first term at Durham University. Monroe was impressed by the organisation. He'd expected chaos—hundreds of first year students and their parents all turning up at the same time, trying to negotiate the tiny streets and find a non-existent parking spot. Instead, the university had issued everybody with allocated times. Police and traffic wardens had controlled the flow of cars into the unloading spots, where volunteer students had quickly and efficiently emptied the cars.

Monroe had been to Durham many times. On every occasion the architecture of the ancient city had never failed to impress him. Earlier, they'd entered the city from the east and enjoyed a spectacular view of the historic cathedral and the noble castle looming majestically over the hilly, cobbled passageways and the narrow streets to one side, the River Wear to other. He called it an oasis of history amidst the bleak beauty of County Durham countryside.

Greg had returned from South East Asia only a few days earlier. He'd seemed refreshed, strengthened by the fellowship of his friends and the travel experiences. Monroe and he had arrived back in Padstow at 2 a.m. after a seven-hour drive from Heathrow during which Greg slept all the time. The next morning, after a brief chat over breakfast, they both got stuck into two frantic days of washing, preparing and packing everything that Greg would need at university.

Monroe looked up as he saw Greg approach. He was carrying two pints of beer, weaving his way, trying his hardest to avoid spilling a drop, through the densely packed room.

'Sorry, mate,' someone said as they stepped back, narrowly avoiding knocking the drinks from Greg's hand all over some people at a nearby table. Monroe watched proudly as Greg turned to the guy and smiled.

'No problem,' he said, casually.

He's different, Monroe thought. Confident, assured—not tentative, like he was at the airport after Juliet's funeral. His transformation warmed Monroe. He felt he'd be able to rest, happy in the knowledge that he'd made the right decision in suggesting that Greg returned to the Far East.

'Here you go, dad. A pint of Black Sheep. Supposed to be good stuff according to a bloke I spoke to at the bar.' Greg stretched forward and placed the straight glass on the table in front of Monroe.

'What?' he asked a girl who'd nudged past him in the crowd. She muttered something in his ear.

'Fine, yeah. I'll be there.' He smiled at her and nodded his head.

'Who's that?' Monroe asked as Greg sat down.

'Can't remember her name. I just met her. She's doing the same course as me…' He looked away. A black guy wearing long baggy khaki shorts and a plain red t-shirt was pushing through the crowd, waving and trying to attract his attention. Greg listened to what the guy had to say.

'Sorry, mate. I didn't hear you before. I'm Greg. My number's 07786 567043.' Greg, still holding his glass in one hand, put up his other hand quickly in a goodbye gesture and turned to sit again with Monroe.

'Sorry, dad. It's mad around here. I've made about half a dozen friends already.'

'Doesn't bother me, I'm pleased for you.' Monroe looked up. A girl with two plates of food was pushing through to reach their table. They both moved their drinks to make way for two healthy portions of Cumberland Sausage, mashed potato, onions and gravy. Monroe looked at Greg and smiled.

'Looks as though we made the right choice,' he said, as the both started their food immediately. Neither spoke for a bit. They were hungry from carrying all the bags, boxes and cases up several flights of stairs to Greg's accomodation.

'Dad?' Greg looked up from his nearly empty plate.

'Go on.' Monroe looked up, expectantly. He sensed from the tone of Greg's voice he was going to ask about Juliet. He continued eating, trying to anticipate the question.

Greg finished wiping a piece of bread around his plate to mop up the remaining gravy, held it in his hand, looked at Monroe and said, 'Didn't really want to bring this up.' He paused to eat the piece of bread. Monroe emptied his glass.

'Have they found anyone yet?' Greg put his right elbow on the table, lifted up the remains of his beer in his left hand and looked at his father.

'No,' Monroe replied quickly, hoping that they weren't going to get too embroiled. Greg hadn't mentioned his mother since he had come back. If he started, it would be unsettling, he thought.

'Haven't they any idea?' Greg looked down at his empty glass and twisted it around on the table.

'Another one?' Monroe asked, seizing the opportunity to change the subject.

'Yeah, but let me get it, dad. It's dirt-cheap here.' He stood up, reaching forward to take Monroe's glass. 'You having the same?'

'Just a half. I've got to drive home.' Monroe watched as Greg disappeared into the crowd, hoping he'd forget what they had been talking about by the time he returned. From where he was sitting he could make out Greg's head in the queue. He was chatting away, shaking hands, writing—presumably names and numbers—on scraps of paper and pieces of card torn from cigarette packets while waiting to be served. He'd laugh, wave, and give the impression that he had known everyone around him for some time. Monroe sat back and waited patiently for Greg to return, relieved that he seemed to be making plenty of friends and appeared happy.

\* \* \*

The day after Monroe returned from Durham he started writing his book. He'd wake at seven, throw on either a pair of jeans or combat trousers and a sweatshirt and make a cup of lapsang souchong tea. Breakfast would be a bowl of muesli, taken while walking around the kitchen and doing various chores to the background sounds of Today on Radio 4. By eight he'd be at his computer, tapping away. There he'd stay, lunching on a hunk of cheese and some fruit or a quick sandwich, occasionally finishing off the previous night's leftovers. Come four in the afternoon, his brain would have seized up. He'd take a shower, shave and rush off to the shops to buy whatever supplies he needed before jogging around the harbour wall. Most evenings he'd read a book, stopping to watch the news before clearing up and dropping into bed around 11 to 11.30. In some ways, he thought, he'd become somewhat of a hermit.

Friends hadn't been queuing up to see him, almost the opposite, he told himself, thinking he was being sensitive. But on a couple of occasions when he'd gone either to the butcher or the supermarket, he found the way people he knew reacted to him seemed as if they were trying to avoid him, keeping their distance. Even Johnny and Les had only been to see him on a couple of occasions, both times together. To begin with, after all the letters and phone calls he received after Juliet's death, and the many one to one expressions of sympathy he received at her funeral, he found the sudden change in attitude upsetting, particularly from Johnny and Les. After a while he came to understand and rationalise people's behaviour. He accepted that in a small community people gossip and while nobody had been charged with Juliet's murder, questions would be asked. He guessed, inevitably, some people would be pointing the finger at him.

The two detectives on the case had been to see him a couple more times; asking him to go over his recollection of the evening of her death again. Each time he told the same story. They'd had a row, Juliet had walked out on him, taking a case and not saying where she was going and, after a few drinks, he'd gone to bed early to be ready for the fishing trip the following morning. He'd asked them if they had any leads. They'd told him they hadn't. And that was how he'd left it.

Snatched telephone conversations and the odd e-mail gave Monroe the impression that Greg's first few weeks in Durham were anything but dull. He'd met many friends; joined up for squash, rowing and debating; partaken in the normal amount of student drinking and surprisingly found some time to do some work. He seemed happy. Monroe's communications with him were irregular and brief, but they convinced him that all was well.

* * *

On the last Saturday in October, Monroe decided he should venture out. Rumour had it that the new chef at the sailing club cooked good food. He thought he'd test her reputation. Wearing a pair of black jeans, a knitted Armani black top, a denim jacket and a checked navy cashmere scarf, flung loosely around his shoulders, he wandered out of his house at 8 p.m. carrying a small rucksack containing a pen, his paper and a book. A strong autumnal wind blew a pile of fallen leaves by Monroe's front door into his face. He brushed them off his jacket, tied his scarf tightly around his neck and stepped over the remainder.

'Hi, James,' Monroe said as he nestled up to the bar to order. James turned to look who'd called his name. Monroe thought he'd detected a surprised look on his face. 'How you're doing?' he added.

James seemed taken aback, lost for words.

'I'm, err, fine,' he said quickly, picking up his drink from the bar.

'And you?' he asked hesitantly, looking as though he wanted to make a quick getaway.

'Don't let me keep you. I'm just ordering a single beer.' Monroe nodded towards James's full glass. 'You OK?'

'Oh, err. Yes thanks. Em, I'm with a crowd over there. If you'll excuse me. Nice to see you again.' James looked over the top of Monroe's head and started to push through the crowd.

'Be my guest. Don't let me keep you.' Monroe nodded to James and turned to wait his turn at the bar. *Well*, he thought. *I'm obviously a problem.*

'A wee drink for you?' a voice said in a broad Scottish accent, directly into his ear.

He looked around to see who'd spoken. He turned. Standing behind the bar, looking at him, straight in the eye, was a tall, noticeably thin woman with unusually short blonde hair and piercing blue eyes. She wore a long sleeveless cotton grey top and matching trousers that accentuated her height. She wasn't pretty, but her strong features and pale skin, made-up to tone with her hair colour, made her strikingly attractive. Monroe guessed she was around twenty-eight to thirty. For a moment he was mesmerised.

'Yeah, I'll, err, have a Beck's.'

*She's new*, he thought. 'Oh…' He stopped, aware she was starring at him. 'In a glass, please.'

'OK,' she smiled in a way that radiated across her face. 'Just a wee minute.'

While she poured, Monroe turned again to check out the crowd. A few heads turned in his direction, and unless he was imagining it, turned back quickly when he tried to catch their gaze.

'Here you go,' she said, pushing his drink across the top of the bar.

'You new? I haven't seen your body and soul before.'

*Unusual way of putting it*, Monroe thought.

'I was going to ask you the same. I'm an old member, but haven't been around for a while,' Monroe replied, thinking there was something earthy and intriguing about the girl. He wanted to know more about her.

'Been banned by the wife, have you?'

Monroe noticed the girl looking down at his wedding ring.

'No,' he replied, with a smile. 'I don't have a wife. I just wear that for old times.' *Sometime soon*, he thought, *I'll stop wearing it.*

'Don't let me keep you,' Monroe said, noticing a man next to him, trying to get attention.

The girl looked at the man and then back at Monroe and said, 'I don't serve behind the bar.'

*Strange,* Monroe thought, returning the girl's gaze. *Why did she serve me?*

"Scuse me,' the man next to Monroe said, clearly irritated at not being served.

'Don't do drinks, mate. I'm the chef,' the girl replied with an impassive expression and her Scottish accent more obvious.

'Come on, girl,' the man replied, obviously not happy at what he thought was a put-down. 'I just saw you doing this guy's beer.'

*Some cool chick,* Monroe thought, wondering what would happen next.

'I'm off duty now,' the girl replied to the angry man. 'So you can…'

'Hey,' Monroe said with an authoritative smile and beckoning with his finger. 'Get the guy a drink, he's thirsty.'

The girl starred at Monroe.

'I'll do it for you.' She turned to collect the man's order.

'What's up with her, then?' the man said to Monroe as he waited for his round.

'Don't know,' Monroe replied, shaking his head. 'I've never met her before.' He shrugged his shoulders. 'Don't complain. I've got you a drink.'

After the girl had served the man his drinks she disappeared. Another, more easy-going girl took Monroe's order for food. Having decided that he was being somewhat paranoid about being ignored by people, who he reckoned where just plain embarrassed, he looked around for a quiet table where he could read his paper while waiting for his meal. After successfully completing three Times crossword clues in succession he reached out for a celebratory sip from his beer. He felt a slight nudge on his shoulder. The tall blonde Scottish girl was standing with his food.

'Mind if I join you?' she said, putting a plate of steaming steak and mushroom pie in front of him and sitting down opposite. 'I know it seems a bit forward of me. But I'm off duty now and you looked lonely.'

*Interesting,* Monroe thought. Better than being on my own.

'No problem. Be my guest. Want a drink?' he said as the girl sat down, opposite him.

'Don't drink. This glass of water's fine. Thanks anyway.' The girl leant forward and looked right into Monroe's eyes.

'Name's Stevie, what's yours?'

Monroe returned her stare, smiled and said, 'Monroe, and can I have permission to start.'

'Don't bother about me, get stuck in.' Stevie laughed and added, 'I made it so you'd better tell me what it's like.' She watched Monroe cut open the pie.

'Mind if I tell you my life story?' She paused, flung both her hands in the air. 'Sorry, clean forgot. I owe you an apology for that scene at the bar.'

Monroe, his mouth full, looked up.

'That geyser who wanted the drink? Do you know him?'

Monroe shook his head.

'Last week there were plenty of people serving behind the bar. He knew I was the chef, but he called the manager over to complain that I hadn't served him quick enough.'

'He's an arsehole,' Monroe chipped in between mouthfuls. 'This is spectacular. It must be the best I've tasted.'

'Yeah. That's what they all tell me. Don't say the same in the morning after they've shagged me.'

Monroe was slightly taken aback. He wasn't sure if she was being outrageous just for effect. Maybe he should call her bluff.

'Is that something you do a lot of?'

'What shagging?' Stevie asked with a seemingly innocent look on her face. 'No, not really. But that's what guy's do, don't they? They butter you up. You know, all sweetness and such. Get you to sleep with them and then they…'

'Disappear,' Monroe said, finding Stevie's forthrightness attractive. 'You got it.' She looked intently at Monroe. 'Are you like that?' Monroe shook his head.

'I don't know,' he replied and shrugged his shoulders.

'I'm a bit old for all that. I suppose I might have been in the past.' He scooped the remaining juice from the pie onto a piece of French bread and put it in his mouth. He waited until he finished it.

'You sound as though you've had a few bad situations.' He looked at Stevie for a reply.

She had placed both her elbows on the table, resting her chin in her hands and was starring hard at Monroe.

'Yeah, well that's another story. You see, I leant to cook by travelling around the world. I was the only girl with a bunch of guys, they couldn't cook so I had to learn.'

'They took advantage of you, then?' Monroe had leant forward, his elbows on the table like Stevie.

'No,' Stevie shook her head. 'You've got it wrong. They were OK. It was later when…' She stopped. She looked as though she wanted to change the subject.

'Your turn. Why you're on your own? Bet you've a wife back home, or away, or something.'

Monroe hesitated. He hadn't come out to talk about Juliet and didn't want to start. He looked away, swirling the remains of his beer.

'Touched a raw spot, have I?'

Monroe turned back and looked Stevie straight in the eye. 'Sort of,' he replied firmly. 'If I tell you, will you promise not to ask any questions?' His eyes remained fixed on Stevie.

She didn't answer at first. She looked hard at Monroe, as if she was trying to penetrate his mind.

'I've seen you somewhere before. Weren't you in the paper a couple of months ago.' A shocked look came over her face. Her hand went up over her mouth.

'I'm so sorry, I didn't…'

Monroe put up his hands to stop her.

'Don't. You weren't to know. I wasn't wearing a badge saying, "Wife murdered."'

'I'm really sorry, Monroe. I'm always putting my foot in things. Not one of life's natural diplomats.' Stevie put her hand out and placed it over Monroe's.

'It's quite appealing,' Monroe replied, relieved. He figured the possibility of any discussion about Juliet had passed.

'What's appealing? My big mouth.' Stevie pulled her hand back and smiled.

'Well sort off. I call it a forthright manner.' Monroe leant back in his chair and grinned.

'Can I buy you a drink?

Before Stevie had time to answer, the young manager, wearing black trousers, a white shirt and a plain dark green tie, appeared behind her. Monroe looked up and said, 'Hi, Guy, how you doing? I haven't been here for some time.'

'I'm fine, Mr Lidlington.' The manager paused and looked away for a second. He turned back to Monroe. He looked a little concerned. 'I'm sorry about Mrs Lidlington.'

'Thanks, Guy. So am I,' Monroe replied quickly, trying to stifle any further conversation about Juliet.

Guy avoided further eye contact with Monroe. He turned to Stevie. 'Could I ask you a favour?'

Stevie laughed. 'I knew it.' She shook her head back and forwards and looked at Monroe and then back to Guy.

'OK, Guy. I'm coming,' she said with a resigned look.

'Sorry, Monroe,' Guy added and turned to walk back to the kitchen.

'Someone's gone sick. Guy's on his own and needs some help in locking up. I'd told him before I'd do it if he had a problem.' Stevie stood up. 'That's why I hung around.'

Monroe raised his nose and said jokingly, 'I thought you wanted to talk to me.'

'I did,' Stevie replied, catching Monroe's gaze.

Monroe stood up and met her eyes. He rubbed his chin.

'You could come back to mine,' he said without thinking, and then realising what he'd done. He'd asked someone he hardly knew, who he'd only met an hour earlier, back to his house, late on a Saturday night.

Stevie starred at Monroe. She didn't say a word. After several seconds she started to nod her head.

'Is that a yes?' Monroe asked, fidgeting from one foot to the other. 'I'll wait for you.'

'OK.' Stevie said. Her eyes still fixed on Monroe. She had a thoughtful expression. 'Be about half an hour. I'll try to be quick.'

* * *

Monroe awoke at eight. He turned his head to watch Stevie sleeping, wondering for a moment what emotions he should be experiencing. *Should I be shocked, feeling guilty, ashamed?* he asked himself, aware that he felt quite normal, good in fact. Gently he manoeuvred himself out of bed, pulled on his boxer shorts and jeans, dumped by the bed, and grabbed a plain navy sweatshirt. He stepped into a pair of old loafers lying around the bedroom and tiptoed out of the room and made for the kitchen where he was welcomed by the sounds of heavy rain rebounding off the patio.

'Shitty,' he said aloud as he waited for the water to fill the kettle.

'Hi.'

Monroe turned sharply around, his back to the sink. He looked intently at Stevie. She was wearing one of his sweatshirts and a pair of his jogger bottoms, standing in the kitchen doorway, one hand on the wall, smiling.

'Do you do talk in the mornings?' she asked as she started to move towards the kitchen table.

'I'm sorry.' Monroe remained standing. He was having trouble with his conscience. Stevie standing by the door, wearing his clothes, with no make up had lifted his soul. *Surely I shouldn't be feeling good?* he asked himself.

'You're not going to start apologising, are you?' Stevie was sitting on a chair, looking at Monroe.

Monroe shook his head.

'I meant, I'm sorry I didn't say something. I was in a bit of a trance.'

'Well,' Stevie said, putting her hands through her short hair. She grinned.

'In the movies, they say things like, "Darling, you were wonderful" and he replies, "You too, sweetie."'

Monroe laughed and came away from where he'd been standing to sit on the chair next to Stevie.

'Do you want me to say that? You won't like it. I was thrown out of drama at school.' He looked up at Stevie.

'How about, would you like some breakfast?'

'Yeah, that's better. Sort of more practical and English. Plus…' She put her hand around Monroe's neck and pulled his face close to her and said with a broad grin, 'I'm starving.'

They cooked the breakfast together. The plan, at first, was for Monroe to cook and Stevie would lay up. But Stevie interrupted Monroe so many times to ask where various items of crockery could be found that it turned into a duo act. Monroe would dash off to locate a plate or something similar, while Stevie took over to turn the eggs, flip the bacon or move around the tomatoes. Both shouted light-hearted instructions to the other, making for a slightly chaotic and witty situation. But it broke the ice. Amidst the debris of it all they sat around Monroe's kitchen table, reading bits of the Sunday papers to each other and engaging in low key banter. At one point Stevie picked up the remains of a piece of cold toast and scrapped it all around her bacon and egg plate. She looked up at the window.

'God, it's still pissing down,' she said while glancing at her watch.

'Shit.' She looked across at Monroe.

'Will you take me in? I'm due at work in half an hour. I've got Sunday roast to cook.'

\* \* \*

For the next few weeks Stevie and Monroe became inseparable. In Stevie, Monroe found someone contrasting in every way to Juliet. She was straightforward, outspoken and fun. She wore funky clothes with chunky jewellery and didn't care a damn about what people thought. Every character trait that had irritated Monroe about Juliet was absent in Stevie. She'd told him about her working class, Scottish background and how she'd fallen out with her mother who'd turned into a complete snob, renouncing her upbringing and paying a speech trainer to change her accent. Monroe told Stevie about his crumbling relationship with Juliet and all about her death.

He'd found a friend, someone he could talk to with ease and who encouraged him to open up, question every preconceived angle on life that he'd come to accept after living with Juliet. He was happy beyond anything he expected or could possible have imagined.

But the locals were displeased. There was gossip about the speed of their relationship so soon after Juliet's death, the age gap between them, the perceived outrageousness of Stevie's behaviour and the continual rumours about Juliet's murder.

# 8

Monroe stopped typing. From the upstairs room he used as his work place, he watched Stevie as she walked down the small broken brick and slate path that led to the front gate. She turned and gave him a wave; a random act, not routine and dependant on her mood. He waved back and noticed her baseball cap, jauntily covering her head.

*It's almost a month,* he calculated, glancing at his watch to check the date. I suppose I should ask myself what I think about it all. But why? I'm happy, I'm content and I love her. We get on well, have similar tastes and share common interests. I don't think I can recall feeling as good about anything for a long time.

Monroe shrugged his shoulders, put his glasses back on and returned to his laptop. He was constructing his third sentence when he saw the unmistakable features of Detective Inspector Symes walking towards his front door.

'Shit,' he said aloud. He stood up, straightened out his old grey sweatshirt and tracksuit trousers and went to the front door.

'Mr Lidlington,' she said coldly, looking him straight in the eye. She was wearing a black, crew-neck woollen top, a pair of dark grey loose-fitting leggings and black canvas slip-ons. Her hair was tied in a ponytail.

'Can I come in?'

Monroe looked her up and down, For a joyous split second he toyed with the idea of saying no. Standing in front of him was a high-ranking, career policewoman who he didn't think would see the humorous side to his objection.

'Follow me,' he said, turning to lead the way to the kitchen. *Probably*, he thought, *the tidiest room in the house.*

'Have a seat.' He nodded his head in the direction of the kitchen table as he walked towards the kettle in the far corner.

'Tea or coffee?' he snapped, turning around and pulling his glasses to the front of his nose to look down at the female detective.

Inspector Symes expression didn't change. Keeping her steely gaze firmly fixed on Monroe's every moment, she pushed the crumpled newspaper to one side, moved a mug containing the dredges of cold coffee away from her and rested her hands, clasped together, on the table and said, 'Our enquiries have drawn a blank, Mr Lidlington.'

Monroe removed his glasses from the end of his nose.

'I thought,' he said, placing the end of one of the frames in his mouth. 'I thought it strange that you hadn't come before.'

'Did you?' snapped Inspector Symes. 'Then why didn't you ring us up?' Symes stood up and took two paces towards Monroe.

'A progress report...' She starred hard into his eyes. 'You know, that sort of thing.'

Monroe turned his back on the detective and flicked on the kettle.

'I take it you didn't want a drink?' he asked facing the kitchen wall. While he waited for her answer he wondered why she'd come. What was her real motive?

*She thinks it was me*, he told himself. Slowly and thoughtfully he poured boiling water onto the coffee granules in the bottom of his mug, added a dash of milk and turned to face the policewoman.

'Is that what I'm supposed to do—ring you up every day and ask if you've found the person who killed my wife?'

'It's normal. The relations of a murder victim to want the murderer brought to justice quickly.' Symes had returned to her chair around the kitchen table. She clasped her hands together and formed an arch with her arms by resting her elbows on the surface of the table. Her knuckles touched the bottom of her mouth, over which her piercing eyes continued to look at Monroe.

'Can you, Mr Lidlington, think of anyone who'd have wanted your wife murdered?'

Monroe was stunned. He felt as though an icy blast had just blown through his brains, disturbing the cosiness of his relationship with Stevie and returning his mind to the grim facts of Juliet's death. He looked at Symes suspiciously.

*Is she really asking me this?* he questioned.

'I don't, Inspector,' he replied.

Inspector Symes positioned her two forefingers on her bottom lip and keeping the tips of her other fingers together fanned them out, tapping their ends purposefully together as she thought.

'Can you tell me again where you were on the night your wife was murdered?' she asked.

Monroe rested back on the work surface. With his left hand he gripped the surface's edge; his right hand covered the top of his mug. He could feel himself bristle.

'I've told you,' he replied, aggressively.

'I know you've told me. But I wanted to hear it again.'

Monroe told Inspector Symes for the fourth or fifth time—he couldn't remember exactly how many times—about the row between Juliet and himself, how she walked out on him and, as a result, how he spent the night on his own. At the end he turned to face Inspector Symes and said, 'What about the fingerprints on the gun. You took mine.'

'Negative, Mr Lidlington. They're not yours.' Symes seemed to have a mocking look on her face.

'Come, come now. If they were yours, we would have had you in well before now.'

\* \* \*

'Hi, bun.' Stevie dropped the carrier bag she'd been carrying by Monroe's feet and put her arms around his waist. Monroe jumped, let go of the knife he'd been using to chop onions and turned around.

'How the hell did you creep up on me like that?' He smiled, wiped his hands on a piece of kitchen paper and put his arms around Stevie's neck.

'Always full of surprises, bun.' Stevie looked into Monroe's eyes, met his mouth and kissed him.

Their embrace lasted for about five minutes. Their lips never parted, but they moved and wriggled and fumbled in a frenzied effort to undress. Items of clothing lay all over the kitchen floor and worktop. When naked they both pulled the other close, each of their hands moving quickly, eagerly over the other's body until they slowly dropped to the floor and made love.

Later they sat around the kitchen table. Empty dishes from the spaghetti Bolognese pushed to one side, a bottle of red wine and a nearly empty jug of water in the middle. Stevie, with her legs resting on another chair, broke off a crusty chunk of bread from the French stick and topped it with a small wedge of Brie. Monroe topped up his glass and poured the remains of the water into Stevie's tumbler. He looked up at her. She was wearing one of his old polo neck jumpers and a baggy, grey tracksuit bottom. Still attached to her ears were a pair of chunky earrings, around her neck hung a chain of rings of many different metals, colours and sizes. During their meal they'd talked endlessly about books, a film they wanted to see and their plans for the weekend. Now they were silent.

'What did you do today, bun?' Stevie asked, as she looked up and caught Monroe's gaze.

He didn't answer immediately; just smiled at her, his lips closed, his chin supported by his thumbs from his clasped hands.

'I wrote all day. Once you'd gone I started and didn't stop until about five, when I popped out to get a few things.' He kept his eyes firmly fixed on Stevie.

'Did it go well?' she asked in an upbeat tone.

'Yeah. Did about 1500 words.' He paused and looked away for a couple of seconds. 'No interruptions. That helps.'

'You genius.' Stevie pushed her chair back, rose and came around the back of Monroe's chair. He raised his hands up to meet hers. Standing behind him, she started to massage his head.

'How long have we been together, bun?' she asked twisting Monroe's head to one side.

Monroe tried to remember when they met.

'I guess about two months,' he replied, looking up. 'Maybe a bit more. I think we met on November 3rd, didn't we?'

'Don't ask me, I never know what the date is.' She turned Monroe's face forward and continued rubbing his scalp.

'Why do you ask?' Monroe asked, curious.

'Don't know really. Just came to me. Sort of feels good being with you. I mean...' Stevie shrugged her shoulders. 'We've done all that, love you business. We know we're an item.'

Neither Stevie nor Monroe seemed in any way fazed by their relationship. Together they appeared relaxed and happy, spontaneous in everything. When one of them wanted to talk, the other listened. When either of them felt tired the other would do the chores. They made love often, impromptu and unpremeditated, whenever and wherever they wanted to with no recourse to whatever event they may have interrupted. They had many common interests, but respected entirely each other's peculiarities and individual tastes. Often they'd disagree, but would agree to differ. In just over two months they had fallen frighteningly in love with each other.

* * *

In early February, with little debate, Monroe and Stevie decided to marry. They didn't want any fuss—just a small ceremony, and as soon as possible. It was at that stage in his relationship with Stevie that

Monroe thought it about time he told Greg. It wasn't that he had been holding back the news through any fear of indifference or negativity from Greg—quite the contrary. He knew that Greg would be pleased and happy for him, as excited as he was. Perhaps he should ask Greg to be his best man, he thought, as he picked up the handset and dialled Greg's number. Filled with eager anticipation at Greg's reaction, he walked to the french windows and starred out at the bleak and empty garden. Long shadows from the winter sun, disappearing behind the rooftops, formed stripes of light and shade on the tiny lawn. As Greg's cheerful, optimistic voice answered, Monroe's eyes were taken to an oasis of brightness at the foot of an old, stone birdbath. All around, in a great clump twinkling in the fading sunlight, was an uplifting show of snowdrops. He felt his heart beat faster.

* * *

Greg tossed his phone onto the floor. He didn't care if he'd broken it. It was of no consequence. He felt empty, disorientated, cut loose, as though someone had just put him through a rapid process of deflation, like he'd imagined the basket of a hot air balloon would fall to the ground if it was suddenly detached from the large gasbag above.

'A replacement for mum,' he'd said to his dad. 'How could you do that? Mum's only been dead a few months.'

*Since mum died, I've tried so hard to be positive,* Greg told himself. I've made lots of friends, joined every club and society possible, played masses of sport—all to keep mum out of my mind. Now he tells me he's met someone who has made him happier than ever and is marrying her in three weeks time. I haven't even bloody well met her. Greg got up from his bed, stumbled on his phone and kicked it across the room.

'My God,' he said aloud. *He must have been seeing her at Christmas.* He didn't let up, at all.

'Shit.' *Does he think he can just ring me up, out of the blue, and tell me his selfish plans and expect me to be brilliantly happy?*

He paced furiously over to the window of his room. Beneath him stood a spectacular view of Palace Green in front of Durham Cathedral. A scene he showed to all his visitors and told them that not many people get the opportunity to live in a 12$^{th}$ century castle. He didn't see any of it. It was all just a blur. A feeling of despondency swept over him, the likes of which he hadn't experienced since the dark days surrounding his mother's death and her funeral. He bit his lips, but couldn't stop the tears that started to roll down his cheeks.

\* \* \*

Stevie wore a plain rubbed silk grey jacket, worn over a black t-shirt, and a matching skirt. Around her neck hung a simple pendant made from a Thai pewter miniature fish hanging on a thin black silk cord. Her blonde hair was cropped tight to her head. Monroe, dressed in a raw silk navy suit and open neck white silk shirt, gasped as she came through the door of the local restaurant they'd chosen for the occasion, accompanied by her mother. He thought she looked beautiful beyond his wildest dreams. Standing next to Monroe in a smart navy suit and tie was Joe Walters. Monroe and Stevie had only wanted the legal minimum number of people to attend the wedding. Stevie's mother, Jennifer, although somewhat estranged from her daughter, seemed the natural choice as one of the witnesses and, by Stevie asking her, would provide something of an opportunity for a reconciliation. Monroe chose Joe Walters after Greg had told him flatly that not only would he not be best man, he also wouldn't attend. Monroe, although not a close friend with Joe, had always had respect for the guy, both as Juliet's boss and in the way he'd handled her death and then continued to communicate with Monroe on a fortnightly basis afterwards—just to make sure he was OK. Apart from the registrar, nobody else attended.

From The Net was probably the best fish restaurant in the country, certainly the best in Padstow. Monroe had persuaded the owner to open the restaurant to the public at 1 p.m.—normally it opened at noon—on their wedding day, giving them time for the ceremony and some drinks in private. The restaurant, originally a large family house built about 1850, overlooked the harbour and was split up into several medium size rooms, each large enough to house about four or five tables of varying size.

And so, at 12.15, on the last day of February, in a light and airy room with a sea view and a dusty pink terrazzo tiled floor they were married. Apart from the makeshift registrar's desk and chair and four chairs for the bridal party, no other furniture filled the room—it all had been cleared out. Perched on the desk was a simple flower arrangement of local daffodils and snowdrops mingled with Cornish heather gathered from Bodmin moor. Both Monroe and Stevie looked sublimely happy. Afterwards, at an intimate table in the restaurant, the wedding party of four ate a meal of oysters, fruits de mare and a wedding pavlova. Monroe, Jennifer and Joe drank a bottle of Bollinger Grand Cru and a bottle of 1990 Chablis. Stevie had a sip of champagne and then drunk water.

The taxi taking Monroe and Stevie home drew up at Monroe's house at 4.30 in the afternoon. The house was in darkness and heavy rain pounded the narrow path to the front door. It didn't bother the newlyweds. They jumped out of the car and raced each up the slippery and wet stones.

'Supposed to be lucky,' Stevie said as Monroe fumbled with the lock.

'What is?' Monroe asked, turning the key.

'Raining on your wedding day.'

'Oh yes,' he replied positively. 'I remember somebody telling me that year's ago.' He pushed the door open and took Stevie by the hand.

'If we're talking about traditions, I think I'm supposed to carry you across the threshold.' He smiled and arranged his hands and arms in such a way that Stevie could drop into them.

'Come on, then,' he added.

Stevie gave him a slightly mocking look and laughed.

'I think I'm taller than you. Do you really want to?'

He flashed her a warm smile and stood up, putting his arm around her waist. 'Come on, let's go in.' Arm in arm, they walked in, turned and starred into each other's eyes.

'Welcome to our home, Mrs Lidlington.'

'Thank you, bun.' Stevie put her arms around Monroe's neck and looked at him. 'What's wrong? You seem a bit distant.'

Monroe was looking away. He'd caught sight of the picture of Greg and himself hanging beside the door into the kitchen, reminding him that Greg hadn't sent a single message. Apart from during the actual ceremony, Monroe had kept his phone switched on all through the day expecting Greg to call. Earlier, the euphoria of the occasion, his heightened emotions and the alcohol had helped to lessen his disappointment until that moment.

'Sorry,' he said turning back to face Stevie. 'That picture of Greg.' He motioned with his head towards the picture and then screwed up his face.

'He hasn't rung, has he? 'Stevie took both his hands in hers. She looked into his eyes.

'Monroe, he's upset. It's quite understandable.' She pulled Monroe closer. 'Look bun, he'll come round. But it might just take a little time.'

Monroe looked into her big blue eyes, firmly fixed on his. He thought he saw a hint of moisture. 'I know, but…'

'Come on,' she said, using her hand to wipe a small tear from her cheek. She took Monroe by the hand and started to lead him towards the staircase.

'We've things to do, bun.'

# 9

Monroe lifted Stevie's legs from his lap and rose from the corner of the chintz-covered couch that he'd been occupying for the last two hours. He dropped the paper he'd been reading onto the bare floorboards to join the pile of other randomly discarded Sunday papers and stretched his arms above his head. The bottom of his old navy jumper exposed a little of his midriff above his faded jeans. He was barefoot.

'Is that a feeding time sign you're making, bun?' Stevie put the paperback she'd been reading, open pages down, on the couch and stood up to join him.

'Not necessarily, hon.' He smiled and caught Stevie's glance.

'I was going to get another drink, a little relief from...' He looked towards one of the speakers and pointed with his thumb in a slightly disapproving way.

'Want one?'

'You don't like rap, eh?' Stevie walked towards the CD player.

'You fix the drinks and I'll put something of yours on.' She looked at Monroe. 'Get me a glass of water, bun.'

'Thanks, hon,' Monroe said, smiling at Stevie as he set off in the direction of the kitchen. Her consideration pleased him. He knew she didn't care much for his taste in music.

'What's Vivaldi like?' Stevie shouted after him.

'Try Four Seasons.'

*Maybe*, he thought, nodding his head to himself. 'You might like it.'

'I'll give it a try, bun,' Stevie replied positively, but with little enthusiasm.

'What do you think?' Monroe asked as he returned with a generous slug of malt whisky, grainy and pale beige in colour, and a glass of water with a slice of lime for Stevie. He looked at her, sprawled full length again on the couch and holding her book above her head.

She sniffed and shook her head, slightly puckering her lips.

'I suppose it's better than some of your stuff.' She took the glass from Monroe's outstretched hand and looked up at him, smiling.

'Leave it on. You put up with mine.'

'Sure?' Monroe reached down to retrieve his paper and sat down opposite Stevie.

'Well sort of...' Stevie stopped. 'Oh it doesn't matter,' she said, throwing her hands apart.

'I'm gonna make a bite to eat. You stay here and I'll see what I can pull together.' Stevie stood up, came over to where Monroe was sitting, leant over him and gave him a kiss on the cheek. She smiled.

'Bun?'

'What?'

'Turn the speakers off in the kitchen.'

Monroe let the paper drop to his lap. He looked up at the old ceiling rose. A hazy, euphoric mood of contentment started to envelop his senses.

*It's nearly a month*, he thought. It seems only a few days ago. Each day is different and varied, a new piquancy about it. We row terribly, but never without making it up. Neither of us wants to be the winner. Sooner or later one of us makes a peace gesture or says something that brings us back together. He thought again about the music, a few minutes earlier. Typical of her generous nature, so prevalent in everything she did, he told himself. When they made love—intensely passionate as they were—she would always look for different ways to please him.

*Is it real?* he asked himself. Should he prepare for a sudden event that could shatter their blissful existence, causing friction and bad vibes between them? He shook his head. I don't think so, he thought, quickly dismissing his fears and happily letting his mind return to the cosy mood he'd been enjoying earlier. Soon his eyelids felt heavy, closing often, his head tilting to the left. Feebly, without any conviction, he tried to stay awake, and failed.

Singing to herself, Stevie started to slice a cucumber, stopping to dart to the fridge and pull out a jar of sun-dried tomatoes and half a cos lettuce.

*He's not like any man I've ever met*, she told herself, shaking a handful of the tomatoes onto her chopping board. He'll always ask me how my day's been, always interested in what I've done.

'Oh hell, have we any feta cheese,' she shouted aloud as she darted back to fridge.

'Good—and some olives.' *A pucker Greek salad*, she told herself as she returned to the chopping board with the cheese and a tub of olives.

*And we talk so much—have so much in common*, she thought. She smiled, as she quickly assembled the salad, remembering the heated disagreement they once had over third world debt and how it all ended up with them going to bed and making love. How that typified their relationship, she thought—moreish and crumbly, flaky bits falling off now and again but the whole thing staying solid. Could be called shocking, the way they got it all together. Sex on the first night and all that. But none of it worried her, and nor did the 20 plus years between them. She put out a tray with two glasses and a bottle of red wine, some mineral water, a large white bowl containing the salad, two hot ciabatta rolls and two plates with cutlery. As her hands took hold of the handles to the tray she glanced round at Monroe's kitchen.

*A gentle glow hangs in the air*, she thought. Rays of light from the ceiling dropped onto the dark green furniture and the scrubbed wooden top, bringing about a warm and comfortable mood. Just as she felt.

\* \* \*

'OK. Have a good trip. I'll come up to see you when you're back. Bye then.' Monroe put the handset down on the table and stood still, staring blankly out of the french windows into the dark night. *That hurt*, he said to himself.

'What's up?' Stevie asked, rising to go to him. Greg's call had come in the middle of their supper. Monroe's plate with his unfinished meal lay where he'd dumped it on the floor by his leather chair. While he'd been talking Stevie had sat silently, listening to his stilted words.

'It was Greg, wasn't it?' she said. Her arms clasped firmly around his waist.

Monroe didn't move. He felt devastated. Greg had just told him that he wasn't coming home for Easter as planned and was going on a trip with some friends to South America. He'd been left some money by his mother and was using that to fund it. Monroe didn't disapprove of Greg's travelling bug, he'd positively encouraged it. But as a way of breaking the ice and trying to build a relationship with Stevie, and having not seen Greg since Christmas, they'd planned to spend some quality time with him. They'd booked theatres in London, hired a cottage in the Scilly Isles for a few days and taken an option on a long weekend in New York.

'Going to tell me about it?' Stevie had moved to Monroe's side. She looked into his eyes. They stared transfixed into the black night outside.

Monroe knew he was ignoring Stevie and that in doing so was

wrong. But at that moment he saw Stevie as the cause of Greg's coldness towards him and was confused, at a loss as how to cope with it.

'I'm sorry,' he said at last.

'He's not coming home, is he?' Stevie said, looking at Monroe's expressionless face.

'No, he's not,' Monroe replied looking away. He couldn't look Stevie in the eye. Irrational as he knew he was, he blamed her for Greg's aloofness. Suddenly he feared that the bonds and ties that held him and Greg together were beginning to untangle to a point that frightened him.

*Might I loose him*, he asked himself? He turned to face Stevie and said, 'I'm going for a walk. I'll clear up later.'

'What?' Stevie responded incredulously. 'Just like that? Aren't you going to talk to me about it?'

'I can't at the moment. Let me just have a few moments alone.' Monroe turned and walked towards the door.

Stevie, with small tears forming in her eyes, leant down to pick up Monroe's plate of half-eaten food.

'OK,' she said, turning her head away from Monroe's view.

\* \* \*

In time, Monroe came round. Stevie saw to that. She let him have his space and then found the right moment to have a discussion. She told him that Greg's behaviour was quite normal and that they'd have to allow him time to sort things out in his mind and at his pace.

'Him going away is probably a good thing,' she'd said. 'If we push him too much, he's likely to run further and farther away.'

At first Monroe had bucked at the idea of Stevie telling him how to deal with his son. 'What the hell do you think you know about it?' he'd yelled at her. 'It's because of you that he's staying away.' Stevie didn't respond to his comment. She simply left him until eventually he came to her, wanting to discuss it all. They agreed that he should plan some time soon to go and see Greg—just the two of them. In his mind he squared his earlier recriminations towards Stevie by telling himself he was just venting his emotions on her as the obvious target. In truth, he admitted, he was grateful for her empathy and understanding.

The day before Monroe was due to go to see Greg in Durham was Stevie's birthday. They dined at a favourite restaurant in a nearby village. As a starter Stevie had local scallops, Monroe had a salad of Cornish mackerel. Both of them shared a small crown roast of new season's lamb followed by fresh fruit salad and two espresso coffees. Monroe had most of a bottle of Frascati, Stevie drunk water.

'Look,' shouted Stevie as their car drew up alongside the gate to their house.

Monroe pushed open the door and ran as fast as he could up the path to the front door, swinging wide open.

'Stay there,' he yelled back at Stevie.

'Don't be stupid, Monroe. If you're going in I'm coming with you.' Stevie shouted back as she followed.

'Wait for me. Don't go in without me.'

Five minutes later they stood together in their living room surveying a scene of heartbreaking untidiness. Whoever had broken in had done so via the french windows; the pane by the handle smashed and the door left open. Drawers had been ransacked, pictures taken from the walls, cushions from the couches flung on the floor. The wilful unmaking of their love nest didn't stop in the living room. As they went from one room to another they witnessed the same destructive sight. Nothing had been left untouched.

'Monroe,' Stevie said, finally, after neither had spoken. Both had just viewed the depressing spectacle. 'I don't think they've taken anything.'

Monroe looked at her and then around their bedroom again. The small TV was still in place. His iPod was in its usual position on the floor, by his side of the bed. Bemused, he went to the drawer where he kept a few of his valuables. The Tag watch Juliet had given him early on in their marriage, a Mont Blanc pen Greg had given him on his fiftieth, a silver framed picture of his parents which he periodically displayed and then took down—all were still in there usual places.

'But they must have been after something,' he said after a while, in response to Stevie's earlier statement.

'Yeah, but what, Monroe?'

'Come on, hon. It's your birthday. Let's leave it and go to bed.'

\* \* \*

Large drops of rain dribbled incessantly down the back of Stevie's neck, gradually enlarging the sodden patch of her black t-shirt until it stretched almost from one shoulder to the other. Her back ached, she felt cold and her feet were sodden. She'd run from where she'd parked the car, encountering endless puddles from the deluges of water that had soaked the uneven stones, forming the path up to their front door.

'Gee man,' she said aloud. 'Could it be worse?' She pushed open the door, leapt inside, flung her soaked denim jacket to the floor and ripped off her soggy top to stand for a moment in only her bra and baggy khaki trousers.

'Oh shit,' she shouted out loudly. All around her was the depressing mess caused by the break-in. She leant against the wall, slide to the floor and burst into tears.

That morning, Monroe had left at 4 a.m. for Durham, leaving Stevie still asleep. He'd rung from his car for someone to come and fix the door and board up the broken glass, which was completed by nine. Stevie had to leave early for work, telling herself she'd clear it all up when she returned. She'd gone in to the yacht club to prepare for a beginning of season sailing supper and had been so busy that the burglary had slipped her mind. It was past midnight by the time she came home.

*I wished I drank*, she said to herself as she trudged, her trainers squelching beneath her, to the kitchen. She flicked on the kettle, flopped into one of the chairs and pulled off her shoes and damp socks, leaving them in a dirty, wet pile beneath her chair.

'I think I'm gonna scream,' she said and did, loudly and long.

*That's better. Where do I start?* she asked herself as she poured the boiling water onto a tea bag and let her eyes roam amongst the disorder before her. An upended drawer of crockery, its contents spread across the stone floor, an empty carousel from a corner cupboard with tins and containers of dried food dumped all over the work surface. Wherever she looked there was no mistaking the mayhem. Still wearing only her bra and damp trousers she started to put things right.

She didn't think or question her actions. Nor did she bother to wonder what the perpetuators of the crime where after. That could come later when Monroe and her had more time to think about it. All she wanted to do was to get the house in some order and go to bed. With that in mind she worked tirelessly until she finally reached their bedroom at one thirty and flopped onto the bed.

*I don't think I can do any more,* she told herself as great surges of tiredness swept through her aching body. She slid off her trousers, letting them drop to the floor and gently eased herself into bed.

At 2.30 she woke with a pounding headache. *Where the hell would Monroe keep his Nurofen?* she asked herself, scrabbling in the dark on her hands and knees through the piles of clothes and stuff on the floor. She stood up and shivered, walking to their connected bathroom. The coldness of the tiled floor on her bare feet made her shudder as she grouped for the light switch. The sudden blaze of light from the powerful spots intensified the pain in her head.

*There's a bathroom cabinet in here,* she remembered.

*Please, oh God, let there be some tablets in it.* Her hands tore and fumbled to open it. An old razor, a spare toothbrush, some hair gel, a packet of soap and a few pocket size tissues, but no Nurofen.

'Oh hell, Monroe. Where do you keep the stuff? I know you've got some. I saw you take one the other day.'

In her desperation her eyes focused on the cupboard under the sink.

*Does he keep them there?* she asked herself as she dropped down onto her hands and knees to open the door.

'Fucking hell, it's locked,' she yelled out.

*Who the hell locks a cupboard under a sink?* In her frustration she shook the fragile door several times. To her surprise, it sprung open revealing a shelf of many baskets, all in a broad gauge plastic mesh, containing sun creams, plasters and medicines of various types.

'Yes,' she yelled aloud, reaching forward to grab the pack of Boots Ibuprofen lodged on the top of one of them. The tip of her right forefinger touched something hard and metallic. Uncertain of what she'd find she reached down between the small cardboard packs until she met resistance from a solid object lurking amidst the many containers. Puzzled, she pulled the basket out and hastily discarded the top layer of stuff all over the bathroom floor.

Until that moment she'd never seen a gun close up. She looked at its eerie matt black finish, its small but perfectly formed handle and its seven to ten centimetre barrel; and then she looked at the trigger and audibly gasped. She could feel herself begin to shake. Her mouth felt dry and she started to look around the room at nothing in particular, except the gun.

*What do I do?* Should I pack it up and put it away or leave everything exactly as it is until Monroe comes home and show it to...

Her mind trailed off. She realised that the cupboard had been locked and not touched by the intruder.

*It must have been there all the time,* she told herself. All of a sudden tremors took hold of her body. She was shaking from head to foot, icy cold and desperate for something to drink. Propped up against the wall, her naked legs outstretched in front of her, she let one part of her mind interrogate the other.

*Does he know it's here?* she asked herself.

*Of course he does. He must have put it here.*

*Why? What would he want it for?*

*People do have guns. They keep them for security.*

*Why didn't he tell me?*

And then her mind took a different tack.

*Why hasn't someone been arrested for Juliet's murder? It's months since she was killed.*

Stevie felt the pain return to her head. She looked at her feet and they were beginning to shake again. This time she didn't feel cold, only clammy and nauseous as though she wanted to be sick.

'He wouldn't do that,' she said aloud, trying to raise herself off the floor. She flushed cold water over her face, looked at herself in the mirror and shook her head.

'Not murder, not Monroe.'

In the morning, after little sleep, she plucked up courage to ring Monroe. It was, she thought, her only course of action. She didn't know how he'd react or whether she was acting in a way that would inflict more pain and anguish on herself. In the night, many times, she'd considered running away. But after finally falling asleep at 5.30, tired beyond belief, she awoke at seven feeling surprisingly human and rational.

She felt much better after she'd spoken with him. He had expressed genuine shock and told her to do nothing until he arrived home. He would set off immediately and aim to get home as soon as possible. She trusted him and berated herself for being so fickle and irrational and stupid the previous night. She'd be at work when he arrived home, she'd told him. Not to worry, he'd said. He'd deal with the gun and tidy up. They could talk about it when she came home.

# 10

Monroe steered his ten-year old Land Rover to a halt in the next road to his. The vehicle was passed its visual best. That was how Monroe liked his cars; reliable workhorses, not fashion items. On days when Padstow was crawling with tourists—he guessed it was one of those days—he found it nigh impossible to find a space outside his house or even in the same road. Unsure, not knowing what lay before him, he withdrew his keys from the ignition and climbed out. He took slow and unsteady steps, ponderous, lacking any vitality. He knew he was out of sorts, some of it he blamed on completing a five hundred-mile drive back from Durham in record time and almost without stopping. But what really bugged him was the gun. It had done so throughout the long journey.

*How could Stevie find a gun in the bathroom?* he'd kept asking himself, time and time again; never arriving at an answer he found convincing. He didn't have a gun. He'd never had a gun, so somebody must have brought it in. But who? and why take the trouble of hiding it under all his medicines and first-aid stuff? He reached his front door, his mind full of unresolved questions and doubts. Stevie wouldn't make it all up, he told himself as he twisted his key in the lock.

He dumped his bag in the hall, hitched up his jeans and leant against the wall. Tiredness attacked him with a vengeance, like a laser guided missile, intent only on destroying its target. His head ached, his limbs felt weak, as though they were immersed in a trough of treacle every time he tried to move. He was pooped, fit for nothing apart from a good night's sleep. Gradually he slid down the wall until he lay in a crumpled heap on the wooden floor.

Stevie pushed open the front door just after 11.00, immediately looking down the hall, into the kitchen for Monroe. It was in darkness. Not wasting any time she sped to the closed living room door.

'Monroe,' she shouted loudly 'Where are you?'

'Up here,' came his reply from the next floor.

'Where's up here,' Stevie yelled as she hurtled up the stairs. She ran into their bedroom to find Monroe propped up in bed, reading a book. She came to an abrupt halt just a few paces inside the door and just stared at him.

Monroe looked up. *That's cool*, he thought. Stevie was wearing a red t-shirt, with the words 'no more landmines' blazoned in white letters across the front, and a pair of baggy khaki shorts.

'How's your day?'

'Monroe?' Stevie said with obvious anxiety in her voice. 'What about the gun?'

Still holding his book in his right hand, Monroe replied, 'I've dealt with that.' He thought for a bit.

'And I've tidied up. But I was so tired from the drive…'

'Yes, I'm sure you are.' Stevie was still standing, looking directly at him.

'But what about the gun?'

Monroe sensed her concern. He knew he'd have to explain more, before the matter could be dropped.

'I took it straight to the police. They're looking into it.' He looked at her troubled expression.

'What's up? You look upset, not yourself.'

Stevie strutted from one side of the room to the other, occasionally giving Monroe the odd glance. She flung her bag onto the bed and stopped short of the bottom brass bedstead.

'Why was it here, Monroe?' She leant on the crossbars, ran her right hand across her cropped hair and focused her piercing eyes at Monroe.

'I'm bloody upset. We've been married barely a month and I find a gun in the bathroom. A gun that you must have known was there, and all you can bloody well say is...'

'Stop.' Monroe, wearing just a pair of boxer shorts, dropped his legs to the side of the bed and came up to where Stevie was standing.

'No, Monroe.' Stevie took a couple of paces backwards.

'I need more than that. I need to know why the gun was here in the first place.'

'I don't know, Stevie,' Monroe replied, raising his voice. 'It's nothing to do with me. I didn't put it there.' Monroe could see he wasn't making much of an impression.

'Well, who bloody well did? The cupboard was locked.'

'I don't know, hon.' He moved closer to Stevie again.'

Stevie didn't move. At first she looked away and then, after a few seconds, turned to meet his eyes.

'Monroe?' she asked.

'What?' He put his hand on her shoulder, trying to give himself a little time before her next question.

'Why haven't they charged someone with Juliet's murder?'

'Because they haven't found anyone.' Monroe pulled his hand away from Stevie's shoulder and kept his gaze firmly on her.

'Why did you ask?'

'Because she was shot, wasn't she?'

Monroe staggered back as though someone had suddenly hit him. He reached for the bedstead to steady himself. He likened the experience to the time when the judge sentenced him to two years in prison, as though someone had kicked him in the stomach. Numbed, he was at a loss to reply. After a few seconds, aware that Stevie was looking at him, he said, 'Do you think I killed her?'

Monroe stood still, looking at Stevie's grey and drawn face. He could see moisture in her eyes. Her iips started to tremble and she turned away.

'I'm sorry, Monroe.' She started to cry. 'I don't know what to think. I just know I'm frightened and confused.' With her tear stained face, she starred at Monroe's.

'Bun, just tell me you didn't kill Juliet,' she sobbed, taking refuge in Monroe's outstretched arms.

Later they both lay naked in bed, side by side and alone with their own thoughts. Monroe convinced himself he'd done the right thing by disposing of the gun in the sea. If he'd given it to the police they'd be a great hullabaloo as to how he came across it. And that, no doubt, would bring Detective Inspector Symes back to ask more questions. Someone he found he disliked, intensely.

He'd lied to Stevie about what he'd done with the gun, but that was deliberate. He knew if he'd told her he'd disposed of it in the sea; she would have asked more questions. Besides, when he told her the gun that was used to shoot Juliet was found a few days after her death on a relatively deserted beach near Rock, her concerns seemed to moderate and she became more tranquil, suggesting they both went to bed.

'Night, bun.'

'Night, hon.' Monroe turned over on his side, aware that this was the first night since they'd been married that they hadn't made love.

Stevie had the next day off. She awoke first and went to the kitchen.

'One rasher of bacon,' she said aloud as she checked the contents of the fridge. In minutes, a lone mushroom, half a tomato and an egg accompanied the bacon in a pan.

'Bun,' she yelled up the stairs. 'Come down, I've done you breakfast.' Keeping half an eye on the pan she quickly ground some coffee beans, poured out a glass of orange juice and chucked some bread in the toaster. She heard Monroe's footsteps.

'Perfect,' she said. The bacon and egg, coffee and toast were all coming together at the right time.

Dead leaves left over from the winter, neglected plants and empty terracotta pots surrounded Monroe and Stevie as they ate their breakfast on the patio. Monroe picked up a piece of toast, broke a small piece off it and started to mop up the remains of the fry up.

'This is the best bit,' he said approvingly.

Stevie, peeling an orange and with a large mug of coffee next to her left elbow, looked at Monroe and smiled. 'Glad you like it, hon.'

She reached out and touched Monroe's hand. 'Sorry about last night,' she said as she squeezed his hand. 'I'd never seen a gun before and was so scared.'

Monroe looked away and caste his eyes over the amount of work he had to do to get the garden straight. He thought about his response, knowing that any return to the previous night's conversation would lead to more heartache and was best avoided.

'No problem, hon. Just forget about it.' Monroe shifted in his seat, rested his elbow on the tabletop and held his bottom lip with his right hand. Straightening his t-shirt, he pointed to the garden.

'Look at all that. Want to give me a hand?'

Stevie, wearing a pair of shorts that barely covered her backside and a bikini top, stretched her long legs out on the adjacent chair.

'If you want me to, bun. But first tell me about Greg.'

Monroe turned to look at her. He was pleased she'd asked about Greg. The short time he had spent with him had gone better than expected.

'It was good. You were right. He is coming round.'

Monroe told her about their meal together, the film they'd seen, Greg's friends and the pub quiz when he badly let down Greg's team, giving them all an excuse to celebrate their poor performance by staying in the pub till closing time.

'He's happy for us all to meet up,' Monroe concluded. 'I'll set up a weekend.'

During the rest of the warm May day they worked together in the garden. By seven as the sun started to disappear, a slight chill encouraged them to move inside. Monroe thanked Stevie for her help, offering to cook supper. They ate steaks cooked on the barbecue, jacket potatoes with crumbled Stilton cheese and strawberries and cream. Monroe drunk a couple of glasses of red wine, Stevie stuck to water. They talked a lot, often laughed, and later, made love with their usual abandon and tenderness

* * *

'Shit, I'll be late,' Stevie muttered as she tumbled out of bed. Monroe had left early for a meeting in London and turned off the alarm, leaving her sound asleep.

'That was clever, bun,' she said as she ran naked to the bathroom, turned on the shower, squeezed a blob of toothpaste onto her brush— some of the sticky paste dropping to the floor—and jumped in, toothbrush in hand.

'Hell. Where's the towel?' she yelled, stepping out on the floorboards, drops of water forming puddles alongside her feet. *It's always when I'm in a hurry*, she said to herself as she raced naked and dripping wet to where they kept the clean towels. She grabbed a thick, deep blue one and wrapped it all around her. *God*, I haven't time for make-up, she thought, towelling her hair dry while pulling on a pair of knickers and grey fatigue trousers. She dropped the towel to the floor, grabbed her bra and flung open the cupboard where she kept her tops.

'That's lucky,' she muttered, taking a sleeveless black ribbed vest from the top of the pile. She pushed her feet into a pair of trainers, dabbed on a little lipstick and ran down the stairs. Halfway down the hallway to the door the phone rang. She ignored it.

*They'll leave a message*, she thought and then remembered that Monroe said he'd call. She wanted to talk to him.

'Is Monroe there?' a female voice asked. She sounded young, well-spoken.

'No, he's not. Can I take a message?'

'When is he back?' The caller asked, sounding disappointed.

'Who is that?' Stevie asked, beginning to be curious.

'No problem, I'll call back,' the caller replied, cutting off immediately

'Rude bitch,' she muttered, dialling 1471. It was a London number and not one she recognised. She dumped the phone, hurtled out of the door and ran to where she had parked her car, forgetting about the call until Monroe returned that evening. She'd been too busy.

'I had an odd phone call this morning,' she said after they'd eaten.

Monroe rose from the table, pulled up his trousers, picked up a couple of dirty dishes and said, 'Yeah? Tell me about it.' He sauntered off towards the dishwasher.

'A woman rang asking for you.' Stevie put her feet up on Monroe's chair and pushed off her trainers. She leant sideways to pile up the few things Monroe had left on the table.

'Did you get her name?' he asked, turning back to face Stevie.

'She didn't give one. Said she'd ring back.' Stevie gave Monroe a quick glance while picking the flakes from the piece of Parmesan and dropping them onto the remains of the French bread. 'Quite a posh voice.'

Monroe had his back to her. 'Means nothing to me,' he said, washing the pasta pan. 'Maybe it was one of those financial people. They always use your first names, as though they had known you for ages.

'Hey this Parmesan is good. Where did you get it?' Stevie asked.

\* \* \*

Three days later, when Monroe had gone into town, Stevie received another call. The same voice as before asked for Monroe. Stevie put the phone down and dialled 1471. This time the call came from a mobile.

'You called,' Stevie said when somebody answered.

'I wanted Monroe,' the voice replied.

'He's not here. Who are you?'

'Just an old friend. I've been away and thought it would be nice to look him up. You see, some time ago we had a bit of a fling and…'

Stevie ended the call. The woman's words, 'we had a bit of a fling' filled her mind. When Monroe and her discussed their past, he had said he'd never had any affairs while married to Juliet. She felt confused and upset, finding yet again she was questioning Monroe's honesty.

\* \* \*

At 1.15., when Monroe returned, Stevie was waiting for him. She stood by the table outside where she'd laid up a light lunch.

'Monroe, she said urgently, as he walked up to greet her.

'What's up, hon?' he replied, dumping his bags on the flagstones. 'You look worried.'

'I am, Monroe.' Stevie took hold of his hands and pulled him to her. 'That woman called again today.'

'What woman?' Monroe asked, unaware who Stevie was talking about.

'The woman who called the other day. She said she was an old friend and had a brief fling with you.'

Monroe pulled away.

'Look,' he said angrily, shaking his head. 'I don't know who you are talking about, who she is and I didn't have a fling with anyone. Can we leave it at that?' He went into the kitchen, returning quickly with the phone, a pen and notepad.

'What was her name and number? I'm going to call her.'

'I can't remember. I didn't write it down.' Stevie looked across the table to where Monroe was standing by the kitchen door. 'I'm not making this up, Monroe.'

Monroe reached inside the kitchen, dumped the phone, pen and notepad on the windowsill and said, 'Come on. Let's eat.'

He went to Stevie, putting his arm around her shoulders.

'Yeah, let's do that,' Stevie said, sounding unsure.

* * *

That night, for the second time since they'd been married they didn't make love. Stevie had to work late and complained of being too tired. In truth she was worried. It had been quiet at work, most of her time spent thinking about the past few days. All night she lay awake, tossing and turning and going over everything time and again. She was glad when dawn broke. It gave her the excuse to get up. She pulled on an old grey tracksuit and a pair of plimsolls and padded quietly down the stairs and out of the house for a walk.

*Perhaps*, she said to herself, invigorated by the refreshing breeze that wafted from the harbour, *I'm making too much of this.*

* * *

'Hello,' Stevie answered tentatively, when the phone rang on the next occasion she was in the house alone. She'd just come home from work, tired and hungry and in no mood to talk to some woman who, if Monroe was telling the truth, was out to cause trouble.

*But why was she doing it?* Stevie asked herself, while waiting for the caller to talk. And how did she get the number?

'Stevie?' a man's voice said, sounding slightly unsure.

'Yes,' Stevie replied, equally uncertain. 'Who's that?'

'It's Greg,' he paused. 'I wanted to talk to you.'

'Me?' Stevie answered, deliberately trying to sound as though Greg had made a mistake. In truth, she hoped Greg meant what he'd said.

'Why me?'

'I thought it about time we met.'

Stevie quickly caste her mind back to a conversation with Monroe. He'd said that Greg had suggested a meeting.

'When?' she asked, urgently, keen to keep the momentum going.

'Are you coming down to us or do you want us to meet you somewhere?' she added, unsure of Greg's schedule and not aware if he was able to move around the country.

'It's just you I wanted to meet. Have a chat, get to know you.'

Stevie felt a twinge of caution. Would he just turn it into a lecture about how bad she was for his father? she asked herself.

'I'm a bit…'

'Hold on. I'm not going to give you a hard time. I've talked it all through with dad. I just wanted to build a bridge. You know, get something going between us, all that sort of stuff.'

*Hell, Stevie. Don't be so scared*, she thought. The guy's trying hard. Give him a break. And then she had an idea.

'How about me coming up there. Can you fix me up with somewhere to stay?'

# 11

Full of doubt and uncertainty, Stevie waited outside Café Nero for Greg. Narrow cobbled streets, hilly and unique in character, devoid of much of the usual mass of plastic, neon and glass—proliferate in most shopping areas—led off from where she stood in the market place. Over the years, those responsible for maintaining the historic and traditional features of the city of Durham had done a good job. All the well-known retail brands were represented in the city; but shop designers had been restrained to act in sympathy with local architecture, ensuring their logos and marketing paraphernalia did nothing to diminish the character of the old buildings. Nervously, she caste her eyes over every young male that seemed to be approaching her for someone resembling the photos of Greg.

*What would she say?* she thought. How would they begin? Throngs of student looking people teamed past her, talking and in good spirits. None—she was glad—seemed to notice her inquisitive looks. Would he have friends with him? Maybe he'd bring someone along for moral support? These and many other questions kept reoccurring in her anxious mind.

*It's 12.45,* she said to herself. He said he'd be here by 12. Perhaps she should ring him? No, that would be lame. *Punctuality is a trait of middle-aged parents, and I ain't one of those.* She strolled over to a nearby bench and sat back, hoping the warmth of the morning sun would help ease her apprehension.

Monroe had fixed the trip. As soon as she told him Greg had suggested a visit, he was on the phone checking dates and arranging transport and accommodation. By coincidence both were free the following weekend. Monroe suggested she flew up. She stayed in London with Nina, her Lebanese friend from catering school, caught an early flight to Newcastle, hired a car and turned up in Durham a few minutes to midday.

She had tried to sleep on the plane. But each time she thought she was dozing off she kept thinking about Nina's reaction when she told her about Monroe. At first, when she talked about how they met—sex on the first night, what a great guy he was, the wedding—Nina laughed with her and smiled, and said how happy she was for them both. But then, as she started to recount the tale about the gun, his last wife's murder and the phone calls she had noticed the happy expression on Nina's face change to one of concern. She remembered Nina interrupting, putting her hand out, touching her arm and saying, 'Be careful, Stevie.' It was that comment that kept her awake.

'Excuse me,' a well-spoken male voice said from behind her. She turned to see a tall, blue-eyed young man wearing a long grey t-shirt with several holes around the waist, a pair of faded khaki shorts finishing below his knees and a dusty pair of sandals.

'Are you Stevie?' he asked with a broad smile.

\* \* \*

Café Nero was busy. Most of the small, cosy tables were taken. One large table, suitable for six or more, with a couple occupying one end was all the sitting space available. Greg looked around, catching sight of Stevie's concerned look.

'Too crammed?' he asked.

Stevie shook her head from side to side. 'Don't mind, if there's nothing else. Somewhere a little more private would be better.'

Greg had reached the front of the queue and was facing a girl waiting for his order.

'Yeah, there'll be a smaller table in a minute,' he said, turning back to face Stevie. 'What you having? The cappuccino's good.'

'That'll be fine,' Stevie replied, uneasily. Their conversation so far had been stilted and strained, just short exchanges after their brief introductions. It had started to rain as they met, driving them inside the café where they were jostled and bumped in the slow moving queue.

'There you are,' Greg said, pointing to a small table in the corner being vacated.

'I'll get it,' Stevie said, heading off quickly to the empty table.

Greg watched her. *She's pretty striking*, he thought, following her tall silhouette, her head of cropped blonde hair, weaving through the throng of people. As he manoeuvred through the tables, carrying the coffees and a croissant he noticed her long grey cotton tunic, her grey baggy trousers, her chunky jewellery; so appropriate to her height and vivid features.

He squeezed into his chair. It had been pushed up hard to their table by the person sitting in the seat behind, who despite seeing Greg approaching with his hands full, held high above the heads of the other seated customers, had made no effort to move out of the way.

'Hey, mate,' Stevie said loudly to the guy causing the obstruction. 'Move in a bit, can't you.' The man grunted and moved his chair in a touch.

Greg adjusted to his increased space and looked up at Stevie. Her piercing eyes met his.

'Thanks,' he said, acknowledging the man's gesture. He looked down to spoon up the froth from the top of his cappuccino.

Stevie did the same. 'How's your course?' she said after for a few seconds.

'Fine,' he replied, looking up to face Stevie again.

'Want me to tell you about it?'

Greg found telling Stevie about his life at university easy. Not only was she a good listener, she seemed genuinely interested, often interrupting and asking spontaneous questions. He enjoyed talking to her and sensed she became more relaxed than at first, happy to be listening to him.

'I guess I should talk about you and dad,' he said suddenly, with no warning. Stevie looked shocked. Maybe, he'd jumped in too quickly, he thought.

'What do you mean?' she asked.

Greg looked away for a moment before turning back to face her.

'Why I avoided you both and didn't come to your wedding. All of that,' Greg replied quickly, noticing that Stevie had blushed.

Stevie rested her head in her hands.

'No, Greg. You don't have to tell me that. I came here to meet you, not to make you feel that you have to provide a reason for your actions.'

'Thanks, but I thought it would help to make things better between us all. I, also, didn't ask you up to witness me partaking in a great soul-searching exercise. We seem to have got off to a good start, so I thought I'd try off loading some of my baggage. If you'd rather I didn't...'

Stevie leaned forward and touched Greg's arm.

'Go on. Tell me anything you want.'

Greg wiped his hand across his face.

'I loved mum.'

'I know you did.' Stevie had taken hold of his hand.

'When she died, my world fell apart. I know mum and dad weren't getting along great, but they seemed to jog along and I never dreamed they'd part.' Greg looked into Stevie's eyes. He knew he was rushing everything.

'So her dying and you popping up so suddenly seemed a double whammy. All I could think was couldn't dad have waited a bit? You know, a little respect for mum's past. I was distraught when he told me, couldn't believe he'd do something...' Greg stopped. Stevie was beginning to cry.

'I'm sorry,' he said, feeling guilty. 'I shouldn't have said that.'

'I'm glad you did.' Stevie withdrew her hand and dabbed a tissue against her eyes.

'I prefer to hear it like that. The truth, as you feel it. Rather than be told a cold, contrived version of the events.' She smiled.

'Now you've seen me, am I such a witch?'

'No. You're not.' He looked around at the queues at the door.

'I guess we should get out of here. How about a walk along the river? It's stopped raining, and is really pretty at this time of the year.'

Alongside the River Wear runs a narrow path where, in places, the long trailing branches of the weeping willow trees hang down, clipping the river's fast-flowing translucence water. Greg and Stevie ambled alongside the bank, tranquil and cool, a refreshing respite from the hot afternoon sun. They'd stopped earlier for a drink, sharing a sandwich at a pub at the edge of a bridge that spanned the river.

'That's where I row from,' Greg said, pointing to a boathouse down by the river's edge. Stevie reached down to the grass. It was dry. She sat down and Greg followed.

'I had a fella who rowed once,' Stevie said wistfully, sitting with her back at 45° to the ground, supported by her outstretched hands, her legs straight in front of her.

'Yes,' Greg replied. He was lying flat on his back and staring up at the fluttering branches of a large horse chestnut tree.

'Want some?' he added, pushing a bottle of water in Stevie's direction. Stevie shook her head in a gesture that Greg took to mean no.

'He was OK to start. We'd travelled all through South East Asia together. Him and two other guys. I, like an idiot, fell for him, ended up doing everything for him. Cooking, mending his clothes, sex whenever he wanted it.' She stopped and looked across the river.

Greg sat up. 'What happened?'

'Oh, I fell for him in a big way. He was kind, considerate, fun to talk to. All of that.'

'OK. What's the punch line?' Greg asked, swinging round to face Stevie, his legs crossed at the ankles, sitting up with a straight back.

Stevie grimaced. 'He asked me to join him in being a drug mule. Taking drugs into Thailand for thousands of pounds. Totally safe, he said.'

'And you did?' Greg asked, astonished that someone would succumb to something he considered so foolish. He'd been asked many times in Vietnam, but always remembered being told of the dire consequences if caught.

'Oh yes. Like a fool, and was caught.'

'What? And you're here to tell the tale?'

'I spent six months in the hot, stinking, infamous rat infested women's jail in Bangkok.'

Greg stared at Stevie. Her eyes were fixed at the wind rustling the branches and leaves of a nearby tree.

'Until one day, without notice, they came and said I was free,' she added, turning back to look at Greg, her face tinged with sadness.

Greg took a swig from his bottle of water. He held it out to Stevie, who declined.

'Have you told dad about this?' he asked, astonished.

'Oh yes,' Stevie replied, nodding her head with a serious expression. 'And the ending.'

'Which was?'

'The let me free on some deal done with the British government. The Thai authorities wanted to set an example. So my freedom was agreed providing the Brits didn't make a fuss when they hung my boyfriend.'

'My God,' said Greg, standing up.

'That's horrendous. You must have been shattered.'

Stevie swallowed and shrugged her shoulders. 'I was at the time.'

'Not now?' Greg asked.

'He was married, just using me to look after him.

'A shag whenever he wanted it, and be a mule for his drug business, risking a life sentence or my neck.'

Greg was confused.

'Drug business?'

'Oh yes. It all came out later. He was running the whole show. He'd find innocent carriers by either befriending them or in my case having an affair and promising marriage. Most got through OK, some were caught and languished for years in that God forsaken jail. He hardly ever did it himself, except in the few cases when he was short of a mule. But the authorities had a tip off. It was him they were after, not me, and they got him, determined to make an example.'

'So how did the government get involved?'

'Oh you know the score,' she said disparagingly. 'Any country that wants to hang a British citizen faces the full wroth of the British Government. So to keep Britain fairly quiet—you know, just a gentle protest but no follow up—they traded my freedom for his life.'

'That's terrible,' Greg said, shocked. 'How do you feel about it all.'

Stevie shrugged again. 'I don't. It's over, I'm free and he was a bastard. I don't really think about it. I didn't want him hung, but I wouldn't have wanted to see him again.'

'And he rowed?'

'Yes,' she replied, nodding her head again.

'For Oxford.'

'And dad knows all about this?'

'Yep.' Stevie smiled. 'He knows every bit.'

'What did he say?'

'Oh,' Stevie replied flippantly. 'That was funny. I remember his words exactly. He laughed and said, "So we're a pair of old lags." "Not so old," I replied.'

Greg smiled. 'You knew, presumably.'

'What? You mean about his time in prison? Oh yes. He'd told me that earlier. When he'd finished, I felt I wanted to tell him all about me. So I did.'

'Sounds like the two of you have no secrets?'

Stevie looked up from the daisy chain she'd been making. She looked into Greg's eyes. 'I hope so, Greg,' she replied, sounding a little unsure.

'You don't sound sure?' Greg said, watching her expression.

Stevie frowned slightly, shaking her head a little from one side to the other and said, 'Can we go?' I'd like to see my room.

'OK,' Greg replied, feeling he might have touched on something that wasn't quite right in what he'd come to believe was a relationship made in heaven.

'Here,' he said, stretching out his arm for Stevie to grab onto. 'Let me give you a hand up.'

\* \* \*

Durham Castle is owned by University College, a college of Durham University. Housed in the historic and medieval edifice are those students lucky enough to be allocated a room within its impressive surrounds. The magnificent building, built around 1200 AD, has been renovated to acceptable modern standards while retaining many of the ancient and original features. Greg had booked Stevie into one of the rooms made available for families of students.

They approached the room from an old stone circular staircase encased in grey stone walls from which dusty pictures of university worthies hung in isolated perpetuity. Great vaulted windows, carved and shaped from the same old grey stone, allowed small filaments of light to trickle onto the well-trod steps, concave and dipping in the middle from centuries of wear. The words, Guest Room, were painted in white on the heavy wooden door, stained black and made from large planks held together by strips of metal pinned by big iron studs and shaped at the top to fit the arched surround. Greg pushed the door open to find a light modern room, well furnished and tasteful. In the far corner a smaller wooden door, a replica of the main door to the room, hung half open to allow sight of a small staircase, also built in stone. Stevie ventured up to find a little, adequate en suite bathroom with beech wood furniture, a shower cubicle and a white porcelain bath on feet.

'Cute,' she said to Greg in an expressive gesture, her arms outstretched. Greg made sure Stevie was comfortable, then excused himself, leaving Stevie to shower and change and saying he'd pick her up at 6.30 for a meal.

* * *

'Trevor,' Greg yelled, 'Come and join us.' He was motioning to a tall black guy, wearing a white t-shirt and khaki shorts, who'd just brushed past and tapped him on the shoulder. Stevie looked up from her pizza and smiled. She hoped her inward frustration didn't show. Ever since they'd sat done she'd been desperate for an opportunity to talk to Greg about the gun and the strange phone calls. At first their conversation seemed too spontaneous and vibrant for her to bring up such a serious subject. Greg would have perceived it as being pre-planned and plotted, she thought. Now, just when she thought the right moment had arrived Greg's friends, who she was pleased to meet, had gathered around the table.

'Stevie, meet Trevor, Ed and Charlotte, known as Lotte. Stevie's my...' Greg paused for a couple of seconds. 'My...' He turned to Stevie and smiled.

'I can't call you my step-mum.'

Stevie looked up at Greg's friends and grinned.

'Hi. Pleased to meet you all. Come and join us. I'm married to Greg's dad. I don't really know what that makes me, but let's not worry about it.'

In what seemed like ages, Greg's friends joined them for a couple of beers while Greg and Stevie finished their pizzas. Stevie had invited the three of them to eat with them but they said they were joining up with a bigger crowd for a celebratory meal—someone's birthday—leading Stevie to suspect that Greg had been invited to the party but had probably ducked out because of her.

*I need to get on with it,* she thought.

'Great bunch,' Stevie said as they finally said goodbye and departed.

'Emm,' she started, wishing for once she drank.

'Can I talk to you about something that's been bugging me.' *Oh God,* she thought, that was awful.

Greg looked confused. 'That sounds a bit serious,' he replied.

'Yeah, well, err. Did your dad ever have any girlfriends?'

An immediate transformation came over Greg's face. His cheerful look turned to one of concern.

'What? I don't understand. What're you on about?' he said in a worried tone.

*Shit, I've screwed up already,* Stevie told herself. *But I must go on.*

'Before your mum died, did you know of him seeing anyone else?' she said cautiously.

'What is this, Stevie?' Greg seemed completely thrown off balance. 'Where you coming from? Why these sudden questions?' He picked up his beer and drained the glass.

'I don't know what you're after.'

Stevie caught Greg's eyes. She was touching a raw nerve, she knew, but she had to continue. 'Presumably by you're reaction, if he was seeing anyone else, you didn't know about it?'

'Leave it alone, Stevie.' Greg replied angrily, shaking his head.

'Minutes ago we were all having fun. Now you seem to be coming from another planet.' Greg sat back in his chair and looked away, starring above Stevie's heads to a blank piece of wall.

He turned back to Stevie and said, 'Look, if you've come all this way to cross-examine me about dad, forget it.' He started to get up. 'I'm going to join up with my mates. I'll meet you in the morning and…'

Stevie reached across and put her hand on his arm.

'No, please don't go, Greg. I'm sorry. I was a bit blunt. But there is something about your mother's death I have to discuss with you.'

Greg looked at Stevie warily. Slowly, he sat down.

'What's my dad got to do with mum's death?'

'Can I tell you about a couple of things that have happened.' Stevie was aware that Greg was starring at her suspiciously.

'Go on.'

'A few weeks ago we were burgled.'

'Yes, I know. Dad told me,' Greg said abruptly.

'Did he?' Stevie asked, surprised.

'I said, he did,' Greg replied emphatically.

'Did he tell you that after the burglary, when I was tidying up, I found a gun?'

'What?' Greg said, visibly shocked.

'Yes a revolver.' Stevie paused. She could tell Greg was taking it badly, but thought it better to get it all out. Drip-feeding the information would only prolong the agony.

'A couple of days later I received these strange calls from a woman who said she was an old friend. She wanted to speak…'

Greg stood up. He held out both his hands in front of him, facing Stevie, as though he was stopping traffic.

'Stop. None of this is making sense.' He looked down at Stevie.

'What happened to the gun?'

'Your dad told me he took it to the police.'

'Fine,' he said sharply, shaking his head.

'Did you ask him about the phone calls?'

'He just brushed it off, saying he didn't have any affairs when you're mum was alive.' Stevie looked up at Greg. He was upset and angry. She wasn't sure what he was about to do.

'Exactly,' Greg said loudly, still standing. 'So why do you come all this way to ask me these questions when you've had perfectly satisfactory answers from dad?'

'I don't really know,' she replied, trying to be honest, unsure of where the conversation was leading, acutely aware of Greg's intensity.

'I just thought I wanted to talk to someone about it. You seemed the most likely of people.'

'Oh come off it. You hardly know me. Up until yesterday we hadn't met.' Greg sat down and stared straight into Stevie's eyes.

'There's more to it than that, isn't there?'

Stevie, surprised that Greg was still listening, hoping he might have calmed down, decided to take a risk.

'I'm scared, Greg. I'd never seen a gun before and...' she paused.

'And what?' Greg said, leaning forward.

'And your mum was shot, wasn't she?'

Greg shot up, knocking his glass over with his abrupt movement.

'Get out of my sight. I never want to see you again. You've come here to tell me that my father murdered my mother. You must be out of your mind.' He stopped, fumbled in his pocket and withdrew a crumpled ten-pound note. He tossed it dismissively onto the table, turned, and without uttering a single word, stormed off.

# 12

Barefooted, wearing a pair of dirty shorts and a sleeveless grey vest, usually reserved for rowing, Greg gingerly approached the wing of the castle where he hoped he'd find Stevie. The gravel from the circular path surrounding the castle green made a familiar, slightly painful impression on the soles of his feet. Often he'd overslept in his two terms at Durham, necessitating a similar barefooted bolt around the path to the Great Hall where he'd just catch the last servings of breakfast. Being a Sunday, he had the small green, encircled by the castle, the keep and The Great Hall entirely to himself. A solitary robin watched him, a few fallen petals from the roses fluttered in the light breeze, the threat of rain hung in the air. His lack of sleep and dull headache, the after effects of the many pints of beer he'd drunk after he'd deserted Stevie, made him feel slow and lethargic. A few minutes earlier, at eight, having wrestled with his conscience for several hours, he tumbled out of bed and pulled on the first clothes he could find. He had to see Stevie again. He knew he'd been far too hasty and impulsive the previous night and regretted his actions, wanting, in a less fervent and calmer manner to listen to her concerns and to hear again the details about the gun she'd found.

*I shouldn't have rushed off,* he said to himself as he pushed open the door to the castle keep. She's OK. Good fun. I was out of order. Her concern over the gun was valid, even though I know dad wouldn't have a clue as to how to use one. Perhaps she doesn't know that a few days after mum's death they found the gun that killed her—I can tell her that. But why would dad have a gun? he asked himself, as the door to Stevie's room loomed up in front of him. And what was she saying about strange calls from someone pretending she'd had an affair with dad? Dad didn't have an affair with anyone; I think? With his mind full of similar questions, Greg knocked a couple of times on the solid door. There was no reply.

\* \* \*

Stevie sat crunched into a window seat of the first EasyJet flight from Newcastle to Stanstead. Next to her was an overweight man with thighs the size of the trunk of an old tree and a belly so large that, had she needed to squeeze past him to visit the toilet, it would have been extremely difficult. His voluminous excesses of flesh spilt over from his seat and pushed her legs against the plane's fuselage. She felt like a tinned sardine, squidged and pressed flat inside a metal container, although in her case—alive.

'No thanks,' she said to the male steward who caught her eye while pushing a trolley down the aisle, offering snacks. She returned to gaze vacantly out of the window, watching the white fluffy clouds scoot past outside, and let her mind drift back to her previous state of melancholy.

At first, when Greg had stormed off the previous night, she'd felt nothing but animosity towards him. 'Is that how jumped up bloody students behave?' she'd yelled after him. Annoyed and resentful, she'd paid the bill and left, wondering, as she walked back alone to her room, how Monroe could think so much of someone so rude. Greg invited me up here, she said to herself. Then he walks off in a hump at the end of the meal. *Bloody immature and discourteous,* she muttered to herself as she had climbed the few steps to her room. As she'd started to undress, self doubts and recriminations had started to seep into her mind. She'd sat on the bed, wearing only her bra and knickers and wondered how she could have fouled up so much?

*Of course he reacted like that. If he hadn't, there'd be something odd about him,* she told herself as she reached down to her handbag, dumped next to her shoes at the side of the bed, and started to search around inside for her phone. She had been on the brink of calling Monroe when she'd stopped, rose from the bed and walked to the window. Outside the pale moonlight shone onto the walls of the castle and the steep grass bank beyond, rolling down to the edges of the River Wear, its fast flowing waters dark and twinkling in the weak illumination. The eerie beauty was lost on Stevie. She shivered, starring blankly into the dark night. She could feel her lips begin to tremble and reached out to the wall for some support. Taking in a sharp gasp of air she bit hard on her bottom lip and burst into tears. She clung to the wall for support, sobbing. Slowly she dropped to the floor and lay for a while, weeping and shaking.

When she awoke she had no idea how long she'd been lying in the same position. She felt desperately cold, her mind full of only one thought. The previous night, in a couple of quick, insensitive and ill prepared sentences she'd effectively brought to an end her short-lived, happy and almost made in heaven marriage. How could she ever face Monroe again? She asked herself, knowing that Greg would have called him already, recounting a tale about how she believed his father had killed his mother.

'God, I've really screwed up,' she said, shakily rising to her feet.

'Where do I go know?' she said aloud, as she crossed the bedroom floor to the bed. I can't go home. She put her right hand up to her cheek to wipe away a tear. Her left hand went to her chin, steadying the tremor she felt in her lower jaw. She felt overcome by a sense of helplessness. Her world had suddenly collapsed in a way she had never thought possible. A feeling of emptiness clouded her every thought.

Amidst the shrouds of despair that surrounded her mind she recognised that life had to go on. Cold, dressed only in her underclothes, she grabbed her holdall from the chair and dumped it on the bed. It didn't take her long to throw the few clothes she'd bought with her into the bag. Once she was packed, she took a few more minutes to pull on the same clothes she'd worn the previous night and left.

\* \* \*

Jennifer Philp, Stevie's mother, was unlike her daughter in every way. She was a snob with racist tendencies, had spent large amounts of money to loose any trace of her detested Glasgow accent—replacing it with an Estuary English one—dressed in clothes more in keeping with readers of Country Life than Hammersmith, where she lived, and put money and status higher than personality when seeking a male partner. She was 48 and had never been married. Stevie was born when she was 18 as a result of a one-night affair. Neither mother nor daughter were close. Stevie was quite happy to see her mother as infrequently as possible.

Stevie pulled up outside her mother's house at a few minutes to eight the next morning. She'd flown in to Stansted at six, managed to get off the plane and away from the airport by 6.45 and driven like hell to London. She didn't really know why she'd chosen her mother's house, just that it was the last place she knew Monroe would look. Drained of energy, she parked behind a new looking grey BMW 7series, 100 metres from her mother's front door.

Stevie knew as soon as her mother opened the door that she'd made a mistake. Jennifer—as her mother wished her daughter to call her to avoid giving anyone a clue to her age—had a look on her face that clearly showed her disdain and disbelief. She stood staring at Stevie with one arm against the frame of the door, discouraging any entry.

'Well, what have we here?' Jennifer said, contemptuously. 'This is not a home for the waif and strays.'

'Jennifer, get off your bloody throne and let me in. I'm in trouble.'
Jennifer looked concerned.

'Hold on a minute.' She closed the door in Stevie's face.

Stevie heard her yelling to someone inside and guessed that her mother had another of her temporary live in lovers on site. Presumably the poor guy had to finish dressing or something similar. Stevie sat on the low wall dividing the two small front gardens and waited, wondering if she should just go.

'Come in, Stevie. What's the problem?' A neatly suited man of about 35 to 40 was holding the door open.

'Jennifer's just clearing up a bit.'

Stevie recognised the guy to be Joe Walters, Juliet's boss and someone she'd met at their wedding. *Strange*, she thought. I knew he'd taken Jennifer out a couple of times, but I didn't think anything serious would come of it. Mind you, I haven't spoken to her for some time, and nothing would surprise me with men and my mother.

'Hi, Joe,' Stevie replied, following him towards the kitchen.

'I expect you're surprised to see me here.'

'Kind of. Jennifer hadn't told me you're an...'

'An item, I believe is the current terminology.'

They reached the kitchen. Stevie couldn't avoid looking at Joe any longer. He was wearing a well-pressed navy blue suit, white shirt and navy tie with small red spots. His lace-up black shoes were immaculately polished. She thought she wasn't going to like him.

'Are you?' she asked. 'And how long has that been going on?'

Before Joe had a chance to answer Jennifer appeared looking a little flustered. 'So what brings you here? Fallen out with your convict husband?'

Stevie looked at her mother with disgust. *Why on earth had she come here?* she asked herself. She knew her mother couldn't stand the site of Monroe. This would just give her the chance to gloat.

'Aargh,' she yelled, feeling a sudden sharp stabbing pain in her stomach. The pain came again, causing her to grasp her tummy and fall to the floor. Joe followed by Jennifer came to her aid. They persuaded her to lie down on the sofa in the living room. Minutes later she was fast asleep.

When she awoke a couple of hours later it was Joe who first came to her with a mug of hot tea. He'd changed from his suit into a pair of navy chinos with sharp creases down the front, a checked short-sleeve shirt and a pair of brown loafers.

'How do you feel,' he asked.

Stevie thought for a bit. She felt drained, exhausted, lacking in any vitality or will to do anything.

'Pretty pooped, I'd say.'

'Can I get you something to eat?' Joe asked.

She looked at him suspiciously.

'You looked as though you were going to work before.'

'I was, but it can wait. Jennifer had to go out, so I said I'd stay and look after you.'

'You're some big cheese, aren't you?'

'Something like that.' Joe made a dismissive gesture with his right hand. 'But I've left all that at work. What would you like?'

*Better than first impressions*, Stevie thought. She knew he was putting it on, and she didn't care much for his tidy, precise way of dressing, but he seemed to have a kind way about him.

'I'd love some scrambled eggs on toast, if that's possible?' She watched him as he left the room.

Stevie let her eyes roam around her mother's sitting room. *Same perfectly vacuumed dusty pink carpet, glossy white skirting boards and woodwork, magnolia walls and damask covered matching couches*, she thought. Each windowsill was filled with photos of her mother at various social events. There was Jennifer at Ascot, accompanied by some past employers of hers, wearing an enormous floppy hat and a tight fitting knee-length pink dress with a slit up her thigh. Jennifer at Wimbledon, clearly next to someone who'd been air-brushed out, and a picture of her mingling with a champagne guzzling, well dressed and opulent looking 40 plus crowd at a nondescript summer gathering set in a large garden with a huge marquee. Similar photos were dotted around all the available spots, but none of Stevie or of her wedding. She turned to look at the familiar Monet print hanging in its usual place on the wall behind her. That's always been there, she thought, turning her gaze to the opposite wall to examine a delicate watercolour of children playing in a sun-drenched cornfield with a Victorian looking farmhouse in the background. That's an improvement, she muttered, noting that nothing else had altered from her last visit.

Her quick inspection over, she flopped back in her seat and closed her eyes. She was on the point of drifting off when the doubts and fears, previously so prevalent in her mind, started to return. Again she asked herself why she was at her mother's house, someone Stevie had for some time regarded as a failed parent, her opinion reinforced by the absence of a single photograph of her wedding. She worried about practical things: where she'd live, her job, money, obtaining her clothes. But above all she found she was confused and disoriented about Monroe. She cried when she thought about their closeness, their unions of minds, their intimacy.

'I won't accept it's all over,' she said after a couple of minutes. She leapt up and looked around for where she'd dumped her bag. She'd decided, regardless of his reaction, she'd call Monroe. Hiding and running away from problems had never been her style; better to face up to things head on and deal with the consequences. Cautiously she reached for her phone. Her fingers shaking, feeling sick, she scrolled through her list of numbers until she came to home and pressed the green key. At first, she heard nothing and had to recall the number, adding to her anxiety. One after the other she listened to the ring tones, each time preparing herself more and more for what she expected to be an outpouring from Monroe of his doubtless embitterment towards her. After five rings the answerphone clicked in.

'Oh shit,' she said. She'd remembered he'd told her he was going to London to meet with his publisher. The earlier surge of adrenaline that had driven her to try to contact Monroe sagged. She knew his mobile number, but didn't call it.

'Here you are,' Joe said a few minutes later as he re-entered the room with a tray of hot food and some fresh coffee.

*God knows what I look like*, Stevie thought as Joe placed the tray on the coffee table in front of her.

'Don't look at me, Joe. I must seem like a wreck. Sorry, I've had a hell of a few days.'

Joe looked down at the tray.

'Anything we can do to help?' he said passing a plate of scrambled eggs on toast and a knife and fork.

'This'll do to start,' Stevie replied, surprised she'd managed to say anything coherent. She was confused, unable to decide on her next course of action, thrown by her inability to speak to Monroe. The earlier bout of confidence and her wish to confront the issue had somehow evaporated, given way to all too familiar misgivings and indecision.

'This is good, Joe,' she said, taking a forkful from the plate in front of her. She looked up and met his eyes, conscious that he'd probably been watching her for some time.

'It should be,' Joe replied, smiling.

'Why?'

'Basic bachelor food. You see I've never been married and consequently have had to look after myself.'

'I see,' Stevie said, nodding to show her understanding. Her eyes caught site again of the watercolour above Joe's head.

'Do you know anything about that painting?' she asked, pointing with her left index finger.

Joe shifted in his seat and looked up.

'I do. I gave it to Jennifer as a present. An unknown Victorian watercolourist painted it around 1850. I inherited it from my father. Recently the artist's works have become something of a collector's item. I believe it's worth quite a bit.' He looked across at Stevie.

'Like it?'

'I do,' she replied. 'How long have you and Jennifer been together?'

'Oh,' Joe scratched his head. 'I suppose about six months. We started going out shortly after you and Monroe were married.' He smiled. 'Ironic, really.'

'What is?' Stevie asked, confused.

'What's ironic?' Joe laughed. 'That Monroe should introduce us and then we end as boyfriend and girlfriend.'

'What's ironic about that?'

Joe looked away, as though he wanted time to think out his reply.

'Just that I was Juliet's last boss and end up having a relationship with his new wife's mother.'

Stevie suspected that he was going to say something else but had thought it unwise to mention it.

'I don't call that ironic.' She looked hard at him.

'You stopped yourself. You meant to say that Jennifer despised Monroe, who introduced you both. That's what I call ironic.'

Joe, blushing slightly, met Stevie's gaze head on.

'I don't know what your mother thinks of Monroe.' He paused. 'But I think he's a terrific guy. I think he's been through an awful lot and I'm glad he's got someone like you to make him happy. Have you met Greg, his son?'

Stevie felt at a loss as what to say. Her eyes felt moist. *He's saying things she wanted to hear.* Could she possibly trust him, someone she hardly knew?

'I have,' she replied hesitantly. 'But it's got me into a load of shit.'

Joe leant forward.

'What? Because he didn't come to your wedding? Look, the guy had just lost his mother and suddenly his father…'

'I know,' Stevie said. 'I know all that. I reasoned with Monroe along those lines. It's not that. It's something else. I don't think…' Stevie stopped. She knew, yet again, she was about to loose it.

'Oh hell,' she said burying her head in her hands and bursting into floods of tears.

To Stevie the next thirty seconds seemed like an eternity. She sobbed and sobbed continuously, disorientated and feeling disconnected with the world around her. When she raised her tear sodden face Joe was still sitting in the same position as before, looking away and seemingly oblivious to her dramatic burst of emotion.

*I don't know about him*, she thought. He's seems understanding and kind, but sort of difficult to break the surface. Joe turned to look at her and smiled, triggering an unexpected feeling of impotence, weakness, vulnerability, and an inability to work out what to do or say. After a bit she said,

'I guess you knew Monroe pretty well.'

'Like a brother,' Joe replied, nodding his head.

'And Juliet?' Stevie asked, curious. Her mood more upbeat by Joe's instant and forthright reply.

'Same really. I relied on her entirely. Totally conscientious and trustworthy.' Joe laughed.

'I don't mean like a sister, but you know what I mean. I respected them both enormously. Still do with Monroe.'

'If I tell you what's bugging me,' Stevie said quickly. 'Will you listen, promise not to interrupt, and give me your honest opinion at the end?' As she finished, she wondered if she'd been too impulsive.

Joe leant back in his seat.

'Go on. I promise.'

With her eyes closed Stevie bent her head forward, outstretched the fingers of both her hands against her forehead and dragged her thumbs up and down her cheeks several times. Slowly she looked up at Joe, sitting upright and waiting patiently for her to begin. Hesitantly she started to tell him about the burglary. He didn't comment, just sat still and listened with an impassive look on his face. She found his nonchalant attitude unnerving. Her speech faltered and she became aware that she was perspiring.

'Don't you have anything to say? she asked.

He leant forward and smiled benignly.

'You asked me not to interrupt,' he replied, leaning back in his seat.
*Oh my God*, Stevie thought. Have I screwed up again?

'Go on,' Joe said, in an encouraging tone.

After a moment's thought Stevie continued. At first, a little uncertain, then, as she came to accept that Joe was doing no more than she had asked, she became more fluent, articulately telling him all that happened from the burglary to finding the gun. She explained how Monroe had reacted, and recounted about her abortive visit to Greg. She finished by saying, 'I love him, Joe, but I'm frightened.' Joe looked at Stevie then turned his head away. He rose from his seat and stroked his chin. Stevie watched him, acutely aware how different he was from Monroe, with his tailored shirt and trousers, their front creases neatly pressed.

Joe, still standing, turned to face Stevie. 'I completely understand your concern. Finding a gun must be terrifying. But Monroe's no murderer,' he said emphatically, stopping for a moment. He took a closer look at Stevie, as though he was gauging her reaction to what he'd said.

'Monroe and Juliet weren't exactly hot lovers.'

'I know,' Stevie said, interrupting. 'Monroe told me.'

'I'm sure he did. But that doesn't make him a murderer. Look, you know how close he is to Greg. He's not going to kill his mother, is he?'

'Unlikely. But why have a gun in the house?' Stevie found it easy to believe Joe. He seemed so sure and was saying things she wanted to hear.

'What about the woman who called?'

Joe shook his head. 'I can't make any comment on that. I simply don't know.'

'So you think there may have been an old girlfriend?' Stevie asked, hopeful and expectant for a negative reply.

Joe sat down. He didn't meet Stevie's gaze.

'I can't say, Stevie. Monroe's the same as all of us. He's got physical needs.' He shrugged his shoulders.

'All I can say is that in all the time I knew Monroe and Juliet as a couple I never had any reason to believe anything was going on.' He turned his head to face Stevie. Their eyes met.

'You know Monroe for what he is. Go back and talk it all through with him. Deep down you don't believe he is a murderer? Do you?'

'I don't, Joe. But I was just frightened, as I said.' Stevie felt relieved. *Talking to Joe was right*, she told herself as the clouds in her mind lifted and she could see clearly a route back to Monroe. She'd leave almost immediately, before her mother returned, drive like hell to Padstow and, in her normal way, talk to Monroe full frontal about everything. No pussy footing around, deal with every issue—Greg, the gun, and the girlfriends. Their conversation might be loud at times, painful, awash with tears but it would achieve a result. A good one, she thought, feeling inwardly better. Monroe would explain everything, she'd make good her crass behaviour with Greg and, she was sure, by night-time they'd be tucked up in bed together. She thought she heard the sound of keys turning in a lock. Joe got up and headed towards the door, confirming her suspicion that Jennifer was returning. Horrified, she followed Joe.

'Don't tell her, Joe. She'll gloat.'

Joe turned and seemed to look surprised. 'I've got to tell her something.'

'Not until I've gone. I'll…' Stevie stopped.

Jennifer, carrying a couple of supermarket carrier bags came in the room.

'Stevie, dear.' She said cheerfully. 'You look as though you need feeding up. I've bought some steaks for us all to have for lunch. She turned to Joe.

'You staying?'

Joe looked at his watch. 'If we could eat about 12. I'll have to leave immediately afterwards.

'Splendid,' Jennifer said enthusiastically and turned to Stevie.

'Now you go and have a shower and tidy up and I'll find out from Joe what you two have been up to.'

Stevie glanced briefly at Joe, hoping the quick clenching of her lips was enough of a sign for him to understand her meaning. She knew her mother would seize on the news about Monroe, using it as further evidence in her campaign to undermine him. Joe smiled and nodded, which she took to mean he'd understood.

'OK,' she said nodding to her mother and turning to leave the room.

Jennifer cooked rump steaks, done to order, sauté potatoes and a leaf salad mixed with strips of avocado. They ate on a small round table in the conservatory, draped with hanging plants, every flat surface filled with a tub of either bright red, white or pink geraniums. Cooking and horticulture were two undertakings where Jennifer excelled and Stevie knew it, thus allowing easy conversation about food and the garden.

For pudding Jennifer brought to the table a large glass bowl of fresh strawberries, raspberries and blueberries. She was spooning some into a dish for Joe when she said, unannounced, 'You should go back to Monroe immediately, dear. Patch things up.' She didn't look up, poured cream onto Joe's fruit and passed him the dish. Stevie looked quickly at Joe who winked at her and then held his hand out to take his dessert from Jennifer's outstretched arm.

'You'll have some, Stevie,' Jennifer said without looking at her daughter while filling a bowl with berries.

*What the hell's going on*, Stevie thought.

'Yeah, thanks,' she said taking the bowl, at a loss as to how to respond to her mother's earlier comment.

'Joe told me you two had a bit of a tiff,' Jennifer said, her head down as she delicately spooned her fruit into her mouth.

Stevie glanced at Joe. She was confused, worried about how much he had told her mother and why she was behaving out of character, patronizing her. Joe didn't give her any help. He also had his head down and appeared to be concentrating on eating.

'We did,' Stevie replied, careful to give a minimum response, nothing that could be construed one way or another.

'Take my advice and head off back to Padstow straight after lunch.'

Jennifer stopped to scoop up the last drops of cream from her bowl

'Never let a row fester, I say.'

Stevie became wary. Jennifer was behaving completely out of character.

'Yeah, I'll do that, Jennifer,' she said, indifferently and started to clear the plates.

'Leave the plates, dear,' Jennifer responded. 'Go and look after that good man of yours.'

*This is too much,* Stevie thought.

'Fine,' she said and thanked Jennifer and Joe for their short hospitality and rose to leave.

'I'll come to the car with you,' Joe said, grabbing Stevie's holdall from the floor.

'What the hell is she on about, Joe?' Stevie asked, stopping and turning to face Joe as soon as they were out of the house and on the pavement. 'How much have you told her and what's her game? She hates Monroe.'

Joe slowed his pace but didn't stop.

'I just said,' he replied turning to see if Stevie was catching him up, 'that you both had a row and wanted a little space.'

Stevie looked at him. 'I see,' she said, suddenly full of doubt and concern again.

'There you go,' Joe said as he opened her car door and stood holding it until she was seated.

'Oh, by the way,' he added as she was about to drive away. 'I'd tell the police about the gun.'

'What?' she replied, taking her hands off the steering wheel.

'Just in case they want to investigate it. You know, they might want to know why you hadn't reported it earlier.'

'But…'

Joe patted her on the shoulder.

'It's not a problem. You said Monroe had taken the gun to the police, so all you are doing is adding substance to the story.'

'I see,' Stevie replied, confused.

# 13

Greg, his rucksack squeezed up hard against the driver's back, held on tightly as the motorbike roared away from Hanoi airport, towards the house he had left eight months earlier. Wearing jeans and one of his Durham University rowing sweatshirts, he felt overdressed as the hot sun bore down on his bare head. He guessed the temperature must have been in the upper thirties. Dusty streets full of bustling people, great wedges of cycles and the constant roar from motorbikes together with the sharp horn-honking that accompanies their incessant weaving through the traffic told Greg he was back. They passed alongside a market where the vibrant colours of the fruits and vegetables, so enticingly displayed, and the intoxicating smells from street cooking reminded Greg that this city had much to offer. All that he'd left behind; university, the emotional trauma surrounding his mother's death, Stevie and his dad's relationship and his agonising decision to throw everything up in the air and run, seemed far removed.

The week after Stevie had left so early was unlike anything he'd ever experienced. He attended only one lecture, barely making a note through the full two hours. He didn't row, play squash or go to the bar and hardly ventured out of his room. For one day he just lay on his bed, unable even to find the motivation to take himself to the dining hall. When he did drag himself up, he knew he was being surly and inward with his many friends. It was after one such occasion that he came to his resolution. He'd quit university, go back to Vietnam and find a life away from the impossible turmoil that raged within in his mind since Stevie had visited him. That those seeds were dead and would never germinate, he had no doubt. He knew there was no way that his father would have killed his mother; he accepted that Stevie thought the same way, although frightened and worried. But he believed the only way he could rid himself of the constant reoccurring questions that flooded his thoughts was to go as far away as possible. Moreover, he found he was missing his mother more than he had ever done.

He knew running away was the cowardly option but it seemed the only way he could find some peace, and maybe the chance to rationalise the commotion that was raging in his mind. One night he packed up, took the first available train to London, spent a day waiting for a flight at Heathrow and finally left exactly a week after the morning he'd gone to find Stevie. He dropped a short note to his father, just before he was due to board his flight.

Greg tapped the driver on his shoulder to indicate that they'd arrived at the house. The bike leant to the right, allowing Greg's foot to stand squarely on the ground; a mixture of cracked tarmac, exposed hard core and scorched earth. He swung his left leg over the saddle and stood with his backpack resting against his leg, its bottom sitting in a spot of chalky white stones.

*It seems different, more dilapidated*, Greg thought as he approached the house. He could hear voices inside, but the big steel gates that Matt and he had always kept open, to encourage the locals to visit, were firmly closed. It needs painting, some of the metal surrounding the balconies is rusty, he thought as he waited for someone to answer the bell.

'Yah?' a tall, fair-headed young man with a pronounced public school accent said in a high pitched voice as he peaked through the gap where he'd opened the door.

144

'Hi. I'm Greg. I was living here last year. Can I come in?' Greg stood for what seemed a long time while the young man appeared to be inspecting him from head to toe.

Finally the man leant back and said, 'What for? There's no one here from last year.' He remained an obstruction to Greg entering the house.

'Yeah, I know that. But I've just arrived and thought I could have a bed for a few days,' Greg replied, taken aback by the man's unfriendly manner.

'Stay?' the young man said as though Greg had asked for the impossible.

*What a shit*, Greg thought, remembering how Matt and he had run an open house during their time here.

'You've got room haven't you?'

'Emm. I don't know. I'll have to go and ask my compatriot, old chap,' the man said and closed the door firmly on Greg.

*Who is this guy?* Greg asked himself while he waited for the man to return. Surely he's sponsored by the same organisation as I was. They told us always to offer hospitality to fellow travellers, particularly those from Gap[1].

'He said you can come in. But you have to keep quiet as he's trying to sleep.'

Greg picked up his rucksack by the two shoulder straps and followed the young man into the house. He rested the bag against the familiar black couch, used so often in his time as a makeshift bed for friends, either too drunk to get home or using the house as a staging post on their travels.

'Watch what you're doing,' the young man said, indignantly. 'You're making a mess on the floor.'

Greg looked down. He assumed the guy was referring to the chalky deposit from the bottom of his rucksack. *What a loser*, he thought as he nonchalantly pushed his bag over with his foot to rest on its side.

---

[1]. Gap: Gap activity projects.

'Happy?' he said sarcastically as the young man walked off towards the stairs without another word. Greg flopped onto the couch and glanced around the walls of the room that had been the scene of so many good times. For the first few minutes he couldn't figure out why it all looked so different and unfriendly. When Matt and he had lived there the large wall opposite the couch was the focal point of conversation; covered entirely with posters and cards from places they'd visited, pictures of their lifetime heroes, witty words written by the two of them and their friends, an odd menu or recipe scrawled quickly on a scrap of paper after a successful meal. In the corners and sticking out from behind parts of the intriguing montage they'd stick bits of used card and torn paper with random telephone numbers scribbled on them.

Greg hadn't expected it all to be still there. In fact Matt and he had taken it all down and cleaned the wall before they left. Apparently, so they had been told, it was sort of traditional for the occupants of the house to do similar, using the wall as a living symbol and illustration of the transient tenants' experiences. Several past Gap volunteers had disobeyed the house rules and left their mementoes and paraphernalia on the wall for the next pair of volunteers to hopefully eulogize over.

What he looked at was a clean, empty white wall. *Boring*, he thought as his eyes started to roam around the rest of the room. There were no piles of CD's, no books dumped on the edge of the couch or on the floor, no discarded clothes or carrier bags full of recent purchases. No trinkets, souvenirs or half-drunk bottles of water; none of the usual traits of two male teenagers. All was in order—neat, tidy and devoid of any character or expression. Sad, Greg thought as he dragged his rucksack up the stairs to where he knew he would find an empty room.

At 6 p.m. the next day Greg sat a café besides Ho Hoan Qiem Lake and sipped a cold Tiger beer. His feet were sore, his shirt was wet with perspiration and he felt exhausted. All day he'd trudged between shops and bars he knew in search of a job. None would take him. They told him he needed a work permit—an obstacle he hadn't anticipated. On his last trip he'd met and heard of many non-Vietnamese nationals who'd worked without one. *Has the government changed things?* he asked himself. He became despondent, concerned that he might have made a mistake in coming to Hanoi, indifferent to spending much time in the old house with the two cranky occupants.

The next morning he trudged off to Manger, a French restaurant he'd heard employed westerners if they spoke French. Apparently the owner wanted to recreate the atmosphere of old colonial French Indo China, insisting that all staff spoke French and English first before Vietnamese. The Australian guy who told him about it had reckoned it was illegal, but suggested that Greg give it a try. Greg had passed A level French and therefore figured he stood a good chance of getting job.

Monsieur Lapérouse, as he liked to be known, was thin and erect with swept-back black Brylcreemed hair and a small moustache, waxed and twisted. He was wearing pressed black trousers, shiny black shoes, a white long sleeved shirt and a black bow tie, topped with a full-length neat, dark-navy apron with pencil thin white stripes running vertically down the front. Greg, in his travel weary clothes and three-day stubble, knew he didn't stand a chance and was ready to turn and run when Monsieur Lapérouse said, 'My dear, what a sight. Burn the clothes and spend a day in the bath before you work in my restaurant.' Greg's apologetic reply, in French, seemed to impress Monsieur Lapérouse sufficiently for him to offer Greg a job.

The restaurant was built in an old warehouse, probably used to store rice, renovated and made to look like a fifties Parisian bistro and reached by a creaky outdoor metal staircase. Monsieur Lapérouse managed the front of house with impeccable precision while, ironically, Tam Loc, a young Vietnamese girl did all the cooking. Tam had trained in one of the best catering schools in Paris and worked in one of Gordon Ramsay's restaurant in London before joining Manger. Before Greg started his first shift she cooked for him and all the other waiters the best Marchand de Vin he had ever tasted.

Kim came into Greg's life about a week into the job and when he was ready to jack it all in and return home. He'd noticed her only occasionally in his first week. Their paths crossed when he was about to receive his third dressing-down of the day from Monsieur Lapérouse. Greg was clearing the first course plates from one of his tables, when, to help him, a friendly customer started to stack some of the plates. Greg followed, collecting all the dishes together and scraping all the remains onto one plate. All of a sudden Kim swooped in, taking the stacked up plates away from him and pushing him with her knee.

'Don't stack,' she whispered, urgently. 'He'll kill you.'

As she moved swiftly away, carrying the pile of plates, Greg saw the image of Lapérouse bearing down on him from the opposite direction. *Shit*, he thought. *He's going to fire me.'*

'My dears. I trust everything is all right.' Monsieur Lapérouse waited until he'd received verbal or nodded confirmation from the six diners that everything was all right before turning to Greg and saying sneeringly, 'Well done. Now go to the kitchen and chase up their main course.'

'Saved your bacon,' Kim said when he reached the kitchen.

Greg looked at her, standing against the kitchen wall, small and petite and about a quarter of a metre shorter than him in a short-sleeve black top and a matching knee length skirt.

'Thank you,' he said smiling. 'I thought I was for the chop.' Her warm, sensuous mouth opened into a broad grin exposing a pair of perfect white teeth that shone against her soft olive complexion.

'That's OK, I did the same when I started. Only there was no one to warn me.'

'Did he go for you?'

'Did he, just.' A pained expression came over Kim's face. She laughed.

'Best forgotten, and I didn't want you to go through the same.' She shrugged her shoulders. 'Seeing that you've only just started,' she added, stroking her short dark hair.

Greg's instinct was to stay and talk, but he knew, if he did, he'd be in deep trouble. He looked into Kim's smouldering brown eyes.

'Perhaps we could meet later?' he asked.

Over the next few weeks Kim became lover and best friend to Greg. She was the same age as him and had been backpacking around South East Asia with her boyfriend. They'd had a violent row in Hanoi and he'd walked out on her leaving her to fend for herself. When Greg discovered that both her parents had died in an air crash the previous year, he found he had a sympathetic ear for his own tragedy.

Until he met Kim, Greg's sexual experiences had been limited. None had been a disaster, but equally not particularly memorable. Kim, by no means promiscuous, had been together with her ex for a year and was able to bring to their physical relationship sensitivity and feeling. Often they'd make love for hours and then lie naked in each other's arms, purging their minds of doubt and grief, finding in the other a mental conduit and depository for their worst fears and nightmares until, simultaneously, they both would fall asleep. They became deeply in love with each other and of one mind and body.

They both continued to work for Monsieur Lapérouse, finding the more practised they became the more he would trust them, self-evident in their greater enjoyment and job satisfaction. On the nights they worked together, after the restaurant had closed they would walk through the eerie, dimly lit back streets of Hanoi, avoiding the rats scampering from the large piles of rubbish gathered from the street markets, to their small, one bedroom flat in the Latin quarter. They'd sleep until ten, make love and then spend the rest of the day before going to work, ambling through the many small and intricate streets, eating in street cafés or from the exciting food stalls.

Four weeks passed before Greg thought about his father. He noticed an advert in an English newspaper for father's day. It made him feel guilty.

'I should have sent him a card, or something,' he said to Kim, over a shared bowl of Pho.

Kim raised her head. She looked surprised.

'Buy a postcard from the stand outside and do it now before you forget,' she said and then added, 'If you really want to.'

He hesitated. He felt that if he made a big thing about it he'd upset Kim—her father was dead.

'I'll pick one up later,' he said, quickly turning the page of the newspaper. 'Look, Manchester United have signed another Brazilian player.'

Kim looked down at the article. For a moment they both read it together and then finished their soup, talking about what they'd do at the weekend. When the time came to leave neither of them mentioned buying a card. The significance of the date didn't feature in Greg's mind again until an English family he was serving, later in the day, mentioned it. Two middle-aged parents, backpacking with their teenage children, told him they were having a celebratory father's day dinner before embarking on a trek near Sapa, a town in the mountains overlooking the Chinese border.

'Have a good one,' Greg said smiling at the man as he turned to return to the kitchen. On his way he felt strange. His earlier impulsive feeling of guilt over forgetting his father had given way to a sense of reluctance to do anything about it.

*Better to do nothing,* he told himself. *I'm too late now, anyway.*

He had discussed everything about his mother's death with Kim. They'd talked about it for many hours, on many different occasions. There was nothing that she didn't know. Each time, she just listened, letting him pour out the facts in whatever way he found the easiest. She'd make no judgement, no comment, just gave him sympathy and understanding. When he came to the end of each episode and event he'd feel relieved, as though he'd off loaded a burdensome and painful object that he had been carrying around with him for some time.

After a while he found the burning need to talk about his trauma had gone away. He came to realise that for the first time since his mother had been murdered he could look at the circumstances around her death in a rational and less emotive way, able to examine the facts without blinkers and pre conceived values. One night, when Kim and he were walking home, he was silent, deep in thought.

'Kim,' he said as she turned to see why he had suddenly stopped.

'I think my dad lied to me.'

# 14

Stevie looked at herself in the rear view mirror. She was wrecked, unable to comprehend and take in the events of the last 24 hours. As often as she dabbed at her make up to hide the signs of her emotional stress, she knew she couldn't do anything to relieve the depressing tiredness that had overtaken her body. Only last night, she recalled, she was sitting in a restaurant in Durham talking to Greg, unaware that a series of events, turbulent and wild and similar to a ride on a roller coaster, were about to shake and nearly shatter her brief, idyllic marriage. She pushed open the car door, grabbed hold of her holdall and trudged wearily and with some trepidation to the door of a bleak looking farmhouse.

Ten minutes earlier, after her car had nearly veered of the road into a ditch, she realised she was too tired to drive any longer, deciding to pull into the first place she could find that offered a bed for the night. She stopped near Launceston, right in the middle of Bodmin moor.

Her room was drab and cheerless. The wallpaper, smudged and dirty, was peeling and hanging off in places. A large brown water stain stretched from one corner of the dusty ceiling to cover a quarter of its surface. She glimpsed around the depressing surroundings and shrugged her shoulders, reluctantly accepting she had no choice but to stay. *Safer than ending up on the mortician's slab*, she thought, kicking off her sandals. She unzipped her jeans and let them drop to the floor, pulled her red t-shirt over her head and made for the tiny bathroom.

Relieved to find the water piping hot, she eased herself into the pink, plastic bath, the sides of which bulged and dented with each move she made, until her shoulders were slightly submerged. For a few seconds her numbed body felt relieved, her troubled mind found some respite from the myriad of questions and ambiguity that continuously invaded its sanctums and inner reaches. Then, as though she'd suddenly switched to replay mode, she started to relive all that had taken place since she'd arrived at her mother's house at eight that morning.

Blind desperation must have been her only reason for going there, she told herself. She found the sympathetic reception from Jennifer strangely false and out of character, only to be surpassed by the initially supportive attitude of Joe and then his bewildering comments made on her departure. It was so bizarre, so confusing, she had thought as she'd driven away, heading for home and repatriation with Monroe.

What disturbed her most was why she hadn't gone straight to their house. Instead, as she was about to drive past a police station she heard Joe Walter's voice repeat in her head—'It's not a problem. You said Monroe had taken the gun to the police, so all you are doing is adding to the story.'

Wrapped in a bath towel she sat on the edge of the bed and held her phone in her right hand, scrolling through with her thumb until her home number showed on the screen. She was about to make the call when she hesitated and tossed the phone onto the bed, staring at the rain splashing against the window. A couple of minutes passed before she tried again, ending the call the moment the dialling tone sounded in her ear. For several minutes she paced back and forth in the dimly lit room, stopping to take hold of the back of the only chair. She stood still, letting her eyes roam around the cheerless surroundings.

'Monroe,' she said nervously several minutes later.

'Where the hell are you? I've rung you at least ten times. Isn't your phone working?'

Stevie recognised the desperation in Monroe's voice. She could feel herself begin to shake.

'I'm sorry, Monroe. I fouled up. I shouldn't have said what I did to Greg. Is he mad at…'

'What the hell are you talking about? Where is Greg? I can't raise him anywhere. He's not answering his phone. I've left numerous messages. Where are you?'

Stevie was thrown. It seemed Greg hadn't been in touch with Monroe.

'I'm in some B&B on Bodmin moor. I'm on…'

'What's going on? You're supposed to be in Durham with Greg. Where is he?'

Stevie felt moisture gathering in her eyes.

'I don't know, Monroe. I was with him last night, then we had a row.'

'Oh, hell. No.' Monroe sighed. 'What about?'

Tears where running down Stevie's face. She wasn't sure what to say.

'I started to tell him about the gun…'

'You fucking what?' Monroe shouted down the phone. 'I thought you were going up to see him to get to know him. You didn't need to talk about all of that.' Monroe paused. For a minute neither spoke.

'Did you talk about Juliet's death?' he asked in a worried tone.

'I just said she was shot.' Stevie heard the line go dead.

'Monroe, Monroe,' she yelled.

* * *

Monroe placed the handset on the scrubbed-wood work surface next to his empty glass of wine.

'Hmm,' he muttered, twisting the stem of the glass in his hand a few times before replacing it on the surface and pushing it away from him. He'd bought it as part of a set of six with Stevie on their honeymoon in Venice. They'd woken one morning with no set plans and decided to take the vaporetto to Murano and Burano. He remembered clearly how they walked down the sandy path from the little church on Burano, expecting there to be a water bus to take them to the other island for lunch. Somehow they'd messed up their timings as no bus came for about an hour. When they finally arrived in Murano, hungry and thirsty, they fell on the first restaurant still serving lunch and devoured, with relish, a dish of fried seafood—calamari, prawns, lobster and mussels. All washed down with a cold bottle of Pinot Grigio. After coffee, they ambled in and out of the glass shops that sat either side of the main canal, ending up in the large emporium where they bought the glass he'd just drunk from.

*Why the hell did she do all that stuff with Greg?* he asked himself. All that'll do is stir everything up again, just when Greg was coming round. Monroe knew he'd been wrong in putting the phone down on Stevie, but what she had done had made him angry. He pulled up his jeans around his waist and moved to the end of the kitchen to pour a glass of whisky.

The next morning, at eight, he was awoken by a knock on the door. He hadn't slept well, worried about the whereabouts of Stevie and Greg. He pulled on his old towelling dressing gown, ragged and worn from age, and stumbled downstairs.

Inspector Symes was standing about a metre away from his front door, neatly dressed and expressionless. For a moment she reminded Monroe of a troublesome old girlfriend. *Another reason for not liking here,* he thought

'Yes,' he said, with one arm barring her entry. He noticed she wasn't alone. Standing about a metre and a half behind was Sergeant Wilson, wearing jeans and a navy polo shirt.

'We'd like a word, please, Mr Lidlington.' Inspector Symes took a pace forward and was about to raise her left foot to reach Monroe's front door step.

'Maybe I wouldn't,' Monroe replied curtly, casting a dilatory glance between the two police officers.

'I'm tired, Inspector, and not in the mood for passing the time with you two.' He moved away from his door and started to push it closed.

'Good bye.'

'I can't accept that, Mr Lidlington,' Inspector Symes replied sharply. 'If you won't let us in we'll have to ask for a warrant.' She looked up so her eyes met Monroe's.

'And I believe we'll get that, pronto. So it's a choice between letting us in for a quite chat now, or having us come back.' She paused, increasing the intensity of her stare. 'Your call.'

'What do you want a quiet chat about?' Monroe asked, his arm still barring their entrance.

'Mr Lidlington,' Inspector Symes replied forthrightly. 'We don't do police business on the doorstep. Take my advice and let us come in and talk.'

Monroe looked them both up and down. Inspector Symes hadn't moved; her eyes fixed on him. Behind her, Sergeant Wilson fiddled with his phone. Monroe wanted to put them off 'Can't you come back tomorrow?' he said 'I can agree a time.'

Inspector Symes starred at Monroe coldly and replied saying, 'Yeah, I can, but I'll have an arrest warrant with me.' She looked into Monroe's eyes. 'For hindering police in the course of a murder investigation.'

Reluctantly Monroe moved away from the door and started to walk down the hall to the kitchen.

'This way,' he said gruffly, hearing the front door close behind the two police officers. He sat down in his usual chair at the end of the table, pulling his dressing gown tight around him, and made a gesture with his right hand for the other two to do the same. In the middle of the table sat an empty glass and a bottle of whisky, about a quarter full.

'What do you want?' he asked, making no attempt to clear away the evidence of his previous night's lonely binge.

Inspector Symes rested her jaws in her cupped hands, her elbows resting on the table about a third of a metre apart. Monroe remembered her penetrating stare from the last time she'd come to ask him questions.

'Your wife, Stevie, came to see us yesterday.'

'Where is she?' Monroe asked confused, wondering why Stevie would want to go to see the police.

Sergeant Wilson looked up from his notes. He had an impassive expression on his face.

'She said she came to confirm what you had already told us; about the gun,' he said.

Monroe put his hands down to the arms of chair and gripped them. He felt a thud in his stomach. A clammy sensation came over him. He wasn't at all sure what to do or say next.

'So you see, Mr Lidlington,' Jo Symes chipped in, her steely eyes firmly fixed on Monroe.

'We're a bit confused, as we can't seem to trace an occasion when you came to report the finding of a gun. We thought if we came to see you, you might be able to throw some light on things.'

Monroe stood up. He walked towards the kettle, thinking hard about his response.

'Tea or coffee?' he asked.

'Well? Mr Lidlington. Can you explain?' Jo Symes replied, still holding Monroe firmly in her gaze.

Monroe turned with the kettle in his hand.

'Stevie found it after the burglary.'

'What burglary?' Symes snapped.

For the next ten minutes Monroe, nervously, told them about the break in and how Stevie came across the gun the next day. He tried hard not to miss any bits out and kept his recollection as true to the events as he could remember. At the end, Inspector Symes turned to him.

'So what did you do with the gun?' she asked.

Monroe had been expecting the question.

'Chucked it in the sea,' he replied, watching for the response of the two detectives.

* * *

Au Treu Square, Hanoi, is a mixture of old and new Vietnam. Nestled in the middle, built by the French towards the end of the 19th century in a style reminiscent of European architecture of the period, is the magnificent St. Joseph's cathedral, known as Nha Tho Lou or Big Church by Hanoi residents and a symbol of how far the Church of Rome was spreading its tentacles at that time. Elsewhere, French colonial buildings, three and four floors high with their windows framed by large painted shutters, would house Vietnamese shops or cafés, their owners' families resident in the upper floors, or fashionable European style restaurants. As a result Vietnamese and tourists alike congregated in and passed through the square almost at any time of the day and night, helping to make the location one of the most vibrant parts of the city. Beggars, aware that the area had more money passing hands than elsewhere, would wait outside the more expensive restaurants ready to pounce as the customers left.

Monroe sat in a bar overlooking the cathedral where he'd agree to meet Greg and sipped from his second glass of ice cold water. A large ceiling fan whirled away above him, its draught affording a brief respite from the sultry humidity. His shirt, damp from perspiration, hung limp on his shoulders, his shorts stuck to him and beads of sweat trickled down his face. He wiped his face for the umpteenth time and looked at his watch. It was 12.45 and he'd been expecting Greg since noon.

Despite being told by Inspector Symes not to leave the country, he'd decided to fly to Hanoi to try to find Greg the day after he split with Stevie. After a tearful conversation, when he told her he couldn't face living with her anymore, she'd said, 'What're you going to do about Greg?' He remembered thinking cynically, at the time, that she was trying to sound sympathetic until she added, 'I bet he's gone back to Hanoi, that's were he told me he'd left his heart.' The new inhabitants of Greg's old home in Vietnam had told Monroe that Greg worked in Manger. He called the restaurant and left a message for Greg to meet him.

Greg shuffled into the bar an hour late. He was wearing a pair of dirty, torn and ragged jeans, an off white long sleeved shirt that hung loose around his waist with the sleeves rolled up to his elbows and a pair of rubber flip flops, the ends of which were split and frayed. He looked as though he hadn't shaved for about a week to ten days. Monroe stood up, his heart quickening, as Greg neared the table. He took a step forward to embrace Greg as they always had and stopped. Greg seemed to be avoiding eye contact, standing still and making no effort to greet Monroe in any way. He looked weary, as though he'd made a great effort to be there. There was no sign of pleasure or happiness on his face.

Monroe's heart sunk. Never, as long as he could remember, had he seen Greg like this. Their relationship had always been strong, greeting each other spontaneously with a hug or embrace, today it seemed as though the spark that ignited Greg's happy go lucky nature had gone out.

'What's up? You look depressed, out of sorts,' Monroe said, unsure how to start the conversation.

Greg gave Monroe a quick glance and turned towards the spare plastic seated chair, placing his hands on the shiny metal crossbars that formed the upright back and pulled it out to sit on. Monroe noticed that Greg's hands were trembling. He moved next to Greg and looked into his eyes.

'Greg, tell me what's bugging you. I haven't come all this way after not seeing you for a couple of months, hearing nothing from you for the last six weeks or more to suddenly find that you can't even give me the time of day. Snap out of it.'

Greg slowly turned his shoulders towards Monroe, twisted his head slightly and raised his eyes a little. His hands shook as he gripped the edge of the table. He turned again to look Monroe in the eye.'

'Dad, I think you killed mum.'

* * *

Monroe caught a plane back to London the next day. Greg had walked out on Monroe immediately after he'd made his dramatic pronouncement. Monroe had tried in vain to call him back, left messages at the restaurant where he worked, but heard nothing. After a heart searching night he came to the conclusion that he'd leave Greg for a while, return to England, sort out Inspector Symes and then come back to prove to Greg that he was wrong.

He was the first to leave the plane. To his surprise one of the aircrew had come up to him shortly after the plane had reached its allocated gate and invited him to leave before anyone else. He'd taken a sleeping pill shortly after take off and managed to stay asleep for most of the long flight from Singapore, waking only a few minutes before landing. As a consequence, he found he was still a little woozy and light headed as he descended the steps of the aircraft to the reception committee that awaited him.

They stood about three metres away from where the last step from the aircraft met the ground. A group of four, Inspector Symes, Sergeant Wilson and two uniformed police, one holding a lead at the end of which sat a bristling police dog, panting, with its tongue hanging out. The other uniformed officer, clearly, was armed. To the right of where the four police stood, three police vehicles, a squad car, a saloon car and the dog handler's vehicle were parked in a neat row.

Inspector Symes strode forward as Monroe reached the last few steps.

'Mr Lidlington,' she said, flanked by the other three. 'I have a warrant for your arrest for the murder of Juliet Lidlington.'

Monroe reached out for the support of the handrail. He felt he was going to pass out.

# 15

Greg sat cross-legged on the dusty stone floor. He looked all around the small room that had been his and Kim's home for the past few months. Untidy piles of books, varying in height and some spilling over, filled one corner. Masses of cheap, copied CDs, devoid of their cases, were spread indiscriminately across the glass top of the bamboo coffee table. Semi-orderly accumulations of washed and worn clothes stood waiting to be squeezed into his already full rucksack. Next to him was a large cardboard box of souvenirs, his camera, pens, writing paper, framed pictures of him and his mother, letters he wanted to keep and other bits and pieces that had some sentimental or emotional value to him. He didn't have a clue as to how he would fit it all in to his bulging bag. He shifted his weight onto his right buttock and outstretched arm, straightening his leg in the process. A huge cockroach scuttled from beneath his shorts and ran towards the open window.

'Watch out, Kim,' he yelled as she walked passed him, missing the insect by centimetres, and carrying a pile of her clothes to her similarly full backpack.

She lunged at the insect, no doubt hoping she'd either end its life or speed its progress to wherever it was heading. It escaped and headed off at a greater speed to a distant corner before disappearing into a gap between the floor and the wall. Appearing unperturbed by the animal's plight she dumped her pile of belongings next to her bag.

'How you doing?' she asked as she turned to look at Greg, standing and moving items around inside his rucksack to try to create some additional space.

Greg, wearing a dirty pair of khaki shorts and a tattered navy polo shirt smiled and started to walk towards Kim, scuffing his flip-flops across the floor. The smell of street cooking reached his nostrils.

'Badly,' he replied. 'Lets go get some of that.' He tossed his head in the direction of the intoxicating smell and sniffed.

'Maybe we'll pack better when we're fed?'

At a café in the street below their flat they shared a bowl of noodles and a couple of rice bread rolls and watched the throng of people bustling back and forth from the street market opposite. Many a time they had walked up and down the narrow streets that made up the length and breadth of the market's territory. On each occasion they'd encountered large containers of live fish and eels, clucking chickens, unaware of their imminent death, great mountains of eggs, vivid displays of fresh coriander, fennel, chillies, peppers, garlic and ginger; wooden bowls of cumin seeds, cardamom pods, ground turmeric, nuts and other unusual spices unique to Vietnam. Every day they'd be fruit stalls bulging with ripe pineapples, soft mangoes and papayas, odd shaped coconuts, prickly lychees and small sweet bananas. On the corner of every street a riot of colour would shine from the florid flower stalls that served the love affair Hanoi's residents had with everything horticultural. They sat for nearly an hour, captivated by what shortly would be just a memory.

At ten, Kim and Greg, both hot and tired, left their flat in Hanoi for the last time and set off on a long walk to the train station. It was 11 when they reached the station, in time to board the overnight express to Ho Chi Minh City. Greg felt a tinge of sadness as he climbed the steps to the interior of their coach. He dumped his backpack on the floor of the four berth compartment and turned to help Kim. He noticed a little moisture in her eyes.

'Tell me we'll come back, someday, Greg,' she said, dropping her bag on an empty bunk and pulling Greg close to her.

Shortly after they'd unpacked a few essentials onto the two bunks they'd had allocated to them, an older Vietnamese couple entered the compartment. Kim and Greg, conversing in the limited Vietnamese they had picked up, offered their greetings to the man and woman. The couple looked at them, grunted a reply and then turned away to unpack. After a minute or two the woman placed a couple of wooden bowls, two pairs of chopsticks and a plastic container on the bottom bunk. She opened the container and, using the chopsticks, scraped portions of what looked like fried rice into each bowl. As the train pulled out of the station the couple sat on the bunk facing Kim and Greg and ate their meal, occasionally one turning to the other to mutter a comment. Kim looked at Greg. Without saying anything the two of them rose and moved to the corridor where they watched the lights of Hanoi disappear into the distance. When they returned to the compartment about half an hour later the man and woman were asleep—the man snoring loudly. Kim and Greg kissed each other goodnight, climbed into their bunks and attempted to go to sleep.

Lying on his bunk, Greg wasn't aware if Kim had managed to fall asleep, but he knew for certain that whatever sleep he'd experienced had been little and intermittent. The train's soporific motion had lulled him off many times only to find, on almost every occasion, he would be woken a few minutes later by the increasingly loud noises coming from the Vietnamese man opposite. After several hours of tossing and turning Greg became aware that a silence had descended over the compartment. The snoring had ceased. He turned again onto his side, hoping the train's motion and his tiredness would allow him to fall into a deep sleep for what was left of the night. Half an hour later he woke up, freezing cold. The air-conditioning was icy. He shivered and wearily swung his legs over the bunk, quietly lowering himself to the floor. As he stood completely still the only sound he could hear was deep, rhythmic breathing coming from the other three occupants of the compartment. He figured they were fast asleep. Silently he slid open the door and eased himself into the corridor. For once the warmth and humidity, often heavy and oppressing, was a welcome relief from the chilly conditions of the carriage he'd just left.

The city of Vinh is approximately 200 kilometres south of Hanoi sitting in the middle of the region known as East Central Vietnam. It has a population of around 175,000 and is the commercial centre of a vast agricultural area. At 5 a.m. Greg stood in the corridor and watched as the train crossed over the Song Ca River, leading to the Gulf of Tonkin. He remembered reading in a book about the Vietnam war that this area was the scene of many bloody battles.

Slowly the train pulled into Vinh station and came to a halt. Greg felt a little hungry and thought he would stretch his legs. He climbed down the steps and sauntered off to a kiosk selling croissants and rolls. He bought two cheese-filled croissants and sat on a bench watching the other passengers, who'd also alighted, queuing at the various food stalls on the platform.

His eyes closed, his head started to loll. He moved around to fight off the waves of tiredness that had suddenly started to wash over him. Whenever he moved his arms or shuffled with his feet his limbs felt heavy and immobile, as though he was immersed in a vat of treacle. In his mind he questioned what he was doing and where he was. And then, without any warning, it seemed that someone had pressed a button in his memory. Subconsciously his thoughts had started to rewind, to the time when his dad turned up to tell him that his mum had been killed.

*They'd had a row. Mum walked out on him. He didn't say where she went. He said he went to sleep. In the morning he got up and went fishing.*

Greg shook his head. As had happened several times before he found he was questioning every aspect of his father's story. Each time he did, the more he was certain he was right. Next to him a woman carefully replaced her half-eaten rice cakes in a plastic container and walked towards the train. At the other end of the bench two men, deep in conversation, rose and while still talking moved in the direction of an open carriage. He didn't notice them or the woman.

*He said he pulled her body up in fishing net! My God, everyone would sympathise with that.*

'Exactly,' Greg yelled out. 'And he didn't have an alibi.'

He thought he felt someone touch his shoulder. He looked up to find Kim, a worried look on her face, standing over him and tugging on his polo shirt.

'Quick Greg. The train's going.'

* * *

They found Ho Chi Minh City different from Hanoi. It didn't have quite the same authenticity and intrinsic charm as the northern capital, where the tentacles of globalization had, as yet, not reached. Hanoi was earthy and true to its inhabitants, whereas Ho Chi Minh City was tainted by creeping westernization. Streets were busier. Cars, a rarity in the north, took preference over bikes and pedestrians, and large skyscraper type buildings, like the tall glass-clad headquarters of the HSBC, appeared everywhere. In many ways it was more commercial. At night, bars, restaurants, jazz clubs and an undercover sex industry continued well into the early hours, unlike the 10 p.m. lights out they had been used to in Hanoi. But, despite their comparisons with the capital they found it was a thronging, vibrant Vietnamese city whose inhabitants bustled furiously from one place to another. And like Hanoi, its streets were packed with exciting markets where strong, spicy smells from the nearby street cafés filled the air.

At the end of their third day, tiring a little of tourist trips and sites, they sat in one of the many parks sipping Tiger beer and chatting generally about the city.

'Have you thought about when you're going home?' Kim asked all of a sudden.

Greg, sitting opposite on a white plastic chair, looked blank. Her question had taken him by surprise.

'I don't know,' he replied wistfully. 'How about you?'

Kim picked up her glass, staring into it as she drained the last dregs of her beer. She put it down on the stained white table and looked at Greg. He was watching a large white butterfly that had landed on the edge of the table. For a brief moment it stood still, its wings motionless and perfect, then it fluttered gently and flitted away. He laughed and turned again to Kim. He noticed a small tear in one of her eyes.

'What's wrong?' he asked, reaching out to hold her hand.

'I guess I don't want to be like that butterfly. A brief part of your life for just a moment, then disappearing for ever.'

Greg smiled, still holding on to her hand. He squeezed it.

'That butterfly was beautiful, like you.'

Kim started to cry openly. She wiped away the tears from her cheek.

'Thanks, luv,' she said with a weak smile. 'Have you thought about us?'

Greg thought about what she'd said. He looked away for a moment at the large puddle from the afternoon's monsoon, a little smaller from when they'd first sat down. *Dried up in the sun*, he guessed.

'Not really.' He saw pain in her face. 'I'm sorry. I know I should have done but I…' He paused. Kim had puckered her lips. Her head was down.

'I guess I've been pre-occupied with thinking about dad.'

Kim looked up. Her face was stained and smudged from her tears. 'Where've you got to?'

'What do you mean?' Greg replied, looking a little confused.

'About you're dad. What conclusion have you come to?'

Greg stood up and picked up the two empty glasses.

'Another one?'

'I'm fine,' Kim replied, looking at him.

'Be quick, luv.' She watched him walk to the small queue in front of the kiosk, serving drinks. Her eyes scanned the people going back and forth. Young couples stood around motor bikes and chatted, older men with long white hair and natural goatee beards sat under the big sprawling trees, youngsters badgered tourists continually to buy postcards, t-shirts or copies of Graham Green's novel—A Quiet American. Clearly different from Hanoi were the many Vietnamese people dressed in western clothes: men in smart, well-tailored business suits, woman in knee-length tight skirts and short-sleeved chic blouses. All going about their business, keen to show they had deadlines to meet.

Greg stood several centimetres above the rest of the drink's queue. After a while his turn to be served came and he ordered another can of beer, paid for it and returned to where Kim was waiting for him. Seeing her sitting forward, anxious for him to return, seemed to set up inside him a sort of barrier, a dam that blocked the flow of his innermost thoughts and concerns. He wanted to tell her everything—but he found he just couldn't.

'That's good,' he said as he took a swig from his drink.

'Greg,' Kim said anxiously.

'Your dad? You said you'd tell me.'

Greg took another sip of beer.

*I can't*, he said to himself. He looked away at a woman walking past, selling sliced pineapple from a large wicker basket.

'Greg. What's up with you?'

Greg turned to face Kim. He felt her large brown eyes boring right into the centre of his.

'It's nothing to do with you and I just don't want to talk about it.'

Kim brushed her right hand through her hair, threw her head back and looked at Greg with a shocked expression.

'So it's OK for you to pour your heart out to me after you've slept with me, tell me you love me every day, live together like man and wife and then, when we have to make some decisions about the future, you just shrug it off and say, "I just don't want to talk about it." That simply isn't good enough. I want…'

'Hey,' Greg said seeing the moisture well up in Kim's eyes. 'What's all this about the future. I didn't know we were having some sort of in depth discussion.'

'Do you want notice? Look, Greg. I love you and I want to know what's going to happen to us.' Kim lost it. Large tears started to stream down her face. She bit her bottom lip.

'I'm sorry,' she said quietly as she reached out for his hand. 'I've got used to you. I don't want to loose you now.'

Greg screwed up his eyes. He was confused.

'I'm not going anywhere. What's all this about loosing me?' He held back on embracing her. In the north of the country, displays of public affection were frowned upon. Even if the culture was different in the south, he didn't want to take the risk of upsetting the local population. She was still holding his right hand between hers. He put his left hand on top.

She looked into his eyes.

'You sure?' she said with a questioning look on her face.

'I'm sure. Where did you think I was going?'

'I thought now we're through with Vietnam, you be going back home, to see your dad.'

Greg shook his head. He reached forward and placed his hands around her neck.

'No. I'm not going to do that,' he said forcefully. 'I love you, and am staying with you.'

A huge broad smile came across Kim's face.

'I'm sorry,' she laughed, pulling a tissue from her bag. 'I'll have a drink now.'

They sat and talked for some time about their plans. They figured out that between them they had sufficient money to get to Cambodia, Laos and Bangkok; work for a bit and then go on to Burma and the top right hand corner of India with the intention of reaching Nepal before the winter.

'When shall we start,' Kim asked as they both, simultaneously, drained their third beers.

'Tomorrow, I guess,' Greg answered and then looked Kim straight in the eyes. 'I never want to see my father again.'

# 16

Joe Walters leaned back in his leather chair and swung around a few degrees. He let his hands drop into his lap and clasped them together. He was pleased. His routine search of his computer files had found no trace of anything he thought might be incriminating. Every morning he checked them and each time he found nothing. This morning he'd come in earlier than normal to give them a second and third going over—just to be sure. He rose from his desk, walked to the large window that overlooked Bishopsgate and gazed down as the City went to work. Most mornings at the beginning of his day, before the start of his back to back schedule of appointments, he'd take a few minutes to watch the endless stream of people on their way to their place of work. He found the sight of so many workers going about their business with obvious purpose mildly therapeutic. It reinforced his confidence in the health of the country's financial heartland. Over the years, he'd found he could gauge the strength of the economy by the number of people on the streets. More people meant a strong economy, less a weak one. Today, even at 8 a.m., the pavements were thick, the coffee shops full. Good, he thought, as he moved back to his desk and, while still standing, looked at the single sheet of neatly typed foolscap that sat in the middle of the immaculate expanse of ash wood. He picked it up and took it with him to one of his easy chairs.

He was wearing a faintly checked lightweight navy suit—new for the occasion—a light blue silk shirt and a discreet navy silk tie with random red motifs dotted here and there. His polished black shoes were handmade by a shoemaker in Jermyn Street. He pulled up his trousers, slightly, to avoid them sagging at the knees and sat down. He picked up the typed agenda, headed:

## VISIT OF MR JAN DE BOERS
## CHAIRMAN
## THE MIAX CORPORATION
## MONDAY, JUNE 28th.

Joe let his eyes roam up and down the day's timetable. He'd written it himself and checked the document's presentation many times, making a slight adjustment here and there, either in the substance of the day's events or in the look or layout of the itinerary. He dropped the paper on the table and leant back. He felt good about the day's visit, confident that his careful planning would ensure that it would proceed smoothly without any embarrassing hitches. He congratulated himself on previously spotting a glaring error in the proposed itinerary, where the head of IT had suggested that Jan de Boers had a working lunch— take away pizzas—with all the section heads.

'I know this is the age of enlightenment, get to know your staff and all that,' he'd said when Guy Williams had shown him the draft, 'but Jan de Boer is not a man of the people. He's Afrikaans. They've been used to years of people serving him. He's not one to slum things.' Guy had been visibly taken aback, prompting him to ask Joe if Jan was a racist.

'Of course not,' Joe had replied vigorously. 'The ANC routed all those out some time ago,' he added to ensure he didn't offend Guy, of Afro Caribbean ethnicity.

'How you doing,' Joe said a few minutes later when Anna came in with his diary, some papers and three newspapers: The Times, Financial Times and The Telegraph. She was wearing a smart grey suit, beige silk blouse and matching grey shoes.

'Good,' she replied, giving Joe an affectionate kiss on the cheek and sitting opposite him in one of the other easy chairs. Some years earlier, shortly after she'd split up with her husband, they'd had a mild affair. Joe, concerned that it might have become out of control and affect his work, brought it to an amicable end, but not before he'd set Anna up in a flat and promised that he'd look after her financially, which he did until she met her present boyfriend, a TV producer.

'We went to Paul McCartney's "Back in America concert,"' she added.

Joe smiled. 'Good?'

'Excellent. He really worked hard.' Anna paused and looked at Joe. 'You calm and ready for the day?'

'No problems,' Joe replied confidently. 'What you got for me?'

Anna pushed a few letters across the table for him to sign and placed the three newspapers in a neat pile, overlapping so the name of the paper was visible.

'Just some letters for your signature,' she said. 'Want a coffee, Joe?'

He nodded while attentively reading the first letter. When he'd finished he placed it flat on the table, took out a black Mont Blanc pen from a leather pen and pencil case and signed it. By the time Anna had returned with the two coffees he'd read the other two letters and signed them. She never made any mistakes, but he always read through in detail everything she gave him.

'So,' she said, looking at her watch. 'Five minutes and he'll be here.'

Joe drained his coffee.

'I just need to make one call. I'll join you outside in a minute.'

Joe waited to hear the click of the door closing. He reached for the unopened copy of The Times and turned immediately to page five. Quickly he read for a second time the report of the arrest of Monroe

Lidlington, charged with the murder of his wife, Juliet. He took note of the page number and closed the paper, replacing it back on the pile, exactly as he had found it. He stood up, adjusted his tie, fastened the top two buttons of his jacket and walked out of his office to meet Anna at the door to the lift.

Jan de Boer's silver Mercedes swept to the entrance of Miax UK at exactly 9.30, as planned. A reception party of Joe, Anna, the financial director, the operations director and the sales director were there to meet him. As the car stopped, his driver leapt out to open the back door. Jan was tall, about one metre ninety, and thin. He had swept back blonde hair, a suntan, blue eyes and was dressed in a light grey linen suit, a grey shirt and a navy and grey tie. He strode over to Joe and took hold of his outstretched hand.

'How you're doing, Joe?' he said with a pronounced Afrikaans accent. Joe replied and then proceeded quickly to introduce him to the others.

'You guys have organised some nice weather,' he said, pointing to the sky as they all followed him into the building, Joe at his side.

The day went as Joe had predicted. In the morning Jan spent time with the financial director and the operations director. All those who had been part of the reception party had lunch with him at Jamie Oliver's restaurant, Fifteen. He said he had never eaten so well in such a pleasant environment. Joe skilfully ensured Jan remained the centre of attention, allowing him to monopolise conversation and appear a natural raconteur. In the afternoon he visited all the remaining departments, shaking hands and laughing and joking with all members of staff. By four he'd been everywhere. Anna escorted him back to Joe's office for his last meeting. She was present to take notes.

'How do think it's gone?' Joe asked as their guest visited the bathroom.

Anna looked at Joe with a wry smile.

'Oh, they all think he's wonderful.'

'And you?' he asked.'

'He's a real slime ball, Joe. But you told me that.' Anna looked up. Jan had emerged from the WC.

'Would you like a cup of English tea, Jan.'

'My dear, that would be swell,' Jan answered as he swept passed her to return to his seat.

For half an hour, over tea and biscuits, Joe took Jan through all the company figures, showed him all the favourable press cuttings from the British and American financial press, updated him on the status of current and future projects and discussed the pros and cons of all tendered contracts.

'I must say, Joe, you do an excellent job.' He smiled as he sipped his tea, turning to Anna. 'And so do you, my love.'

'Thank you,' Anna said, returning his smile. 'When do you return to South Africa?'

'Oh,' he replied, pausing and sitting upright in his chair.

'Thanks to the wonderful work you folks do in keeping everything under control, I can go onto Europe and take a little break. My girlfriend is joining me in the morning and we're flying on to St Tropez to stay on her uncle's yacht for a few days.'

'That'll be nice,' Anna replied, noticing a wink from Joe.

'If you both are fine, I have a few things to attend to.'

Jan rose. He walked over to Anna.

'My dear,' he said as he leant forward to kiss her on both cheeks.

'Thank you so much for looking after me. It's been delightful. My very best wishes to you and your family.' He held out his hand for Anna to shake.

'No problem, Jan. Have a good time in France.' Anna withdrew her hand from his, smiled and said, 'Bye then.' She turned and walked out.

Jan de Boer walked over to where the teapot and milk stood.

'May I?' he asked looking out of the window.

'What a swell day, Joe,' he added without looking at Joe.

Joe, ignoring what he considered where fatuous comments, sat down in the chair nearest to Jan. He reached across to The Times, folded it back at page five and pushed it towards Jan. Once Jan had picked it up, Joe tapped him on the arm and then put his right fore-finger to his lip to signify silence. He looked at Jan for some signal of understanding. Jan looked at Joe then nodded his head once before dropping his eyes to read the article. Jan read it, gave Joe a quick expressionless glance, and then read it again. He looked up, nodded his head twice, and closed the paper. Joe folded it away and placed it in his briefcase. Often he would take The Times home to do the crossword.

'Shall we go,' he said to Jan, holding his arm out and sweeping it towards the door.

'Congratulations, Joe,' Jan said loudly as the door opened to the outer office.

'You have things tightly controlled. I'm indebted to you.' He turned to shake Joe's hand, seeing Anna waiting to take him down in the lift to his car.

Joe shrugged his shoulders.

'I'll come down with you,' he said, gesturing Joe towards the lift.

\* \* \*

Jennifer Philp stood back and examined the way she'd laid the table. *That's better,* she thought, having rearranged the crockery and cutlery several times. She'd invited two girlfriends and their partners to come and meet Joe. He wasn't that keen at first, giving as an excuse the visit from South Africa of his chairmen. She was able to talk him round by promising to arrange everything—all he had to do was to turn up. Her current anxiety was caused by her uncertainty over the placement of the wine glasses. Should she put the small glasses in front or to the left of the big ones? She decided to leave things as they were. They were eating in her small, recently converted, dining room. The walls were covered with a regency stripe paper, the carpet dusty pink, the table and chairs polished mahogany with spindly legs. It was clean and tidy, but lacking in character.

A few minutes later, at six, she sat on a chair in the kitchen, a cup of Earl Grey tea with a slice of lemon to her side, The Mail open in front of her.

'My God,' she yelled, feeling a surge of elation and knocking over the cup, the pale scented liquid spilling all over the paper.

'They've arrested him. I told Stevie he was no good.' She leapt up, dabbed a kitchen cloth on the soggy newspaper and reached for the cordless phone. Holding the phone in one hand she furiously thumbed through her telephone book, hoping to find the only contact number she had for Stevie.

*The girl will see some sense, now,* she told herself as she turned from page to page, annoyed that she couldn't remember under what letter she would have written the number. Having searched all likely options she decided to start at the beginning, turning every page, until she came to a name she recognised.

'I can't wait to tell her,' she said aloud, overcome by frustration.

'That you, Stevie? Jennifer here. I've something important to…'

'It's not Stevie. I'm Nina. Who are you?'

Jennifer felt embarrassed. She'd made a fool of herself. *Stevie doesn't sound anything like Nina,* she told herself. Nina's foreign with dark skin. 'It's Jennifer. I'm sorry Nina, I wasn't thinking.'

'OK, but she's not in. She's working. Do you want me to tell her you called.'

'Oh thanks, Nina. Please do, and say it's urgent.'

'If it's about Monroe, I think she already knows. Monroe called her.'

'He called her?' Jennifer asked, surprised and slightly deflated. She wanted to be the first to break the news. 'I didn't think they were talking?'

'I don't know, Jennifer. But I'll pass on your message.'

\* \* \*

Stevie pushed open the door to Nina's flat, dropped her bag on the floor and let herself slide down the wall. She ended up sitting cross-legged, facing the opposite wall with just enough strength to push the door closed with her right foot. For a while she didn't move, hoping the pain she felt in both her feet would subside and, from somewhere, a trickle of energy would miraculously revitalise her body.

Monroe had called at eight that morning. She'd listened nervously to what he had to say, been at a loss as to how to respond and then broken down in tears. Nina had heard her and tried to offer some comfort. Stevie had brushed her away, mumbled a bit about Monroe and said she had to get out. All she'd managed to do was pull on a pair of old tatty jeans, a sleeveless black vest and a pair of flip-flops. She'd run out of the house with no make-up, grateful for her low maintenance hairstyle.

She'd walked all day, endlessly drifting from one park to the other. She started in Kensington Gardens, just across the road from Nina's flat in Ladbroke Square, and then onto Hyde Park, crossing over Park Lane into Green Park before ending up in St James's. She didn't eat, existing only on bottles of cold mineral water bought from kiosks and mobile vendors. In St James Park she sat on a bench for an hour, starring vacantly as London's varied and cosmopolitan population strolled pass her, some stopping to share her bench and enjoy the sunshine.

After a bit, when her feet ached less, she pulled herself up. On the other side of the hall, set aside from the rest of the pile of opened and unopened mail that sat permanently on the hall table, she saw a white unopened envelope with her name scrawled boldly in pencil across the top. She picked it up and read, 'Hope you're OK, see u tonight,' above the neatly typed address. Stevie smiled. Typical of Nina, she thought, checking that the letter wasn't addressed to her. Looks like a bill, she guessed, as she was about to lay it back on the table. At the bottom she saw PTO written in large letters. She picked it up again and turned it over, 'Your mother called! Asked if you'd ring her urgently!—Love N xxx.'

'Fat chance,' Stevie muttered, tossing the letter back on the table. *She's read about Monroe in the papers and wants to gloat, I bet. Well she* can bloody well call me. Speaking to her is the last thing I want to do.

At 1 a.m. Stevie awoke. She'd been asleep in a chair in Nina's living room, for how long, she didn't know. The darkness of the room was a clue, as was the stiffness of her body and how cold she felt. She looked at her watch and gasped. Wearily she pulled herself up and stumbled across to the light switch, pressing it down. She heard someone yell. She jumped. Nina, looking terrified, was standing next to the kettle, gripping the work surface.

'Hey. Tell me next time you going to do that. I nearly jumped out of my skin. I was creeping around in the dark, trying not to wake you.' Nina looked away at the steam rising from the kettle.

'Want a cuppa?' she added, pointing to the two mugs she'd laid out. Stevie nodded, apologised, and they both moved into the living area.

Nina's small basement flat had been cleverly put together. The high tech, utility feel of the kitchen, created by the mixture of matt stainless steel units, topped with a black granite work surface and a limed wooden floor, contrasted with the warm ambience of the adjacent living area, where soft uplighters washed light peachy walls and two large, light grey couches sat facing each other on the same wooden floor as the kitchen.

'Monroe's been arrested,' Stevie said as soon as they both sat down on opposite ends of one of the couches.

Nina, still wearing her chef's overhauls, sipped her tea and frowned.

'Didn't you expect it?' she said, with what seemed like a slightly knowing expression on her face.

Stevie sat back. She put her tea down on the arm of the sofa, her lips were tightly shut. She looked at Nina and made a grimace, her mouth remaining closed.

'Maybe, she said. 'But it doesn't make it any better. I loved that guy. For a short while we had something I've never had before from anyone. I still love him.' She put her hand up to her forehead and rubbed it.

Nina looked confused.

'I thought you…'

'I know,' Stevie said, leaning forward and turning her head to face Nina. 'I know I told you I think he snuffed out his last wife. But...' She put her hand up to her mouth and sniffed. She could feel moisture in her eyes.

'I just don't know, Nina. I'm all confused. When he told me...' She stopped to wipe away a tear and swallowed. '...he had been arrested I just broke down. I sobbed down the phone.'

'What did he say?'

'Not much, really. He was quite calm. He said he was allowed two calls—one to his next of kin and one to a solicitor. So he called me.' Stevie turned to Nina.

'Whatever I think, Nina. And I know it's a terrible thing to say, but if his wife hadn't died, I probably would never have married him.'

Nina looked sceptical. 'I suppose so,' she said.

Stevie leapt up. She paced back and forth across the room. She turned to Nina.

'You don't know him,' she snapped. 'You think he's guilty, don't you.'

'Stevie,' Nina replied, looking stunned. 'Hang on a minute. I know nothing about this case apart from what you've told me. When you came here you told me you were convinced that he'd done it. You said you didn't want to see...'

'Well I was wrong,' Stevie shouted. 'I've been thinking about it all day and I've changed my mind.' She looked hard at Nina.

'Oh, Nina,' she said, suddenly tearful. 'I don't care a shit. I just want him back.'

\* \* \*

Jennifer Philp was feeling edgy. She'd broken a dish, dropped some of the salmon mouse on the kitchen floor and stained her black crepe de chine trousers, necessitating a change into a sleeveless black dress with a plunging neckline. Joe was late and she'd been unable to contact him, Stevie hadn't called back and her guests were about to arrive. She decided to pour herself a large gin and tonic.

'Sorry,' she heard Joe yell as he came in through the front door.

'I had to see Jan off properly.'

Joe kissed her on the cheek. She deliberately held back.

'You could have rung. I've been trying to get hold of you all day,' she said with a frosty tone.

'I told you I couldn't be contacted today. I barred all calls. What's the big deal?'

'Over there,' Jennifer said, still deliberately aloof and pointing to the folded back copy of The Mail on the table.

Joe walked over and picked it up. He glanced down at the bold headline over a picture of Monroe.

## CONVICTED FRAUDSTER CHARGE WITH WIFE'S MURDER

Facing the wall, he read the article in full. Jennifer watched him, stealing herself for his reaction. When he'd come to the end he tossed the paper on the work surface and turned. She smiled.

'They've got him,' she said. 'I knew he was a…' She stopped. Joe was looking stern and serious.

'He didn't do it, you know. I've known him for ages and it's completely out of character. Juliet and he were a devoted couple.'

Jennifer felt crestfallen.

'But I thought you persuaded Stevie to speak to the police?'

'I did, but just to keep the record straight.'

'What?' Jennifer yelled, angry and frustrated by Joe's confusing attitude. The shrill tone of the doorbell brought to an end any further discussion. Jennifer glared at Joe before rushing off to great her guests.

# 17

Monroe shifted slightly in his seat to allow his left hand to reach for his wallet. The taxi had turned the corner at the bottom of his road and was slowing to stop outside his house. He wondered in what state he'd find everything after leaving so quickly for Vietnam, ten days ago. The car rolled to a halt outside his front gate. The driver looked down at the meter, waiting for Monroe to move.

'How much?' Monroe enquired.

'£25,' the driver replied without looking at Monroe. He kept his gaze firmly fixed on the front windscreen.

Monroe guessed the man knew. He had sensed a stand-offish attitude from the moment he'd picked him up from outside the magistrate's court. All the press buzzing around would have started the man thinking. He would have had time during the drive to work it out. And the picture in last Thursday's local paper—that would have confirmed the guy's suspicions. No doubt he thinks he's got a murderer in the back of his car, Monroe concluded.

'Thanks,' Monroe said as he paid the driver the fare plus a tip and closed the door. The man said nothing. He took the money from

Monroe's outstretched hand, wound up his window and drove off, confirming Monroe's suspicions.

*Is this how it's going to be?* Monroe asked himself, his eyes roaming all around for lurking reporters and photographers. Relieved that the street was empty, he made a note to congratulate Tim, his solicitor, for arranging the press statement outside the court. It must have given them something to work on, he thought, as he reached into his bag and fumbled for his keys. All around him parched, wilting plants and shrubs, dry soil, dusty paving stones told him the heatwave that started at the beginning of June had continued while he'd been away. His own front garden seemed worse than others, telling him that Stevie hadn't visited.

*God it's hot*, he thought as he walked to his front door. A trickle of perspiration ran down the back of his polo shirt, his clothes felt dirty, clinging to his body. They were the same ones he'd worn on the plane back from Vietnam. He pushed back his front door, slammed it closed behind him and stood still. He dumped his two bags at his feet, put his hand over his eyes and rubbed his face.

*What do I do know?* he asked himself, dropping down to sit on the top of his big bag. In the last ten days he'd continuously believed he was trapped in a bottomless pit with no chance of escape. His nightmare started in Hanoi, when Greg accused him of murdering Juliet and then subsequently walking out on him, leaving him almost suicidal and needing to be helped into a taxi back to his hotel. At least, he admitted, he'd been able to sleep on the flight, a respite before his arrest.

*I should be thankful I was bailed.* Hell, I thought I'd be in that goddamned cell for the rest of my godforsaken life. Why am I going through so much shit? He didn't try to find an immediate answer. Instead, he thought about the alternative to bail and shuddered, suddenly feeling grateful, finding a chink in the darkness ranging inside his head. He decided to take a shower

At 12, washed and shaved and wearing a pair of navy shorts, a yellow t-shirt and sandals he descended the stairs. He flung open the top of the stable door to the garden and started to hunt around the kitchen for something to eat. He found a can of tuna, some dried penne, one egg, a tin of olives, a stick of frozen bread and some olive oil. After about fifteen minutes he carried a cold pasta salad, a bottle of bear and a hunk of the ciabatta bread to the slate table outside.

He pulled up one of the empty wrought iron chairs, sat down and took a swig from his beer. A ray of sunshine darted through the nearby trees to fall on his hand, a bee buzzed up from the tired pots and landed on the middle of the table. *I've been here before*, he thought.

The yellowing lawn, the thirsty plants and pots, the fading flowers and the roses. Dusty flagstones and bird droppings on the slate table top. All of it reminded him of previous times, but none were more pronounced in his memory than the time, just after Juliet's funeral, when he had sat in the same garden with Greg, a year earlier, when the sun was similarly hot and the vegetation equally tired and in need of water. He thought how he'd tried to help Greg rebuild his life, persuading him to meet up again with his mates and start his course in Durham.

'How I've failed,' he said as he pushed aside his food. He stared at a couple of fallen rose petals, twisting and turning in the light breeze on the grey stones.

'Greg,' he whispered and wondered where in the world his beloved son was and what he'd be doing at present. He prayed he'd be safe.

Later, after sitting silently for some time he wearily collected his dried up meal, his warm beer, the untouched bread and carried them all inside to discard in the bin. He dragged himself upstairs and lay on his bed, hoping he'd fall asleep.

The early afternoon sun woke him. His short bout of sleep had been brought to an abrupt end by the dazzling rays flooding his bedroom and illuminating his face.

'Shit,' he yelled, remembering that on a hot day the front bedroom, facing west, was always bathed in sunshine. *I should have closed the curtains?* he told himself as he forced his tired body to sit upright.

Disorientated, devoid of any purpose, he ambled over to the window and stared out. In the distance a large three-masted schooner tacked and set a course for the entrance to the harbour, its magnificent expanse of sail stark against the deep blue sky. Stretching from the boat's crafted bow a white, foamy wake ran the full length of the vessel and some distance behind it. Small sailing yachts and speedboats seem to hold back in respect of the majesty of the beautiful sailing ship. Monroe shook his head, turned and headed in the direction of the staircase.

He sat in the living room, cold and miserable, with an opened bottle of scotch sitting on the table in front of him. 'Maybe a third will do the trick', he said, pouring a generous amount into his glass. He held the glass to his lips, sipping the liquid until the fiery warmth had reached his stomach. He waited, hopefully, for a feeling of well being to kick in and make his misery disappear. The phone rang. He let it ring until the answerphone clicked in and he listened, first to his own voice and then to Stevie, leaving a message.

'Monroe it's me. I called Tim who'd told me you'd been bailed. I'm really pleased for you. I want to see you.' Stevie paused. Monroe could make out her breathing.

'I know you'll think this sounds crazy—I love you. Please call me at Nina's—0207 652 3863. Please.'

Monroe poured a fourth drink.

\* \* \*

Stevie turned up at seven, unannounced. Monroe opened the door to her and turned around, leaving her to follow him back to the sitting room. It had been some weeks, maybe a month since he'd last seen her and, suffering from the effects of the six or seven whiskies he consumed earlier, felt no noticeable emotion over her sudden appearance. He'd only been awake for half an hour and his head hurt like hell.

She stood quite still, watching him take a seat. She was wearing white baggy cotton trousers with deep turn-ups, a loose fitting white long sleeved cotton shirt, the sleeves rolled back to just above her wrists and a pair of leather flip-flops. A couple of small silver rings ran through the top of her right ear and on each of her wrists dangled an uneven number of large silver bracelets.

'Monroe,' she said, looking straight at him.

'I don't care if you did kill Juliet, I want you back. I wouldn't have married you if she was still...'

The pounding in Monroe's head had become more intense. He felt sick and would have preferred to remain seated but Stevie's words had made him jump to his feet.

'What did you say?' he snapped, resting one hand on the arm of the couch. 'Well I care. I care a lot if you think I killed her,' he said emphatically.

'You think I'd murder someone?' he added with a look of disbelief. 'Now you listen. If it wasn't...'

Stevie took his arm. Her big blue eyes seemed bright and intense, her strong bone structure pronounced. 'I don't know what I think, Monroe.' She shook her head.

'I guess I don't think you did it, but I don't really care anymore.' She grabbed hold of Monroe's other arm, trying to pull him round to face her.

'I love you and I want...'

Monroe shook her arms away. He didn't want to listen to her pleas and excuses. He stood and faced her head on. Only about a metre separated them.

'You thought enough about it to convince Greg that I did it?'

Stevie moved away. She sat down on one of the couches.

'That's not fair,' she replied, leaning forward, her elbows resting on her knees, her head supported by her hands.

'I just told him about the gun and then he walked out on me.'

Monroe walked to the window and stared down at the neglected garden.

'OK. If that was all you said to him, why has he vanished?'

'What do you mean?' Stevie asked with a look of concern on her face. 'I thought you went out to see him last week.'

'He walked out on me.' Monroe said, his gaze fixed on the bottom of the garden. This was the first time he'd spoken about Greg since their abortive meeting in Hanoi. It hurt.

'What do you mean?' Stevie asked, a worried look on her face.

Monroe had turned to face Stevie. He looked down at her. 'He said he thought I killed Juliet.'

She stood up and stood a little distance away. She looked shocked.

'Monroe, that's awful, I'm sorry.'

Monroe's mouth felt dry. The hammers in his head were still relentlessly banging away. He sneered at Stevie, unaware of the moisture in her eyes.

'Well it's too fucking late now,' he shouted. 'He's gone and I don't know were the hell he is. If you hadn't gone up to Durham, he probably would still be here now.' He stood up and pointed his right forefinger at Stevie.

'I hold you responsible for this.'

'No, Monroe, that's unjust. You thought going to Durham was a good idea.' Stevie shouted back. 'He would have found out one way or another.'

'Found out what?' Monroe retorted loudly.

'About his mother.'

Monroe paced quickly to the door of the room. He pointed down the hall with his right hand.

'Get out. I don't want to see you again. Greg's disowned me and I hold you responsible.'

Stevie stood quite still. Then she fell back on the couch, tears starting to well up in her eyes. She put her head in her hands.

'I'm sorry, Monroe,' she sobbed. 'I fouled all this up. Can we start all over again.'

Monroe looked at her. He was shaking all over; perspiration was starting to break out on his forehead, his head pounded and he felt ill.

'No,' he said firmly, unable and unwilling to think of anything else to say and walked out of the room.

* * *

Torrents of rain pounding on the slate roof woke Monroe at seven the following morning. He looked out of the window and saw great deluges falling from the sky. It seemed as though the rain was set in forever and would never stop. Tentatively he checked his physical and mental well being. His head no longer hurt, he wasn't shaking and no dark clouds seemed to lurk around his mind. He felt quite normal. *Not good, but OK*, he told himself. Gingerly he pulled on an old pair of jeans, a white t-shirt and a pair of his vintage sneakers. He made his way to the kitchen in search of food. There was no milk, butter or bread. He discovered a tin of baked beans, which he heated up and ate, accompanied by a dried water biscuit and a cup of black coffee. He came to the reluctant conclusion he'd have to go shopping.

After he'd shaved, ruffling up his short hair in the process, he started on the job of checking the cupboards and fridge for what he had to buy. He was focused, pleased that his mind was free of all the depressing baggage of the previous day. Grabbing a black denim jacket he walked out to his car at 8.10, hoping he'd miss the queues and be able to return home fairly soon.

The supermarket was busy. Many others had the same idea as he did. He found the whole experience disconcerting. People he knew, who he'd normally exchange a nod or pass a verbal greeting, ignored him. Assistants looked at him and quickly looked away; even the manager, who Monroe had often chatted to in the past, dashed to fill up a shelf when Monroe nearly collided with him. He felt like a pariah and suspected that people were saying to each other, 'Look out, that's Monroe Lidlington, the man who murdered his wife, then hitched up with a girl almost half his age. Keep out of his way.'

Some were downright rude, barging in front of him in the queues to the service counters, pretending they hadn't noticed him. He felt like yelling out, 'Hey, a man's innocent until he's proved guilty. I haven't been tried yet.' But he knew he'd be wasting his time. Their minds were made up.

Driving home in the rain Monroe tried to put the hostile behaviour of the other shoppers behind him. He decided to try to bring his life back to some order, establishing a routine to give him a sense of purpose. If he didn't, he believed he was in danger of falling into a quagmire of depression, even becoming suicidal, allowing thoughts and worries about Greg to monopolise his mind. It would all be too painful, destroying any rational, everyday thinking: best erased from his mind. Greg wouldn't be gone forever, he told himself, believing that once he'd been acquitted, the two of them would be reconciled, re-united somewhere.

An hour after he'd turned on his PC he sat staring at a blank screen. However hard he tried, words wouldn't come into his head. He was writing a factual account—truth not fiction—he reminded himself for encouragement. There was no need to invent or imagine a story, all he had to do was write down what had happened to him, using words and sentences that hung well together and jumped up from the page. But no inspiration came; instead he started to question what he'd written in previous chapters.

'Hell, I didn't write that,' he said aloud. He thought about deleting the complete file and all back-up, confining the whole project to the bin. He'd tried all the tricks he'd read for curing word block. Get something on the page or screen, they'd say; take a walk, make a drink. None had worked.

Instead, he found he was gazing out of the window, watching with interest as birds and squirrels scampered around the foot of the old birdbath Juliet had given him some time ago. *It looks dirty and rather out of place now*, he thought. It probably needs to be moved, found a more sympathetic location, one that will hide the unsightly attempted mending of the crack on the base, the result of some gardening Stevie and he had done, he remembered. Whenever his eyes moved away to watch a squirrel or bird gathering food or seeking worms, he found some trick in his memory kept dragging him back to the birdbath, watching senselessly as the rain trickled down the ornamental pillar to the damaged base.

The memories of many happy times; the month Greg was born, snowballing in the winter, the first spring Juliet and he had stood together and looked at the delicate white droplets, still and simple, after they'd had planted the bulbs the previous autumn. He saw the snowdrops clearly now—inspiration after Christmas was over and through the cold months to come. And, he remembered they were there on the day he and Stevie decided to marry—a large clump at the foot of the old birdbath.

*Now it just looks dirty, tired and out of place,* he thought with a heavy heart and shaking his head. That it was July, midsummer, and not the time for winter bulbs, didn't cross his mind, only that there were no snowdrops.

# 18

Kim sauntered slowly to where Greg had come to a standstill, a few paces in front of her. Both of them wore khaki shorts, hers were short and tight around her backside, Greg's long and baggy and touching his knees. He was wearing a sleeveless black vest; she'd chosen a red t-shirt. On his feet he had the same tired sandals he'd worn for the last month; Kim wore a pair of flip-flops. Slung loosely over Greg's shoulder was a small canvas backpack containing their money, passports, room keys and Kim's make up. The camera they shared, hung loosely around Kim's neck.

Neither had spoken for some minutes. Kim came to Greg's side and put her hand in his and like statues; they stood still, with open mouths, and gazed, awe-struck, as the early morning mist rose from the lost city of Angkor Wat. As far as their eyes could see, stone edifices, almost white from age, rose up from the surrounding plains and bush, most of the buildings intact and true to their original form. Long, open-sided cloister like walkways led to large temples topped with tall, spherical towers, each one with two or three circular balconies wrapped around the carved exterior. Here and there rectangular lakes, originally made by man and edged all around with neat brick faced lawns, separated one village or compound from the next. Built between 980 and 1220 AD the sprawling mass of temples that made up Angkor spread out over some 40 miles around the village of Siem Reap, about 192 miles from the Cambodian capital, Phnom Penh.

All day they ambled along stone terraces, in awe of the several 1000-year-old giant carvings of the Hindu God Vishnu, and amused by the many statues of sacred elephants. They entered holy tombs, lit candles and incense, wondered at the intricacy of stone sculptures of the God Vishnu and other ancient idols. Bullet holes and pockmarks, evidence of the civil wars that raged in the country until 1991, were everywhere. Towards the end of the afternoon they found themselves in the inner city of Suryavarman's Angkor, built by Suryavarman 1, the king of Kambuja, who reigned from 1006 to 1050 over an empire covering much of southern Vietnam, Thailand, Laos and the Malay Peninsula. In Angkor, he created a carefully planned system of plazas, avenues, temples, terraces and causeways in which he, his court and nobility lived.

At seven, standing together on the wide steps that led from one of the giant terraces, they watched the sun slowly drop below the top of the tallest temple, leaving for a moment the smaller ones silhouetted, their magical cones golden against the blackening sky, until they too became gradually shrouded by the deepening darkness.

'I think that's it,' Greg said, his tone a touch melancholic.

Kim had been standing with her legs slightly apart. She placed both her hands deep in her pockets, tilted her head slightly back towards the night sky and shook it several times, her dark hair catching the trickle of the evening breeze.

'I guess so,' she said forlornly.

'I've never seen anything like it.' She thought for a bit, admitting she was never likely to see anything else in her life that could replicate the sense of history and majesty that rose up and seemed to radiate through the old buildings and everything in the vicinity.

'Agree,' Greg added,

'It's so beautiful and mystic.' He turned away as the ancient buildings were finally hidden from view by the black of the night. They walked silently, hand in hand, for some time along the wide flagstone causeway, laid ten centuries earlier, until they were close by a small kiosk selling iced drinks and snacks and lit by a neon light strapped to a bamboo pole ascending into the sky. Greg bought a coke for himself and a bottle of water for Kim. They sat facing each other, cross-legged on a grass verge and sipped their drinks—both overwhelmed.

After a bit Kim leant back on the ground, her knees arched, and stared up at a black sky pierced by many twinkling stars. They're seemed more stars here than at home, she thought, until she realised she couldn't recall the last time, in England, she'd laid in the open and looked at the night sky. She felt she was under some sort of spell. The wonder of Angkor and all its mystery, the warm starlit night made her feel calm and tranquil, as though fate had at last decided to give her a break. She thought about Greg; his laugh, his carefree and easygoing manner, his love of life, the way he talked non-stop, his irritating but loveable habit of always loosing things. She laughed aloud, mindful of his disastrous time keeping and untidiness. How kind he'd been when they'd talked about how her parents died in the air crash, the way he listened patiently and so often. All of a sudden she bit her bottom lip—she felt a tiny tear form in her left eye. She stretched out her arm, touching the grass several times with her hand to find him, expecting he'd be lying by her side, absorbed as she was with the illuminated planets and blazing suns of the vast universe way yonder. He wasn't there. She sat up and saw him sitting at a nearby table reading a newspaper.

'Come over here,' he said, beckoning her to join him.

'What is it?' she asked, leaning on his shoulder and staring down at whatever had him transfixed.

'There, look, read it,' he said, jabbing his finger at the folded paper in front of him.

## PLAYBOY CHAIRMAN DEPARTS AFTER DEATHS SCANDAL

Millionaire resigns after announcement of Government investigation into mining disaster where 30 miners died

Jan de Boer, flamboyant 30-year-old playboy who inherited The Miax Corporation from his father Van de Boer, the son of the founder Frederick de Boer, a legend amongst the Afrikaans, unexpectedly resigned yesterday from the position of chairman of the company. Jan de Boer, who remains the owner and majority shareholder, handed all control of the company over to Joe Walters, an Englishman and currently chief executive of Miax UK.

Thirteen months ago 30 miners were killed in a disaster in one of the company's diamond mines 280 kilometres south of Johannesburg. An underground explosion, 850 metres below ground, caused by methane gas, tore apart a development area where men were working. The Miax Corporation immediately announced an internal investigation, which later, although blaming the explosion on a broken ventilation fan, exonerated the management from any blame and praised their speed in evacuating the other 2500 men who were working in the mine at the time. The South African government, under pressure from the families of the deceased, who believe the internal investigation was nothing but a whitewash, has recently announced a full government investigation into the disaster.

Jan de Boers, in announcing his resignation, categorically denied, when asked by a reporter, any connection between the explosion and his departure. 'I'm leaving my grandfather's business to those who know it better than myself, particularly the highly capable Joe

Walter's who now becomes chairman and chief executive.' Pressed on what he was going to do with his life, being relatively young, de Boers said, 'I'm going to be spending most of my time travelling the world, experiencing life in it's most basic forms.' Jan de Boers is reputed to be one of the richest people in the world. Most people suspect the 'experiences of life' he talks about will be spent in five star luxury.

Joe Walters, when contacted in London, wished Mr de Boers the best for the future, saying his contribution to the company would be missed. Mr Walters confirmed he would be running the company from his London office. Business analysts believe de Boers has let Walters run the company for some time. The announcement will make little change, apart from allowing de Boers to be well clear of the scene if and when, as widely expected, Miax comes under criticism from the government inquiry.

Kim looked at Greg. He looked serious and disturbed. The article meant nothing to her.

'What's it all about?'

'Sit down.' Greg took Kim's hand and gently pulled her down so she was sitting facing him. The paper sat on the table between them. Greg touched the article a couple of times with his right index finger.

'Mum knew all about this,' he said, tapping the paper a few more times.

'What,' Kim asked, bewildered.

'This disaster.' Greg jabbed the paper again with his finger. He seemed a little frustrated.

'Look, mum told me all about it. She said it didn't look good for Miax.'

Kim turned the paper back towards her. She looked up at Greg staring hard at her, impatient for her response.

'Look luv, I'm non-the wiser. Let me read it again,' she said.
Greg leant back.

'Go ahead,' he paused, pushing the newspaper a little nearer to Kim.
'But I can tell you all about it.'

Kim pushed the paper away. She saw in Greg an eagerness and sense
of purpose she hadn't seen before.

'I'm all ears,' she said. Greg sat up and looked at her. She thought he
was checking he had her full attention. A long flickering shadow from
the fading neon light hung across his face. Kim waited for him to speak.

'Mum told me that Miax had been instructed by the health and
safety executive, after a previous accident, to install back up fans in
every mine.'

'So?' Kim asked, still not sure where Greg was coming from.

'So,' he said, seemingly a little annoyed. 'They didn't do it in this
mine.'

Kim wriggled a bit. The wooden seat was beginning to feel a little
uncomfortable. She remained confused.

'Mum told me, just before she died.' Greg stopped and gripped the
table with both his hands. 'Because of budgets and all that stuff, they
hadn't got round to doing it in this mine,' he added forcefully.

'I still don't see what you're getting at.' Kim shook her head. She was
trying hard to grasp what he was talking about.

Greg stood up. He paced back and forwards and sat down.

'Look,' he said loudly, looking across at Kim. 'Mum was in charge of
all Miax's communications—she was a sort of spin-doctor,' he said
quickly and resolutely.

'We were speaking on the phone—I was in Vietnam—just before
she died. She told me all about this disaster and was seriously worried
they'd try to hide the truth.'

Kim had read all about big companies covering things up. *Is this one
of those?* she asked herself 'Who would have wanted to hide it?' she said,
looking up into Greg's eager eyes.

'Miax.'

'Miax? I thought they were squeaky clean?'

Greg looked away quickly and then back at Kim. 'Not really,' he answered with a sarcastic sneer. 'But what's worse is that mum used to work for Joe Walters.' Greg was thumbing through the article again. He stopped and pointed.

'Look,' he said pushing the paper back to Kim, his finger still pointing. 'He's now the chairman.'

Kim raced through the article and then dropped the paper on the table. She brushed her fingers through her hair and looked at Greg. She felt a shiver run through her body.

'What are you suggesting, Greg?' she asked, in awe of his answer. She didn't really understand what Greg was going on about, all she knew was he seemed uncharacteristically focused. She knew she was being irrational, but the thought of Greg revisiting his mother's death and his father's involvement frightened her.

Greg reached across the table and took Kim's hand.

'I guess I'm no longer sure that dad killed mum.'

Kim was stunned, unable to make any comment. She felt as though she'd been knocked sideways, nauseous and shaky. She looked into Greg's eyes and saw real pain.

'Oh God, Kim. If I was wrong.'

\* \* \*

The hotel they stayed at in Siem Reap, Grand Hotel de Angkor, lived up to its listing as inexpensive and basic. Their room was so small that they had to move around the bed in single file. Nestled between the bed and the outside wall a cracked, stained wash basin hung precariously from two bolts, looking as though it would fall to the floor if touched. Greg carefully turned on both the taps. Cold water ran from each. At the end of their corridor a small shower, with a stained, torn plastic curtain for privacy, served them and the occupants of the other nine rooms. Returning from dinner, they pushed open the door of their room to be greeted by a couple of large cockroaches, unlike any they'd seen before, scuttling across the bare wooden floor.

During their meal they hadn't spoken about the article in the paper or anything remotely connected to it, instead they conversed like a couple, long married and rather bored with each other's presence, commenting on things around them just to break an otherwise deadly silence. Later, after they'd made love, they clutched each other for some time, silent and still until they spontaneously and in harmony fell apart, lying on their backs and holding each other's hand.

'Don't leave me, Greg,' Kim said softly after a while. She listened and waited for many minutes for Greg's reply until she felt his hand fall away from hers, followed by the sound of his deep breathing. She turned away, closed her tear-drenched eyes and hoped she'd soon fall asleep.

Greg wasn't in the room when Kim awoke. The sun was up, people where moving around but he was missing. His backpack was sealed, propped up against the wall by the door. Trying not to read anything into his unusual readiness, she left their room for the shower. On her return, as she pushed open the door to their bedroom, she saw him sitting anxiously on the bed.

'I want to go to South Africa,' he said, before she closed the door.

'I've checked flights this morning and we can get a cheap flight from Bangkok the day after tomorrow.'

'Why?' Kim said, looking down on Greg. She wasn't sure why she'd asked—she knew the answer.

Greg stood up. He looked a little uncertain.

'I can't really explain it properly. I've been up since five thinking the whole thing through.' He came closer to where she was standing and looked her in the eyes.

'I think my mother was murdered.'

'We know that, Greg.'

'Not by my father, by someone else.'

Kim sat on the bed and looked away. She was confused. Ever since they'd made love the previous night she'd expected Greg, in the morning, to announce he'd be going to South Africa—on his own. Instead, he'd just asked her to go with him. She loved him and didn't want to leave him, but the thought of being around when he immersed himself in his quest for the truth about his mother's death filled her with dread. How would they both cope? The pain would be akin to cutting open a recently healed wound.

'I don't know, Greg. I'm not sure,' she said, looking up at him, resolute and looking eager for her reply.

# 19

Greg could see Kim clearly, standing on the platform at Siem Reap, wearing the same tight shorts she'd worn at Angkor Wat, a white vest and her trademark flip-flops. He'd been leaning out of the train window, his hands clasped behind her neck, looking into her big brown eyes, moist with tears.

'This isn't goodbye for good, Greg, is it?' she'd pleaded.

He'd shook his head.

'I'll be back as soon as I can. I promise.'

'When, Greg?' she'd asked as the train slowly started to move.

'I don't know, luv, but as soon as possible.'

They both had to release their hold on each other. The train was gathering speed. Kim ran alongside, waving and gradually falling back as the carriage pulled away. Their gestures continued until neither could see each other, anymore.

* * *

Greg twisted in his seat in an effort to find a more comfortable position. He watched the plane's wing dip and wondered what Kim would be doing, where she'd be? She said she'd go back to Hanoi and see if she could get a job again at Manger. *She'll be there now,* he thought, comfortable that she'd be in a familiar environment. But then she'd walk home from the restaurant at night, alone, in Hanoi. In the unlit, rat infested streets. Why wasn't she with him? Why didn't she understand his reasons for going to South Africa. He had tried to explain.

\* \* \*

'I can't do it,' Kim said, her eyes red and moist, the front of her white vest wet from her tears.

'For both of us,' she sobbed, 'there's too many wounds—stitched and settled. If we start to open them, it can only cause us pain.'

She'd just re-entered their room in the hostel in Siem Reap. Earlier, after Greg had announced his intention of going to South Africa, she'd walked out, saying she needed some time on her own to think. Greg had been confused, wanting her to go with him, at a loss as to her concern.

'Look, luv. I've said I think I might have been wrong about my dad. Surely you can understand that I can't rest until I've found out the truth.'

He wiped a tear away from her eye.

'If I'm wrong. I must know,' he added, plaintively

Kim sniffed and wiped her eyes. She turned to look at Greg. 'You think there's a conspiracy, don't you?'

Greg withdrew his hand and stood up. He walked up and down. 'I don't know. I'm not sure. But look.' He sat down again next to Kim.

'Mum told me Jan de Boers was a slime ball, never doing any work, leaving Joe Walters to run the company while he spent his time freewheeling around the world.'

'How does that help?' Kim asked. She'd stopped crying. Her eyes seemed brighter.

Greg turned to face her. He thought he saw a glimmer of understanding in her face.

'It's just too much of a coincidence,' he said, standing up again.

'What is? Kim asked, looking up at him.

'It's like this.' Greg was standing still. *It's all so logical*, he thought.

'Mum told me about the mine disaster. She said she thought Miax would try to hush it all up, and then.' He stopped and hesitated. 'And then she was killed.'

He bit his lip, shaking his head slowly back and forwards.

'Kim,' he said vigorously. 'Since then. Until now, nothing else has been heard about it.' He looked down at Kim. She had started to cry again.

'I'm sorry,' she said tearfully. 'You'll have to go on your own, Greg. I understand. I know what you must be going through. I love you, but I'm frightened. I think raking over the past will just be too awful. I don't think I can take it.'

Greg felt angry. He thought he'd explained and couldn't understand Kim's reluctance to support him. He grabbed tightly onto both her arms and shook her.

'What do you mean you love me? Do you think I should just walk away from it? Allow the truth about mum's death to go untold? If you really cared you'd come,' he shouted.

'Greg, that's not what I said.' Kim shook him off and walked away to the far corner of the room. She watched while Greg stood still, his head bowed, arms dangling at his side. After a couple of minutes she slowly walked out of the room, holding back her tears until she was out in the corridor. She wasn't crying when she returned a little later, just standing at the door with a desolate expression.

'Let's go,' she'd said sadly. 'I'll come to the station with you.'

\* \* \*

Halfway down Cleveland, in the Sandown area of Johannesburg, Greg found the small and unimpressive offices of The Miax Corporation. He was surprised at the size. All around him imposing, glass fronted office blocks rose to the sky. The area abounded with swanky shops, smart restaurants and four and five star hotels, each boasting haute cuisine of the highest standard. Based on the vastness of Miax, its tentacles and influence stretching in all parts of the globe, Greg had expected their headquarters to be the best and most prestigious in the area. Instead, he was met by a single scratched nameplate, amongst 16 others, next to an intercom system on the front door of a nondescript, tired, old building.

He pressed the buzzer and waited; glad that he'd been able to buy a fleece lined corduroy jacket in Bangkok. A cold wind blew, sheets of rain pounded the street. Vietnam and South-East Asia seemed miles away. After 30 seconds he pressed again.

'Yees,' a female voice, unmistakably Afrikaans, answered.

'I want to talk to someone about the explosion in Welkom about 13 months ago,' he said authoritatively, having rehearsed the line many times.

'What explosion? Don't know what you're talking about.' The intercom clicked, followed by silence.

Greg looked around him, watching the taxis drop business people at the entrance to the various offices and convention centres. The rain was pouring out of the sky by the bucketful, sluicing across the roads to flow down large drains. Everywhere he looked people carried umbrellas.

*Have I got the right place?* he asked himself, as he studied closely the small name adjacent to the button he'd just pressed. Clearly, it read The Miax Corporation. Maybe this is a just a subsidiary office, he thought, not the main one. He waited for an answer to the intercom.

'Yees,' the same voice said.

Greg summoned up all his courage.

'Is this the headquarters of The Miax Corporation?'

'Who are you?' the voice snarled.

'Greg Lidlington. My mother used to work for you in England. She was Joe Walter's…'

'We know all about her,' the same voice said, less aggressively than before. 'What do you want?'

Greg shivered. The wind seemed to have increased in its intensity. The bottoms of his jeans were damp from the blustery downpours, blown his way with increased regularity. He turned up the collar of his jacket.

'My mother told me all about the Welkom disaster. I want to ask…'

'Come in, come in quickly and take the lift to the sixth floor. Someone will meet you there,' the voice said, rapidly.

Greg heard a metallic click as the door's lock was released electronically. He stepped inside, glad for the shelter, and entered a small uninviting entrance hall with a single desk to one side manned by a uniformed security guard. He walked across the tiled floor towards a couple of elevators on the back wall, expecting to be challenged. The man looked up from his desk, nodded at him and returned to whatever he was reading. *Strange*, Greg thought. *Casual, bit low key for a big company.*

The lift door opened to reveal a small lobby with a two-seater couch and grey painted walls that led off to a narrow corridor. By the couch was an empty desk. In the middle of its wooden top a single grey telephone sat next to a white card, propped up by a strut attached to its back. On the card, typed neatly, was a short message, USE THE PHONE TO ASK FOR WHO YOU WANT TO SEE. Greg reached forward to pick up the receiver.

'That will not be necessary, Mr Lidlington,' a voice said from behind him. He turned to see a tall, well built man with thick black hair and dressed in a modest grey suit, white shirt and conservative tie, wearing polished black shoes. Greg guessed he must be in his mid thirties. The man took one pace forward, looked Greg up and down and stretched out his hand. Greg felt his hand being crushed by the man's pulverising grip.

'Come this way,' the man said with a stony look on his face. He turned and walked down a narrow corridor with closed doors, each with a small brass nameplate on it. *Sinister*, Greg thought, following the man.

They entered an office at the end of the corridor. The man walked around the far side of a white laminated desk, empty and missing anything that would indicate anyone worked there, and sat down. Greg figured he was supposed to sit in the vacant chair opposite.

'Mr Lidlington,' the man said without looking at Greg directly.

'You may not be aware but this small office is just the legally registered office of The Miax Corporation. All operating files and records are kept in the functional headquarters in Bishopsgate, London. All we do here is safeguard the company accounts and file whatever documents are required by businesses registered in South Africa.' He stopped for a moment and looked at Greg.

'Do you understand? Nobody here could answer any question about the company's activities, past or present.'

Greg was aware that this guy, with his Afrikaans accent, unwilling or too rude to introduce himself, was at last looking at him, waiting for him to speak.

'Well, why does the plaque on the door say, The Miax Corporation, South Africa? Mr…, I didn't catch your name.' Greg watched for the man's reaction.

The man stood up. He held up his large hand and started flapping it, dismissively, in Greg's direction. Greg read the gesture to mean—go, get out. The man started to move towards where Greg remained seated.

'If you'll excuse me, Mr Lidlington. I have to go.'

Greg shifted in his chair so the man couldn't pass him.

'So you're not prepared to tell me how 30 miners lost their lives in one of your gold mines in Welkom?' Greg focused his eyes on the man's face. It remained expressionless.

'I have no comment, Mr Lidlington. You'll have to direct your enquiries to our headquarters in London.' The man moved to the other side of the desk.

'Now,' he said insistently, 'I'll have to escort you to the lift.'

'So you accept there was a disaster, then?' Greg watched as the man remained still, his face expressionless, at the far end of the desk.

'Whoever answered your door bell denied there ever was one.' For the first time in the short discussion with this nameless person Greg reckoned he saw a flicker of emotion in the man's eyes. The man had moved his head and for a brief moment seemed a little concerned. It didn't last long.

'Please, Mr Lidlington,' the man said, his now familiar deadpan expression covering his face, holding out both his hands and raising his arms simultaneously. 'I have to ask you to leave.' He pulled his lips back in a quick, sudden smile and then let his impassive expression return almost immediately.

'I'm sure London will be able to help you with your enquiries.'

Greg didn't bother to say good bye. He rose from his seat, turned and walked out of the office, heading for the lift, aware that the man would follow him until he left the building.

\* \* \*

Greg opened the door of Robby's Place in Pimville, Soweto and gasped. The air was thick with smoke, a local jazz band thumped out lively authentic tunes, fantastic and unusual food aromas wafted around and people were clearly enjoying themselves. Greg, aware he was the only white face, gingerly edged towards the bar and ordered a beer. He paid for his drink, found an empty stool and waited, savouring the intoxicating atmosphere.

Not much time passed before he was interrupted. A light tap on his shoulder brought him face to face with a short, balding guy wearing a pair of pressed dark navy jeans, a navy suede jacket with a zip down the front that had been fastened up to his neck and a pair of white trainers. Greg guessed his age to be early thirties.

'You must be Greg,' the man said with a broad grin. 'I'm Ayanda Ledwaba from the Sowetan.'

Greg took the man's outstretched hand. His handshake felt firm and solid. 'How did you know it was me?'

Ayanda smiled again and looked around.

'You look English, you're white and about 19. Can you see anyone else who fits the description you gave to the office?'

Greg smiled and nodded.

'You're right,' he answered. 'What're drinking?'

'Thanks, man,' Ayanda said a few minutes later as Greg placed two beers on a table in a quiet corner of the courtyard.

'First, can I ask you a question?' Ayanda said as Greg sat down.

'Go ahead,' Greg replied taking a sip on his beer.

'Why did you contact The Sowetan about the mine disaster?'

Ayanda sat back and listened while Greg took a full 15 minutes, taking care not to exaggerate or leave out bits, to tell first how his mother told him about the Welkom disaster, the circumstances surrounding her death, his suspicions of his father, the article in the Australian newspaper and finally his meeting at Miax. When he'd finished Ayanda leant back in his seat and laughed.

'Look, man. You're wasting your time talking to Miax.'

'I got that impression,' Greg replied, wondering what Ayanda was smiling about.

'They're Afrikaans. Jan de Boers is from one of the families that founded apartheid. He's a paid-up member of one of the right wing parties that laments the ending of the regime.' Ayanda picked up his bottle and drained it.

'If they had something to hide, you're not going to get it out of them. Nobody in management works for them unless they subscribe to white supremacy.'

Greg was shocked. He thought the end of apartheid and Nelson Mandela's presidency had routed out all the racists. From what Ayanda was telling him many were alive and kicking. He wanted to hear more.

'So can you tell me what happened in Welkom?'

Ayanda stood up. He pulled an A4 sheet from under his pad and gave it to Greg.

'Read this. I'll get you another drink. Same again?'

Greg nodded and started to read what Ayanda had given him. It was a copy of an article in The Sowetan, just after the accident.

## THIRTY DIE IN GOLD MINES
## MIAX DENY MISTAKES

Thirty mineworkers were killed in an explosion at the Miax Butix gold mine on Tuesday July 8, in South Africa's worst mining disaster in two years.

The explosion at the mine near Welkom, 280km south-west of Johannesburg, occurred about 850 metres underground and tore apart a development area where the men were working. Two more miners suffered serious burns, one of whom is in a critical condition in a local hospital. Six others escaped unharmed. Four thousand men were working in the mine at the time of the explosion and all have been accounted for. As news of the disaster spread, hundreds of anxious relatives telephoned to find out whether their loved ones were safe.

The immediate cause of the disaster is thought to have been a methane gas explosion. A broken fan had been reported the night before, which would have reduced air circulation and increased the danger of a gas build up. Four senior members of staff—two electricians, a vent officer and a production supervisor, who had been sent down the mine to investigate the breakage, were among the dead. The other 26 fatalities were construction workers repairing tracks. The disaster comes 51 weeks after a similar explosion killed seven at the same mine on July 15 last year.

In a statement, The Miax Corporation's divisional manager, Peter Rutts claimed that the lessons of last year's disaster had been learnt and the four senior members of staff were equipped with devices used to measure the presence of methane gas. He said that the deadly gas is "lighter than air and so in a haulage area methane can be quite high overhead and difficult to detect". He added that the lack of circulation caused by the broken fan could increase the danger of a methane build up.

The government has announced that there will be an investigation into the explosion. One question that must be addressed is why work at the mine had not been stopped, at least in the vicinity of the broken fan, when the danger of a build up of methane was known. With 4,000 miners underground at the time, the disaster could have been far greater.

South Africa's deep-level gold mines are among the most dangerous work environments in the world. The death toll last century is reported as anything from 69,000 to 100,000, with more than 1m workers injured in South African gold mines.

The gold is reached by blasting, which destabilises the overhead roofs and creates a constant danger of rock falls. Methane gas explosions and fire are also serious hazards, causing many deaths.

'What happened to the government investigation?' Greg asked as soon as Ayanda had rejoined him.

Ayanda looked serious for the first time.

'It didn't happen. Called off after Miax's own internal investigation.' Ayanda looked across the table and met Greg's eyes.

'Do you have any evidence about the back-up fan not being fitted?' Ayanda asked after several seconds.

Greg covered his mouth with his hand. In his mind he saw a picture of his dad, his eyes full of pain, sitting in the bar in Hanoi when he'd just told him he believed he'd killed his mother. Greg looked away. He noticed a large shadow was creeping across their table.

Ayanda tapped him on the shoulder.

'The back-up fan?' he asked.

'What?' Greg asked, his mind far away. He looked at Ayanda.

'Can we go inside, I'm a bit cold?'

\* \* \*

Ayanda dropped Greg at a recommended hostel in Johannesburg at around 10.30 p.m. Earlier, over a few more drinks and a meal, they'd agreed a course of action. Greg would return to the UK and go through his mother's papers and computer. He would look for evidence to substantiate his claim that no back-up fan had been fitted at the mine and that Miax had deliberately hushed it all up. Ayanda would keep in touch with the new government enquiry, aware that Greg's findings, when they became available, could be explosive.

Greg sat on the edge of his bed, uneasy and deeply disturbed. He couldn't speak to Kim. It was 5 a.m. in the east and she'd be asleep. *Should I call dad?* he kept asking himself, but each time he picked up his mobile phone he stopped, not sure how to start the conversation. Ayanda, with whom he'd quickly built a rapport, had explained to him that a few white supremacists still existed in South Africa, and were able, in some circumstances, to exercise some power and influence. Greg became convinced that Miax had hidden the truth behind the disaster, leaving serious questions in his mind about his mother's death. But despite Ayanda's logical and clear plan Greg was unsure as to how to proceed.

He stood up and paced back and forward around the tiny room, missing Kim and doing little to stop himself sliding into a mental state of remorse. At 11.30 he called his dad—there was no reply. Immediately he tried Kim, holding his phone close to his ear, hoping desperately as each ringing tone continued her voice would suddenly click in. Instead, his call was directed to her voice-mail. He lay on his bed, fully dressed, worried about her, where she might be, how she was coping? But repeatedly, almost insistently he found his mind was becoming saturated by a deep desire to see his father again. He tried, once more, to ring him.

* * *

Jan de Boer, wearing a long pair of Bermuda style bathing shorts and a Ralph Lauren yellow polo shirt, moved from the poolside chair he'd been sitting in to eat his breakfast, to one in the shade. In his hand he held a copy of an e-mail he'd just received. As he read it, his usual carefree expression changed.

'Darling,' a near naked young blonde woman said to him. 'You haven't eaten your breakfast.' In front of where he'd been sitting was an untouched bowl of sliced papaya, melon and pineapple. Next to the bowl was a wicker basket, brimming with croissants, Danish pastries, freshly cooked toast and slices of rye bread. A tall glass of iced orange juice, almost full to the rim, stood to the right and a glistening cafetière of freshly brewed coffee sat adjacent to a large white bone china cup and saucer.

He looked at his watch. It was afternoon in South Africa, he thought. They were about ten hours ahead of California.

'Sorry, sweetie. I'll finish it in a minute, but I have to make a call. Pass me my phone, please.' He took it and rose, walking to another chair, out of his girlfriend's earshot. He dialled one number and listened until someone answered.

'Is that you Albert?' he asked.

'Listen,' he continued after Albert had confirmed it was he who had answered.

'You've read the e-mail, no doubt. I'll pay you a couple of million rands to fix it.' He listened while Albert spoke and then he said, 'I'll take care of that. Just make sure that Miax is cleared of any wrongdoing.' He listened again.

'OK, I'll deal with that right away.' He ended the call and dialled another number. It rang for some time.

'Jabu, I've got a job for you.'

Jabu listened as Jan gave him his instructions. .

'Yes, in the next two or three days. Make sure it looks good. I'll pay you half a million rands. What?' Jan listened.

'I can't over the phone. I'll send you an e-mail with his details. I'm going to do it now. Confirm you've got it. And remember, if you mess up—no money.' He waited until Jabu had confirmed the instructions and rang off, going directly to his office to e-mail Jabu the details.

# 20

After a week in which Monroe moped around the house, unable to concentrate on anything for long enough to stop him sliding into a pit of self-pity and depression, he had a visitor. At first, when the trill metallic sound of the doorbell woke him, he ignored it, hoping whoever was at the door would go away. The sound seemed to become insistent, demanding his attention. Fearing it probably would be Inspector Symes or one of her lackeys, he pushed the newspaper, crumpled across his chest, to the floor and dragged himself to his feet.

Signs of his despondency were evident in every room. Books lay where they'd been discarded; on the living room floor, in the corner of the two couches, one of them halfway down the hall, open and page side down on the floorboards where it had been dropped. Used crockery, cutlery and glasses—the remains of food and drink clinging to their surfaces—festered in the kitchen alongside the empty bottles. Throughout, dead leaves from the garden, blown in through the open doors, mingled with the dust and made small bundles in odd corners. Each day, Monroe had crept out of the house at 7.30 in the morning to collect food and bare essentials from the supermarket, managing to complete his shopping in 15 minutes and without opening his lips. With leaden feet, he trudged towards his front door, dreading the prospect of having to make some conversation with a person or persons, however short it might be.

Monroe eased back the door. Johnny, looking almost raffish in a pair of aged navy chinos, a red polo shirt with frayed edges and wearing a pair of salty looking navy deck shoes, leaned against the porch wall. In his left hand he held what looked like a bottle, wrapped in paper.

'You going to let me in, so we can sort this one out,' he said, motioning to the bottle.

For a moment Monroe felt unsure. He hadn't seen or spoken to Johnny since a couple of days before his wedding. He thought Johnny had given up on him, on account of all the rumours about Julie's death and his speedy re-marriage.

'Come in, Johnny,' he finally said, a little sheepishly.

'You don't sound bloody sure, old chap,' Johnny replied, looking a bit put out. 'I've come to see if you're OK.'

'Sorry, Johnny, it's me,' Monroe said quickly as he fully opened the door. 'I'm not myself. Good to see you.' He put his hand out to take Johnny's. As they shook hands, Monroe met Johnny's piercing blue eyes, unflinching, but undoubtedly taking in his dishevelled appearance.

'I must look a bloody mess,' Monroe added, aware he hadn't shaved for five or six days or changed out of the same pair of jeans and t-shirt.

'Come on, old boy. What do you take me for? You know I don't care a jot about appearances. Are we going to get into this malt?' Johnny started to remove the red tissue from around the bottle he'd been holding, revealing a ten-year-old Arderg whisky. He pushed it in Monroe's direction.

'Let's do just that,' Monroe quickly replied, suddenly aware that the house must look badly neglected.

'We'll go in the garden.' He nodded his head towards the end of the hall. 'The house is in a bit of a state.'

'Doesn't worry me, old chap,' Johnny said as Monroe led the way down the hall, into the kitchen and through the stable doors that led to the patio.

'Plonk yourself down, Johnny. I'll get a couple of glasses.'

Monroe went to the dining room. All the everyday stuff needed washing. He returned, suddenly conscious of the sprawling mess all around his kitchen, with two of his treasured, antique, cut-glass whisky tumblers. They chinked slightly as he put them down on the slate-topped table, next to the already opened bottle. Johnny showed no outward signs of noticing the unusual display of best glassware. He poured large measures in both glasses.

'To you, Monroe,' he said, raising his glass in the air.

'You too,' Monroe responded, taking a large slug. The peaty taste stimulated his palate, a warm glowing sensation spread to his brain. He took a smaller sip and put his glass down.

'Reliably good, Johnny.'

Johnny leant forward, brushing a few leaves from the table top, squinting slightly from the early evening sun. He rested his chin in his right hand and looked at Monroe.

'Rose died a couple of months back.'

'My God, Johnny,' Monroe responded immediately, shocked to the core. 'Why didn't you tell me?'

Johnny stood up, picked up his glass and turned away from the table. He took a large sip and said, facing down the garden, 'She's not suffering anymore. It's better really. But, by Christ, Monroe…' He turned to look at Monroe face on. A small tear dribbled from his right eye. 'I miss her like hell.'

'Johnny,' Monroe said, standing up and putting his arm around his old friend's shoulder. 'You should have told me.'

Johnny sucked through his teeth. He shook his head.

'Nooo. Nooo,' he said slowly. 'You had your own problems. It was all going on about the time when Greg disappeared.'

Monroe looked at Johnny. 'How did you know about that?'

'Gossip, Monroe. Nothings secret in this town.' Johnny sat down next to his old friend.

'Anyway, enough of that. I didn't come round to tell you all my woes, old chap. I came to see how you're coping and…' He poured a second generous slug into their glasses.

'And to provide some sustenance.' He pushed Monroe's replenished glass towards him. 'Here, have another wee dram.'

Monroe studied Johnny's lined and weathered face. The aristocratic air that went with his fine bone structure, his sparkling bright eyes, his full head of flowing silver hair, his whimsical but reassuring smile.

*This is a man*, he thought, who'd probably grieve for the loss of his wife for the remainder of his days, but would do everything in his power to hide any outward signs of his emotion. He had genuinely come round to see how an old friend, going through a hard times, was coping; to cheer him up and offer any help. *Why have I been so self-indulgent, wrapped up in all my own crap?* Monroe asked himself.

The sun dipped slowly, the shadows became longer as Monroe told Johnny, from the beginning, all about the mess he was in, his worries and fears. He told him about the break in, Stevie finding the gun, her visit to Greg and his subsequent disappearance and her actions. He didn't miss anything out and Johnny didn't interrupt. Not once. He listened, topping up Monroe's glass so many times that Monroe had to put his hand out to say no. At the end Johnny looked at Monroe, brushed his right eyebrow with his right hand and said, 'Who do think killed Juliet?'

The sun had set. Fading twilight hung over Monroe's back garden. It started to feel a little cold. He shook his head back and forth, rubbed his stubbly chin, put his hand through his hair and stood up.

'I don't have a clue,' he replied and then added, holding onto the neck of whisky bottle, a third full.

'But it wasn't me.'

\* \* \*

Greg found the sloping narrow streets, small slate walls and stone fronted houses of Padstow comforting. This was his home. His earlier anxiety and tension had seemed to have given way to a sense of renewed identity. Shortly he'd be reunited with his father and that excited him, dismissing doubts and expectations of a possible uncomfortable meeting to focus only on the joy, he knew, they'd both feel at seeing each other again.

For almost all the time during the flight from Johannesburg, the long train journey from London to Bodmin and the coach to the local bus station he'd worried about their meeting. *How would it be?* After the heart wrenching way they'd split two months earlier, in Hanoi, he felt unsure, fearful of an unbridgeable gulf between them, destroyed by his hasty actions. When he wasn't thinking about the reunion, trying to turn his mind to other things, he found his thoughts returned to Kim, wondering how she was, what she'd be doing, when they might see each other again. Many times he'd tried to sleep, woken often by cramp and discomfort and finding his mind tripping back to where he'd left off.

The noise from seagulls overhead, familiar streets, a whiff of the sea air spurred him on as he walked up the hill from the harbour to his house. He felt good, confident and sure that past differences with his dad were over. Shortly, he'd be telling him about Miax and the mine disaster. He was certain, from that moment; both of them could start to rebuild their lives together, returning to the close, happy father and son relationship they always had. Stevie worried him. Their meeting in Durham was a disaster and would have to be sorted. He didn't dwell on her, convinced that if he made up with his dad, she'd follow on.

He didn't notice that there wasn't a window open in the house. He didn't look at the neglected front garden, the untouched splurges of seagull droppings covering the slate path. He only thought of seeing his dad's face and the two of them embracing in an undoubtedly emotional hug. He pressed the front door bell, dumping his backpack on the tiled porch while he waited for the door to be answered. *They could be out*, he thought, giving the bell another push. He'd called ahead a couple of times but nobody had answered. He tried the bell a third time. Deflated a little, he started to think where he'd left his keys, hoping they'd be somewhere close to the top of his bag.

*It sort of feels cold*, Greg thought, as he stood in the hall and let his eyes roam around. Christmas was the last time he was here, eight months ago, and he looked to see what had changed. He left his bag propped up against the front door and ventured down the hall towards the kitchen. It smelt musty, as though the windows had been closed for some time. He went to the stable door and pushed it open, poking his head out to look at the garden. He was shocked. All around were dead, dried up plants, parched, he suspected, by lack of water. Dusty leaves covered the tabletop, the small lawn was uncut and yellow, also desperate for a drink. Straggly, dried up remnants of geraniums, petunias and trailing lobelia hung miserably from all the pots. It looked unloved, he thought, surprised that his dad would have let things go— and why?

Greg looked around the kitchen. *That's an improvement*, he thought. A new green toaster—a wedding present, he guessed—had replaced the old shiny Russell Hobbs one that kept burning the toast. Different mugs hung from the mug tree, smart knifes of various sizes with black handles stuck out from a block of wood, two green solid-looking frying pans hung from the wall. Elsewhere all looked much the same.

*They've probably just popped out*, he thought, feeling hungry. He expectantly pulled open the door of the large American fridge that sat in an old disused fireplace, glad that his old friend, his source of instant nourishment and mood enhancement in his school days, still remained and had not been replaced by a newer, unfamiliar model. He audibly gasped.

'What the hell?' he said, aloud.

'What're they up too?' The fridge, normally brimming with every conceivable food, quick snacks, various alcohol, chocolate bars and bags of sweets, and an appliance that could be relied upon to satisfy any and every demand, whether it be a sudden attack of the munches, a meal or a drink, was completely empty, bar a solitary unwrapped pack of cheddar cheese. Greg was stunned. He'd never seen it like that.

Questions started to trickle into his mind. The bubble of euphoria that had cocooned him earlier had burst. He checked the dishwasher. It was empty and looking unused for a while. In a corner, by the microwave, he noticed two piles of unopened mail. One pile was for his dad and Mr & Mrs Lidlington, the other was for Stevie. Hers had the Padstow address scrawled through in his father's unmistakable writing and readdressed to a house in London.

*Separate addresses*, he thought and ran upstairs to his father's bedroom and flung open the cupboards. They seemed eerily empty, as they were after his father and he had removed his mother's clothes. Just a few of his dad's things hung sparsely in the space designed for two. The drawers contained only his father's belongings. His mother's old dressing table, where he'd expected to find Stevie's make up and stuff, was piled high with books and newspapers. The bed was unmade, left looking as though only one person had last slept in it. He charged to the other bedrooms, faintly hoping he'd find some evidence of Stevie's habitation. There was none.

Greg felt his mind about to explode. The happy, even emotive reunion he had expected with his father had not occurred, instead he was thrown again into confusion, not sure what was going on. He sat on the stairs in despair and looked out of the side window. There, in the distance, parked up on quay where he'd left it, was his old battered and rusty red Mini. He looked at his watch.

*If, with a bit luck, it started, I could be in London by the evening. It was worth a try*, he thought. He ran to his bedroom and started to hunt for the keys.

\* \* \*

Stevie stretched out along the full length of the couch and reached down for the latest edition of Harry Potter. She'd bought it a couple of days after returning from her sudden trip to see Monroe. *Something to get stuck into*, she'd thought. An anaesthetic from the pain she'd felt ever since she'd driven back. It was nearly midnight; she was totally absorbed in the story, close to the end and wanted to finish before her eyes gave up on her.

The previous night, after a long day helping out at the Lebanese restaurant where her friend Nina was chef, she'd fallen asleep with the book over her face. Sunlight, peeping through the curtains, had woken her. She'd jumped out of bed, taken a quick shower, pulled on a pair of shorts and a sleeveless vest and headed for the tiny brick patio that led off from the kitchen with the thick tome of Harry Potter under her arm. Passing the fridge, she had managed to grab a small carton of orange juice and a croissant from an opened packet.

Sitting in the shade on an old wooden bench, she read until six; when, reluctantly, she thought she should try to fix a quick supper. She put some bread, a small plate of Parma ham, some olives and a large glass of water on a wooden tray and carried it back to the patio, eager not to loose the thread of the story. With the tray balanced on her lap, a fork in her left hand she flipped open the book and scanned down to the last sentence she'd read. A word, a sentence, an expression in the prose, something broke her concentration. Instead of thinking about magic and spells, she found her thoughts had turned to Monroe.

*He's too wound up*, unable to think things through, she thought, as she placed a slice of ham on some bread. She put the book down, realising that this was the first time she'd thought rationally about Monroe, able to be objective. Maybe, she told herself, I should leave him for a bit, let him sort things out in his mind. It seems he's got a good lawyer in this guy, Tim. She returned to her book.

At 1 a.m. she awoke, startled by a loud knocking on the front door. She'd fallen asleep on the couch in the living room, her book, spread out, on the floor. Still drowsy, she dragged herself up, glanced quickly at her watch and wondered what she should do.

*Who could it be*, so late? she asked herself before doubts and worries started to take over her thoughts. She knew it wasn't Nina, she was staying over at her boyfriend's house. Perhaps someone in trouble, or just a drunk or a prankster? Whoever it was, she didn't feel inclined to go and see. She looked across the room to the curtains, glad she'd drawn them when she came in from the garden. Briefly she thought about sloping off to bed, turning the lights out and going to sleep. Too irresponsible, she told herself. I'm in somebody else's house; it could be the police. They'll knock again, she thought, and waited nervously.

# 21

'Come on, open up,' Greg shouted, impatiently. He was standing a few paces back from the front door, leaning at an angle of about 15° with his left arm outstretched, his hand flat against the door.

*What's going on? Why are they taking so long?* he asked himself, desperate for the door to suddenly swing open and Stevie to be standing in its frame, an end to the fatigue and anxiety he was suffering. He'd come all this way, travelled across two continents to find his access to someone he believed would give him a clue to his father's whereabouts barred by a sheet of solid black wood; a symbol, a manifestation of all the varied, competing emotions, the physical exhaustion and outright hunger that was raging through his mind and body. He raised his right arm, heavy like a leaden weight, and managed to lift the big brass knocker, bringing it down on the metal stud with a deafening thud for a second time.

'Who is it,' he heard from inside. It sounded like Stevie, but he couldn't be sure.

'It's me,' he yelled through the brass letterbox. 'Greg. Can I come in?'

Keys sounded in a lock. A metal sliding noise, which he took to be a security door chain, followed. *What if it's not her?* he asked himself. *What do I do?* He felt his heart beat faster. His mind flashed back to the last and first time he met Stevie in Durham, such a painful, abortive encounter. Would she want to talk to him? Maybe her relationship with his dad was so bad that she wouldn't want anything to do with him. He wondered if his rush to London, his tempestuous actions were reckless, lacking in serious consideration.

The door started to open. He had to move his outstretched hand quickly to avoid falling flat on his face. As he straightened up he found he was looking directly into Stevie's eyes, surprised and seemingly wary. He tried to find some words, but they didn't come.

'You'd better come in,' Stevie said after a bit and turned for Greg to follow.

They went into the living room. Stevie walked towards the couch, Greg remained standing, unsure what to do or say.

'Sit down, Greg,' Stevie said, quite coolly, gesturing with her hand for him to choose from either an old deep-seated wooden chair with an African style rug draped over it or a grey disfigured beanbag resting on the dark, stained floorboards. He chose the beanbag, his long legs crossed in front of him.

'Why have you come?' Stevie asked, resting her chin in her left hand, her index and forefinger covering her mouth.

Greg looked across the room to face her. Her face seemed pinched, her eyes narrow and suspicious.

'I guess,' he answered, unsure of how to start. 'I guess,' he continued, shaking his head from side to side, 'I wanted you to help me find dad.'

Stevie took her hand away from her mouth. Her face seemed to harden. She leaned forward and moved her head up a bit so her eyes met Greg's.

'Why do you want to find him? Your actions and attitude, in the last few months, didn't exactly do anything to help him. In fact, quite the opposite, Greg,' she said angrily.

'Do you have any idea how much your dad thinks of you? Do you know what you did to him in Vietnam? You very nearly sent him off the rails. You…'

Greg didn't hear Stevie's next comment. He was furious. 'Hold on,' he said loudly. 'That's hypercritical. You're the one who first accused dad. You came up to Durham, remember.' He turned his head in Stevie's direction. 'And started to sling the shit.' He stood up and started to pace around.

'Look,' he added loudly. 'I've come all the way from Cornwall to find dad. I've found some information about a mine disaster that I believe has something to do with mum's murder. Where is he?'

'You what?' Stevie retorted disdainfully, sitting back on the couch.

'Sit down Greg and listen to me. You haven't been in touch with your dad for ages. Now you suddenly appear, in the middle of the night, and expect everything to be hunky-dory. Painting yourself as some big knight on a white horse, floating down from on high. Come on, Greg. You need to do better than that.'

Greg didn't say anything for a few seconds. He just looked at Stevie, her back resting on the back of the couch, the tips of her fingers pressed covering her mouth and pointing upwards, her bright blue eyes boring right into him. He stretched out his legs.

'OK,' he said calmly. 'Let me try again.'

'Go ahead,' Stevie retorted, letting both her hands drop to rest together in her lap.

For the next ten minutes Greg told her everything he knew about the Miax mining disaster. He didn't miss anything out or add embellishments. Just the facts as he'd found out. He mentioned his meeting with the Sowetan journalist, Ayanda, the government enquiry and how whatever he found from his mother's records or files could have an explosive effect on the outcome. When he'd finished he looked to see Stevie's reaction. She looked pensive, stroking her chin with her hand and rubbing her face.

'He's been charged, Greg. He's out on bail.'

223

'With what?' Greg snapped indignantly.

'Murder. Murder of your mother.'

'Oh God, no,' Greg said, covering his head with his hands. He rubbed his face for several minutes, massaging his eyebrows, in what he knew was a hopeless attempt to wipe away some of his tiredness.

'But I think he's innocent,' he pleaded, looking up at the wall above Stevie's head.

*Is this my fault?* he asked himself. Would everything have been different if he hadn't flown off the rails in Durham and fled to Vietnam? Perhaps if he had stayed at home he could have been more help to his father, perhaps he could have stopped Stevie leaving him? Many more doubts and self incriminatory thoughts rankled in his mind. He blamed himself for everything; sad and sickened by his impatient, self-indulgence.

'I guess if I'd stayed at home, things would have been different,' he said tearfully. Through the hazy moisture that had formed in his eyes he saw Stevie get up. She stood over him.

'Don't blame yourself,' she said putting a hand on his shoulder.

He looked up. Stevie smiled at him.

'Why did you come here, Greg? Why didn't you stay down in Cornwall? Did you think your dad would be here?' Stevie, her eyes fixed on Greg, lowered herself into the straight-backed chair next to him.

Greg took a deep breath and straightened up.

'I don't know really,' he said quietly.

'I guess it was some sort of panic reaction to not finding dad at home and no trace of your belongings,' he added, feeling a little less despondent. He shook his head.

'It was pretty obvious that you'd gone. I was so keyed up in wanting to make things up with dad and tell him about the Miax disaster, that when he wasn't there I became frightened, desperate to unload my feelings on someone.' Greg frowned. He was annoyed by his impulsiveness.

'I saw your redirected letters.' He looked away, irritated that he'd left them in the car.

'And I thought I'd come and see you and find out what was going on. I...'

'But.' Stevie interrupted. She was leaning forward with a curious look on her face. 'Surely you didn't think Monroe was here?'

'I didn't,' Greg replied, feeling more in control of his emotions.

'I could tell you two had split up. I guess I sort of had to make contact with someone connected to him.' He stood up.

'Stevie, I'm going to do whatever is necessary to clear his name.'

Stevie's expression changed. She smiled. Her blue eyes looked alive.

'I'll help you, Greg,' she said, scanning his dirty, tired looking clothing.

'Greg? When did you last eat?'

They raided Nina's freezer to find a pizza and some garlic bread. Greg almost tore off the wrappings and put the food in the oven on the highest setting while Stevie made a couple of large mugs of coffee and plonked them down on the black granite work surface. They sat either side of the worktop on the two bar stools and stared for a moment at the oven, both resting their heads in their hands, their elbows on the breakfast bar, like a couple of penguins.

'It won't cook any faster,' Stevie said, laughing.

'No, but it smells good,' Greg replied, and then he turned to face Stevie.

'Let's say Miax deliberately didn't fit the back-up fan?'

Stevie looked at him.

'What're you on about?' she said looking bemused by his sudden change of subject.

Greg stood up, moved around the work surface and placed both his hands on the end, his arms outstretched. He felt focused again. The motivation that had brought him back from Vietnam to find the truth had returned. He looked at Stevie.

'The mining disaster. They would have wanted to save money.'

'Greg,' Stevie said urgently, pushing back in her seat. 'Slow down, you've lost me.'

Greg sat back on the stool. He rested his forearms on the edge of the worktop and opened his hands in a gesture. His eyes locked onto Stevie's. 'Look. Suppose they thought if that got out...'

'What got out?' Stevie asked, looking confused.

'Not fitting the back up fan to save money. In the post apartheid South Africa, it would do them immense harm.' He moved the fingers on one of his hands around on the granite surface for a few seconds, looking down and then returning his gaze to Stevie.

'Jan de Boer is a white supremacist. He couldn't care a fuck if a few black miners were killed in his mines—as long as it didn't affect his profits.'

'I get it,' Stevie said, looking shocked. She put her hands down to the side of her seat and tucked them under her bottom. She looked across at Greg.

'You think this is all some conspiracy, a cover up?'

'Mum told me on the phone, when I was in Vietnam, that she thought they'd try to hide it up, but...' He stopped. He felt a bit shaky, as though he might lose control, be unable to say what he was thinking, properly and concisely.

'She told me she'd stop them.'

Stevie moved her head sharply to the left to focus on Greg. The look on her face seemed full of doubt.

'She told you that? How was she going to do it?'

Greg shifted in his seat. He rested his elbow on the worktop, his left hand supporting his chin, his index finger against his cheekbone. He turned to Stevie.

'She said that if they wouldn't publish the report, she'd post it herself on the web.'

'Surely she would have lost her job if she done that?'

Greg shook his head a few times. He held his lips together. His eyes felt wet.

'Maybe,' he said, falteringly. 'Maybe, but she lost her life instead.' He put his hand up to cover his mouth. Tears started to roll down his face.

Stevie put her arm around his shoulders. She pulled him to her. For a minute or two they sat with their heads together in silence.

'Can I ask you a question?' Stevie asked after they'd both sat up.

'Please do.'

'Why haven't you said any of this before?' she said, a curiously intent look on her face. 'It changes everything.'

Greg stood up again. He needed a moment to consider his answer. He pulled down the oven door and looked at the pizza.

'I think it's OK,' he said, pulling it and the garlic bread out of the oven and onto a wooden chopping board.

'Shall I divide it up?'

'You have plenty, Greg,' Stevie replied, listening to him from the far side of the breakfast bar.

Greg turned to look at her, a large kitchen knife in his hand. 'I guess I forgot about it.' He turned back to the food and started dividing it up, placing a few slices of both the pizza and the bread on each plate.

'I was so unhinged by everything,' he said as he sat down.

'When dad came to Vietnam and told me about mum I felt my world had collapsed. He was wonderful. He brought me home, sorted me out and sent me back out there to finish my trip. By the time I went up to uni I was feeling pretty balanced. I thought I'd managed to put it all behind me.' He stopped and took a mouthful. Both ate in silence for a bit.

'Can I go on?' he asked, 'You won't like it.'

Stevie nodded.

Greg thought he detected a look of resignation on her face.

'When dad told me he was marrying you, I just couldn't believe it. How could someone I cared for so much, completely flush away mum's legacy so soon?'

He paused then continued quickly, 'I know they didn't get on, but they had something. And then...' He stopped again. He looked at Stevie to check how she was taking it all.

'And then you came up to Durham and told me he murdered mum.'

He looked away, picked up a piece of bread and started munching on it. When he turned back to face Stevie, she seemed to be waiting for him to continue.

'I'm sorry, I reacted badly. I shouldn't have walked out on you like that.'

Stevie put her hand out to take his. 'Don't go on, Greg. I think I know the rest.'

Greg turned his hand around and squeezed hers. He was grateful for her gesture. He looked at her white face. There were small drops of moisture in her eyes.

'I'm sorry,' he said. 'All this must be awful for you. If mum hadn't died…'

'Stop, Greg. I've been down that road. It's horrible.' She smiled for a moment and turned her head away. After a few seconds she turned back, her expression determined.

'Look,' she said urgently. 'I'm here. It sounds as though we've got work to do.'

Greg looked into her eyes. They seemed intense but a little forlorn.

'Greg?' she said, with some urgency. 'You're probably not going to believe this, but I love your dad more than anyone in the world.'

Greg put his hand over his mouth. He looked at Stevie. He wasn't sure how to respond.

'And there's something else,' she said, leaning forward, looking serious. 'My mother is having an affair with Joe Walters.'

* * *

For once Stevie was grateful for her height. It allowed her to keep up with Greg's frantic pace as he pounded the hill that led up to Monroe's house. They'd risen at four, each showering in a few minutes before piling into Stevie's car for the long journey to Cornwall. At first, words between them were sparse. Greg held the flask of coffee and the slices of toast, spread with marmalade and butter, and dispensed them when convenient while Stevie drove. After an hour Stevie asked Greg about his time in Vietnam and found he was eager and keen to tell her as much as she wanted to know.

The last half-hour of the journey was silent. Greg fidgeted, often moving from side to side in his seat, stretching out his legs as far as they would reach. He didn't say anything, just seemed to be immersed in his thoughts, starring straight in front of him. Stevie knew he was anxious, worried about finding his father and what reaction he'd get. She gripped the steering wheel and concentrated on the road ahead, wondering all the time how she'd find Monroe. She hoped that after he'd heard what Greg had to say he'd be more welcoming, perhaps allow her to stay in the house.

*I don't expect much, but he might let us start afresh,* she thought, remembering how angry he was with her last time, telling her to leave and not even saying goodbye. Her eyes felt moist, she felt a familiar wetness on her left cheek. She hoped Greg wasn't looking.

Greg started to increase his pace. She couldn't keep up, letting him stride ahead, almost breaking into a run. He pushed open the gate and raced to the front door, banging the knocker, while simultaneously pushing on the old brass bell.

*Please God, let him be in,* Stevie thought.

'There's no reply,' Greg yelled. 'He's bloody well not here. Where is he, Stevie?'

Stevie met the face of a tall, fit, twenty-year-old male close to the point of mental and physical destruction. He looks at the point of exhaustion, she thought, recognizing that his non-stop travelling for the last 36 hours, lack of sleep, and intense anxiety had finally caught up with him.

'I don't know,' she replied, putting her arm around Greg's shoulder. 'But let's go inside.'

\* \* \*

*It all looked the same as yesterday*, Greg thought. A couple more letters had dropped through the front door and lay untouched on the mat. There were no obvious signs of his father having returned, no rapidly discarded clothing, no hurriedly dumped bags of shopping or belongings. The dishwasher remained untouched, the fridge contained only the solitary, unwrapped packet of cheese, perched alone in the middle of the top shelve. Fear and panic raged inside his head. He felt confused and at a loss as to what he should do next. He turned to Stevie, gazing through the window to the unkempt back garden.

'Do you think he's back in prison?' he asked.

\* \* \*

Detective Inspector Jo Symes sat in the leather chair that Monroe normally used and stared, first at Greg and then at Stevie. She was wearing a black knee length tight skirt, a v-neck short sleeve beige blouse and a pair of flat leather shoes of a similar tone to her top. She stroked her hair, appearing to give herself some time before she spoke. Greg and Stevie, sitting on opposite couches, watched her intently.

She turned to face Greg.

'Where's your father, Mr Lidlington?' she asked curtly.

Greg was taken aback. Stevie had phoned the local police station shortly after they'd checked the whole house for any sign of Monroe. Inspector Symes had come to the phone and asked them to stay put until she arrived. Stevie had told Greg that it wasn't a request, but an instruction, which they could ignore at their peril. Greg wasn't prepared for Inspector Symes's gladiatorial manner.

'I don't know,' he answered, slightly unsure where this aggressive female detective was coming from.

'Don't play games with me, Mr Lidlington.' Symes turned her steely eyes to Stevie.

'Your husband has been charged with murder, he's out on bail and he's broken his bail conditions and you expect me to believe that you don't know where he is. Hmm.'

Stevie leant forward. Her eyes closed up. She placed both her hands on each of her knees and stared hard at Jo Symes.

'Inspector Symes,' she said slowly with a determined tone. 'Greg has just come back from Africa. He came straight here in search of his father and had no idea, until last night, that his father had been arrested...'

'He's innocent, detective,' Greg said, interrupting and shifting in his seat to move a little closer to where Jo Symes was sitting.

'I have evidence to prove it.'

'That, Mr Lidlington, will be for the courts to decide.' Symes looked at Greg with a discerning expression. She sneered. 'I suggest you give your evidence to your father's defence lawyers.'

*Who is this woman?* Greg questioned. She storms in, hardly a courteous word and starts to confront us both in such a combative manner. He didn't like her.

'Inspector Symes,' he said, raising his voice. 'Is my father back in prison?'

Symes appeared slightly surprised.

'I ask the questions around here, if you...'

Something inside Greg snapped. He stood up.

'Don't be so bloody rude,' he said forcibly, looking across at Stevie.

'I asked you the same question Stevie asked you on the phone. If my father is in police custody we are entitled to know. It's a common human right. Please answer my question.'

Symes looked him up and down. She put her left hand to her chin, seemingly considering her response. She stood up to stand about a third of a metre short of Greg.

'I don't have a clue as to where your father is. He's not in prison or police custody.' She turned towards Stevie, exchanging glances with her and then back to Greg.

'If either of you hear from him you are bound by law to inform us.' She paused for a few seconds. 'Otherwise you could be charged with aiding and abetting.' She returned her stare to Stevie. 'Do I make myself clear, Mrs Lidlington?'

Stevie remained seated. With her eyes still clenched she fixed her focus on Symes for a few seconds before answering.

'You do, Inspector Symes, totally clear. Have you finished?'

'I have, and I'll let myself out.'

Greg stepped in front of Inspector Symes, walked down the hall and opened the front door for her to leave. Neither spoke. He slammed it closed behind her. From the living room he could hear the deep heart-rending sounds of Stevie crying.

'She's a bitch,' Stevie sobbed when Greg returned, sitting next to her.

'This is all my fault.'

'Why?' Greg asked, putting his arm around her shoulder.

Stevie looked up at Greg with tears rolling down her face.

'Because I went to the police and told them about the gun.' She put her head in her hands and let out loud, deep sobs, her shoulders shaking.

Greg withdrew his arm. He wondered if he'd heard correctly. He looked at Stevie, reduced to a quivering wreck.

'You what?' he asked indignantly.

# 22

Greg emerged from the Bank tube station amidst the throng of people making their way to work. He started to make his was down Gracechurch Street towards Bishopsgate. Men and woman bustled besides him. Many, he noticed, seemed oblivious to much around them, programmed to reach their offices or place of work, intent only on arriving on time. He remembered how his mother would do anything to avoid an early meeting. 'Hell,' was how she used to describe the morning rush hour. As he bustled and pushed along, doing his best to stay on the pavement, he found he was thinking more about her. She seemed to be all around him. Women's clothing, faces in the crowd, the odd overheard snatch of conversation—all conjured up vivid images of her in his mind. He darted into a small alleyway to wipe away the tears that had suddenly formed in his eyes.

He put The Times down on the coffee table, stood up and brushed off the tiny white specks from the newspaper from his crisp new suit trousers. He fastened the two top bottoms of the navy jacket and followed Anna towards the open door. *This is it*, he thought, hoping that his new found self-control was not about to desert him. Five minutes earlier, when he arrived at the ground floor reception, he felt sure he was going to fluff it. After the insignificant head office of Miax in Johannesburg, he wasn't prepared for the blatant expression of capitalism that greeted him that morning. Intimidated by the revolving glass door, he found the frantic flow of chicly dressed men and woman rushing to their place of work, their heels clicking on the marble floors and the sheer opulence of the entrance hall too much. He'd become overwhelmed by the ominousness of it all, prompting a resurgence of his anti-capitalist views and an intense feeling of wanting to run and hide. He was there for a purpose, he told himself, and focused his thoughts on what he'd come to achieve.

In front of him, framed by the door, stood a man who Greg assumed to be Joe Walters. He stood still, expressionless, and appeared to be inspecting Greg from top to bottom.

'Anna,' the man barked in a startled tone. 'Who is this man?'

Greg raised his right hand and put one finger in the air to stop Anna saying anything.

'Save your breath. Let me do the introductions. I'm Greg Lidlington, Juliet and Monroe's son. I guess you're Joe.' Greg didn't move. He was watching intently the faces of Anna and Joe. He likened their swift change of expression to those of people being told of the sudden and unexpected death of a loved one.

'I'm sorry, Mr Walters but there must have been some mix up,' Anna stuttered. 'In the diary it says Mr…'

Greg took a deep breath and smiled at them both and then looked at Anna.

'Don't bother to explain. I gave a false name when I called yesterday. I reckoned if I said that I was a friend of Jan de Boers I'd get an audience.'

Joe Walters's ashen grey face changed to bright red.

'How dare you. Who do you think you are, barging in like this under false pretences…'

Greg held his hand up like a traffic policeman.

'Stop. You'll give yourself a cardiac arrest.' He looked around to see who was listening.

'I guess it's better if you ask me in, Joe,' he said in a raised voice. 'You wouldn't like me to talk about my mother's death out here where all can hear, would you?'

Joe looked quickly at Anna. A couple of heads in the outer office turned away smartly and returned their attention to whatever they'd been doing before Greg's loud voice had disturbed them. Without saying a word, Joe turned and gestured to Greg to follow him into his office.

Greg walked about half a metre behind Joe. He'd never been in a chief executive's office before. The size and excessiveness of it all grated on him. *Why does he need so large a room?* he asked himself, as Joe led him to the four armchairs arranged around a polished occasional table. Joe went straight to one chair, undoing the middle button of his suit before sitting down.

'Sit down, Mr Lidlington,' Joe said gruffly, motioning with his hand to the chair opposite him.

Greg, keeping Joe in his sights, dropped casually into the chair indicated.

'What can I do for you?' Joe asked, meeting Greg's eyes as he made himself comfortable.

Greg looked at Joe. In the short walk from where they'd met by the door to the office he appeared to have regained any lost composure. The apparent consternation he openly exhibited, earlier, over Greg's sudden appearance seemed to have passed, or he was practised at hiding it. Greg guessed him to be late thirties, fit and neatly dressed in what he imagined to be an expensive hand tailored suit from a reputable West End tailor. His fingernails were well manicured, his tie was perfectly knotted, his black shoes sparkled.

Greg swung his long right leg over his other thigh and pressed himself against the chair's deep back. He was aware that Joe was staring at him, waiting for him to answer his question. But he wasn't going to be fazed, pushed beyond his rehearsed agenda. Inside he felt like jelly, outside he hoped he looked calm and in charge.

Stevie and Greg had hatched the idea of a visit to Joe Walters the previous day. After Stevie had admitted to telling the police about the gun, Greg had cooled, not wanting to be in her presence. But they had to return to London together and towards the end of the journey Greg floated the notion of talking to Joe. The concept took hold and by the end of the day, after Greg had dashed out to buy a suit, some decent shoes, a belt and a shirt, and Stevie had prepared a quick supper, they'd conceived a plan.

Greg learnt forward and looked Joe straight in the eye.

'Do you know anything about the death of my mother?' he asked, watching Joe's every movement.

Joe's forehead wrinkled. A puzzled expression showed on his face. He didn't move in his seat.

'Why should I?' he answered shaking his head. His eyes met Greg's. 'I presume you know…'

'About my father, yes I do.' Greg interrupted, fingering the left wing of his shirt collar. He wasn't wearing a tie and wanted to make sure his shirt stayed tucked behind his jacket's lapels.

'But I wanted your view. I understand that you know my father well. Do you think he's a murderer?' Again Greg looked at Joe for a reaction.

Joe shifted a little in his seat. He fiddled with each of the cuffs of his shirt, turning the cuff links round a little.

'I'm really sorry, Greg. I was as shocked as no doubt you were when the police brought charges against your father. He was the last person who I thought could have done something like that.' Joe shook his head.

'But we'll have to let justice take his course.'

'Would you be willing to stand up in court and give a character reference?' Greg kept his gaze firmly on Joe.

Joe moved again in his seat. He looked away from Greg and gazed towards the window.

'Is that why you came?' he asked, sounding slightly irritated.

'No,' Greg said standing up and walking around to face Joe.

'I came to ask you about the mining disaster at your gold mine in Butix when 30 miners died a year ago.'

Joe Walters's face turned white. His eyes locked onto Greg's. He parted his lips slightly showing his clenched teeth.

'How dare you. You force your way into my office on the pretence of talking about your mother's death and then you bring up something totally unconnected. Who do you think…'

'But they are connected, aren't they. My mother knew all about the disaster, she told me…'

'Out, out.' Joe was charging across his office, pressing buzzers and bells and pointing furiously at his door with his hand outstretched.

'Leave my office immediately or I'll call the police.'

The office door opened. Anna together with a couple of security guys entered. Greg knew his time was up. He started to make his way to the door.

'Bye then Joe. So I take it you won't be making a character reference at my father's trial.'

'Get him out of the building. Make sure he leaves the premises,' Joe shouted as the two security men closed on Greg.

'If they so much as touch me, I'll sue for assault. I'm leaving right now.' Greg stopped and turned back to face Joe, incandescent with rage.

'Oh. Where can I get a press release on the Butix disaster? The Sowetan asked me to obtain one.' Greg smiled as he walked slowly to the lift, followed by the two security men and Anna. He looked back. Joe's office door was securely closed.

\* \* \*

Twelve people sat round the meeting table. Joe sat at the head. While most of the attendees listened attentively as one of the companies senior field managers provided an upbeat progress report on a Brazilian dam project that Miax had tendered for, Joe had other things on his mind. Careful that nobody would see him, he gently pushed back the cuff of his jacket so he could see his Omega wrist watch. He glanced quickly down at the face, released his hold on the sleeve and rose from the table.

'Please carry on without me,' he said and left the room with no further explanation.

'No calls please, Anna,' he said curtly, without any expression as he walked past her workstation and into his office. Closing his door firmly, he went straight to his desk, unlocked a drawer at the side and removed a mobile phone. He scrolled down to the number he wanted, hesitated for a second and then called the number. He felt a sudden looseness in his bowels and wanted to urinate.

'That you, Jan?' he asked, nervously.

'Yeah, of course it's me, Joe. What the hell do you want at such an ungodly hour? It's only seven here. I'm still in bed.'

Joe knew Jan would be in bed. He wasn't worried about that. It was what he had to tell him next that was causing his anxiety. He breathed in hard. He'd felt a sharp, stabbing pain in his stomach.

'I know it's early. I'm sorry to disturb you but I've something important to tell you.'

'Can't it wait? I'm busy,' Jan mumbled, then seemed to say something to another person.

Joe became angry. He knew Jan was in bed with a girl. He was whenever Joe called early in the morning.

'No it can't. It's about the Butix disaster. Greg Lidlington, Juliet's son has been sniffing around. He came here today.'

The 5500 miles that separated Joe and Jan seemed to shrink to nothing. Joe felt Jan's change of attitude like an electric surge running along the phone lines. In the background he could hear Jan telling whoever was sharing his bed that she would have to wait, followed by her loud complaints. From that moment, Joe found he had Jan's full attention.

'I don't want you to do anything, Joe. Act as though nothing had happened. I'll deal with it all from this end. I'll call you tomorrow and tell you what I've put in place,' Jan responded forcefully when Joe had finished.

'Is that clear?'

'Fine, Jan. I'll await your call.' Joe waited for a response. None came. The line had gone dead. Joe replaced the phone in the drawer and locked it. He leant back in his chair. *What an arsehole,* he thought. *Why did I ever allow myself to become beholden to that shit?*

At five Joe called down to reception. He told the guy on the desk that he didn't require his driver, he would drive his car home himself. His next call was to Jennifer to tell her he would be in the office until about 7.30 and then would drive home. They agreed to eat out later at a local Italian restaurant. He spent the rest of the time in the office catching up with some of his correspondence, clearing his e-mails and finally checking the bank balances of the various Miax accounts around the world—a routine that he carried out at the end of most days. At 7.40 exactly, he turned off his computer, locked all his drawers, set the alarm in his office and closed the door. He took the lift to the ground floor where he said goodnight to the security guard on the front desk and started to descend the stairs into the basement that led to the underground car park.

Most nights Joe was driven home, using the journey time to read and catch up on paperwork. On the occasions he drove himself, he did it to relieve the tension of a stressful day. He found the concentration required in driving took his mind off the work pressures. After half a dozen steps he pushed open the squeaky door at the bottom of the stairs and looked for his car. The car park was poorly lit with a low ceiling and many pillars making it difficult to view every parking space from one spot. He walked around for a bit until he thought, in the dim lights, he could see his car in the far corner. He strode off in the direction of where his car was parked. As he reached it, he heard the sound of the door into the car park close. He looked back to see who it was. Who else would be working as late as him?

*Strange,* he thought. He couldn't see anybody. Perhaps he was mistaken. He turned back and reached into his case for the keys, pulling them out and pressing the fob to deactivate the alarm and open the doors.

\* \* \*

Gregory Ivanovitch pushed past the throngs of office workers making their way in drones down Bishopsgate to whichever bus or tube station they used to take them home after their daily toil. From time to time he ran, aware that he should have been in position by now. He was a thick set, tall man. Anyone who he inadvertently knocked out of his way would have felt it. He was solid as a rock, over two metres tall and weighed 112 kilograms. He was wearing black cargo trousers, a short sleeve black t-shirt, a pair of trainers and carrying a small canvas rucksack, strapped firmly to his back.

Working under pressure was not the way he liked to operate, but needs must, he told himself. The price was exceptional. Normally he'd have plenty of notice: time to prepare, reconnoitre a few possible places from where he could do the job, study the target several times and arrive in good time to set up his spot. This time, he'd received the instructions only a couple of hours earlier. At first he turned it down, until his go-between came back to him with a fee he couldn't refuse.

On his left he saw the sign he'd been told about, warning of the exit and entrance into the underground car park. He looked at his watch, ten minutes to spare. He found the fire escape and ran down it to the lower ground floor. The target's car was exactly where the security man from Miax had told him it would be. Five minutes to work out a plan. He'd hide behind the concrete column in the far corner, over in the shadows and by the door to the stairs. He could see the guy pass on his way to his car, let him reach it and then give it to him. *Easy,* he thought, taking out his gun from his rucksack and assembling it.

On cue the door opened. A man about the same build as his target passed through. Ivanovitch cursed to himself. He hadn't seen the man's face. He couldn't risk a shot without positive identification. But the time was right, the man's shape and hair colour fitted the description, he was even heading for the right car. *Shall I risk it?* Ivanovitch asked himself. His training kicked in. He could hear the words of his instructor at the Russian sniper school.

'Never, never squeeze the trigger unless you are 100% sure you have the right man.' *How can I be sure? The guy is almost at the car. There is little time.* And then his eyes focused on the door. He ran to it and pushed it open. It slammed with a bang. The man turned to look.

*Oh yes, that's him.* A surge of pleasure ran through Ivanovitch's body. He took aim. The guy was moving slightly and then stopped. Ivanovitch squeezed the trigger with a firm, controlled experienced action. He knew the barrel of the gun would not move a fraction of a millimetre from his chosen trajectory. The man's head exploded, blood gushed all over his car and his body crumpled to the ground.

# 23

Monroe nestled himself into the corner of the cockpit, his right arm resting along the narrow deck that ran between the boat's side and the cockpit's edge, his leg stretched out on the slatted seating running around the perimeter. He pulled his sweatshirt down a bit to below his waist and clasped his left knee with his other hand.

'First time this summer I've felt a slight chill in the air,' he said, looking towards Johnny, busy steering the fishing boat into the harbour.

Johnny, standing upright with his hands clasped firmly on the wheel, kept looking ahead and nodded.

'We've had a good one, though,' he replied. For a couple of seconds he took both hands off the wheel and tightened the small red and navy spotted cotton scarf he had around his neck. Its colours matched both his old navy chinos and the red polo shirt he'd been wearing, continuously, for the last three days.

Johnny had suggested the boat trip shortly after he'd last seen Monroe. He called Monroe within minutes of leaving the house. At first Monroe had declined his offer. He didn't have a reason, just bloody-mindedness. When Johnny almost insisted, saying he'd organise all the necessary food and drink and be around early in the morning, Monroe agreed. Later, as he threw a few things into his old grip, he found he was looking forward to the trip, grateful to Johnny for asking him.

Monroe leaned his head slightly to the right. A light breeze, cooled slightly by the onset of autumn, touched his cheek, a few drops of spray moistened his face. *I'd be happy*, he thought, if the moment could last forever. After a bit he looked across at Johnny, standing upright and seemingly concentrating on the short distance before they would pull alongside the quay. As he watched his old friend, undoubtedly going through his own pain and grief after the death of his much-loved wife, he felt a surge of gratitude.

'Johnny,' he said resolutely. 'Thanks.'

'What for? old boy,' Johnny replied in his familiar vague tone and without altering his gaze.

'You know bloody well what for,' Monroe replied, laughing at Johnny's typical nonchalance.

'I don't.'

Monroe stood up and took a couple of paces to stand behind Johnny. He put his arm around Johnny's shoulder.

'Johnny Edwards, you're a sly old fox. You bloody well know what I'm talking about. If you hadn't pushed me into this trip, I would be sitting at home moping and worrying about my problems. As it is, I haven't given them a moment's thought.'

Johnny turned quickly to look at Monroe.

'Good, old chap. That was what I hoped. Now, if you don't mind I have to concentrate. There are quite a few other vessels around, some behaving like bloody amateurs.'

'Probably holidaymakers,' Monroe replied moving back to his seat in the corner. He agreed with Johnny. Ahead of them, craft of all sorts were bobbing and weaving with little regard to the established rules of the seaways. He had every confidence in Johnny guiding them safely to their mooring and closed his eyes, letting the early evening sun caress his face.

Over the last few days they'd sailed slowly south westwards along the North Devon coast to Land's end, rounded the rock outcrop and gently eased their way towards Helston, in Mount's Bay, before turning round and retracing their passage. They'd moored up each night and gone ashore to pubs where they knew they could have a decent meal and a comfortable bed. Blessed by dry weather, they'd been able to enjoy three days of tranquillity, almost twelve hours of fresh air and an abundance of stunning views of the rugged coastline. They'd talked and laughed a lot. Tearing the government to pieces, offering many suggestions over England's lack lustre performance at cricket, discussing a couple of books they'd both read, exchanging jokes and amusing anecdotes, and never discussing any of Monroe's problems.

Monroe felt the engine slow. He opened his eyes and looked first at the surrounding sea, wondering what had suddenly caused Johnny to ease back on the throttle. He turned to Johnny and saw him, one hand on the wheel, bending over it slightly and peering hard at the quay, a concerned look on his face. He turned and gave Monroe a short glance, turning back quickly to whatever he was watching.

'What's up? Monroe asked, following the direction of Johnny's gaze.

'What the fuck?' Monroe yelled, standing up.

'What the hell are they doing there?' He was confused. Jolted out his carefree mood by the sight of Greg and Stevie, standing next to each other, looking as though they were waiting for him.

'Why, what?' he said, bewildered, looking to Johnny for an answer.

'I guess they've come to see you, Monroe.' Johnny had closed the engine down to an idle. The boat slowed to almost a standstill, its gentle bobbing motion caused by the swell of the sea, the slight forward momentum a result of the incoming tide.

'Do you want me to continue into harbour?' Johnny looked at Monroe for an answer.

Monroe didn't hear. He was staring at Greg and poking his chest and face with his fingers in case he was asleep and it was all a dream, his subconscious playing tricks on him. He saw Greg raise his hand and wave. Monroe found he was waving back. The boat jerked a little and shot forward, bringing his estranged wife and son closer and closer. He stood still and watched. Somewhere, inside him, deep down in the bowels of his emotion, a smouldering ember ignited and, as though it had been fanned by a warm wind, roared through his body.

Monroe remained motionless, his gaze fixed on Greg as the distance between father and son decreased by the second. In spite of being within an audible range, neither of them attempted to speak. Monroe, unsure of what to do or say, kept his eyes firmly on Greg. He looked at his taut and tired face, his dishevelled hair, his typical clothes—jeans, a black lightweight jersey top with a crew neck and flip-flops—and conceded that his eyes were indeed telling the truth.

Greg was the first to speak.

'Dad, you can't go home.'

'What're you on about?' Monroe retorted, glad he had the opportunity to say something, even if it was just a quick response.

'The police, they're waiting for you.'

'They can go to...' Monroe stopped. He saw Stevie step forward to stand next to Greg. She'd been standing behind him.

'Listen to him, Monroe. He's right. They've been after us to find out where you were. They want you for breaking your bail.'

Monroe looked at them both, standing alongside each other. He shook his head from side to side, alternating his gaze from Stevie to Greg.

'What am I supposed to do?'

'Come with us, dad. I've found things out about Miax that could prove your innocence. We have to go through it all with you. We haven't much time.'

Monroe stared hard at his son. He felt disorientated; wanting to run up to Greg with open arms and hug him. Something was stopping him. He turned to look at Johnny, busy securing the boat to the jetty, appearing not to be aware of the high drama being played out. Monroe turned to Stevie.

'What's your angle in this?' he snapped, puzzled as to how the two of them had met up.

'Come on, dad. We can talk about all that later. Jump in the car. We're going to The Smugglers. We can sit outside in the big garden and talk this all through.'

Monroe looked again at Stevie. He couldn't see how he could bring himself to sit in the same car as her.

'I'm not coming,' he said and went to help Johnny with the tidying up.

'Dad,' Greg shouted.

'Don't be so pig headed. I've masses of apologies to make to you. But you don't expect me to make them here, in the middle of the quay, for everyone to witness. If you go back to the house you'll be picked up by the police.'

'Come on, you've just made that up. Do you expect me to believe there's a police car sitting outside the house. I'm not that important.' Monroe felt muddled. He looked away from the two of them to try to clear his mind. He searched for Johnny to see if there was anything he could do.

'You've been charged with murder, Monroe,' Stevie said angrily to Monroe's face. She'd come forward to the edge of the quay, next to the side of the boat where he'd picked up some rope and was coiling it on the deck, and leant over. Nobody else could hear what she had to say.

'Look, I don't care what you think about me. I only care about you and Greg. He's come all the way back from Vietnam, via South Africa, because he knows he was wrong about you, and has found out some facts that will clear you.' She turned her face to look him in the eye.

'Monroe, listen to me. There is a police car outside the house, we've been there. For Greg's sake, get in the car and we can talk about it all.'

'How did you know I was on the boat,' Monroe asked looking at Greg.

'We called Johnny's house,' Greg replied, coming closer to his father.

'Who was there?' Monroe asked, looking into Greg's tired, strained face. His bright blue eyes, a little bloodshot in the corners, shone with their usual intensity. His thick brown hair, tousled and sprouting in its usual free for all way, was as he always remembered it.

*This is my son,* Monroe told himself. *He's back, standing opposite me. I'd thought I'd lost him.*

'A housekeeper,' Stevie replied, in answer to Monroe's question. 'She said Johnny had gone out with...'

Monroe, suddenly overcome by emotion, leapt off the boat and pulled Greg to him, clasping him tightly with both his arms.

'Greg. You're home,' Monroe shouted, tears rolling down his face.

Greg laughed a little, pushing his father back a touch.

'I'm here, dad,' he said, a wide smile spread across his face. He looked Monroe in the eyes. 'I've got a lot of explaining. I'm sorry.'

Monroe wiped his tear stained face with his bare arm, smiled back at Greg and laughed.

'You don't look so bad.'

'You too, dad.'

For about a minute they both stood still looking at each other, Monroe shaking his head in disbelief.

A few feet away, Stevie who had been watching the reunion, gingerly stepped forward. She looked unsure as she tentatively put a hand on both the men's backs. Her eyes were moist, her face appeared pained.

'I owe you both an apology,' she said, and withdrew her hands.

Monroe looked at her, slightly dismissively, and then back at Greg. He wasn't sure what to say.

'Thanks, Stevie,' Greg said, putting his arm around her shoulder. He turned to his father.

'Come on, dad, we've much to talk about.

Johnny watched as Monroe and Greg, deep in conversation ambled away. Stevie followed a pace or two behind.

'I'll be in touch,' Johnny shouted nonchalantly.

Monroe turned immediately. 'Johnny, I'm so sorry. I...'

'Don't say a word old man. I wish you all good luck.'

Monroe opened both his hands in a gesture of helplessness. 'What can I say, Johnny?'

'Nothing, just go on your way and see to your family.'

* * *

Monroe leant back on the old wooden bench and moved his empty beer glass a few centimetres closer to his left hand. He rested both his elbows on the wooden surface, clasped his hands together and made a bridge with them to support his chin. His eyes moved from Greg to Stevie and back again to Greg. Both of them were watching him, waiting for his response. For an hour the three of them had been sitting in a remote corner of the garden of The Smugglers, under a large apple tree, laden with fruit, while Greg had told his father, from the beginning, all about the Miax mining disaster and his meeting with Joe Walters.

'Come on, dad. What do you think?' Greg asked, after his father had stayed silent for several seconds.

'I find it all a bit far fetched. You two, who only months ago where accusing me of Juliet's murder, come up with this imaginary tale of some giant conspiracy in Miax resulting in your mum's death.' Monroe looked at them both, his chin still resting in his hands.

'I take it I'm in the clear with you both?' he added, his eyes moving between his son and wife.

Stevie turned her head to face Monroe. Her eyes sparkled. She looked angry.

'I never accused you of murdering her, just wanted an explanation about the gun.'

'Then, why did you go to the police, why did you charge all the way up to Durham to tell Greg I murdered his mum, if you didn't think I did it?' Monroe was watching Greg as he spoke.

'Dad,' Greg snapped. He shook his head. 'None of that is going to get us anywhere. Look. Mum told me, just before she died that she thought Miax where going to suppress the truth about the disaster.'

Monroe leant forward and looked Greg straight in the eye.

'So, what if they did? That still doesn't prove that they killed her. What possible motive could they have?'

'Mum said she was going to publish the truth on the Internet, herself.'

Monroe jolted in his seat. Greg's words had triggered the depth of his memory; something lurking in his subconscious had suddenly come alive.

'When did she tell you that?' he asked, wracking his memory for the time when Juliet had mentioned something to him about a mining disaster.

'Just before she died. She called me in Hanoi to have a chat. Because of the time difference, she called one morning from the office and told me all about it. She said she was almost ready to publish her report. If Miax didn't come clean, she was going to resign and post her report on the Internet.'

'When? When, Greg? Can you remember the exact day?' Monroe was leaning forward, an earnest look on his face and banging the table. He'd become animated.

'Well, not exactly, dad. Why is the day so important?'

Monroe gripped the sides of the table with his hands. He was still leaning forward, gazing intently at Greg.

'I've suddenly remembered that Juliet was working on a mining disaster report the night she died.' Monroe looked quickly at Stevie, who seemed serious and remained silent. He looked back to Greg.

'She wanted to talk to me about it, but I was busy doing something else. That was what started the row,' he added, excited, speaking quickly. He threw his hands open and said, 'The one she walked out on.' He looked away.

'That was the last time I saw her, alive.' Monroe became aware of someone moving. He turned his head back to Greg and Stevie. She was standing up, clutching her small canvas bag.

'I'll go,' she said, looking down on the two of them, uncomfortably.

Greg reached up with his right hand. He tried to pull Stevie back to her seat.

'Please stay,' he pleaded.

Monroe looked at her. She was wearing a pair of tight navy jeans and black t-shirt with the words 'adopt a minefield' in bold white writing across the front. From each of her ears dangled large dulled-pewter earrings in the shape of Buddhas that blended with her cropped blonde hair. Her big blue eyes looked tired and strained. He thought about what she must be going through. *She's got guts to be here.*

'Stay, Stevie. You look exhausted,' he said, smiling at her

Stevie looked at him silently for a few seconds. She smiled back.

'Thanks, Monroe. I will,' she replied as she sunk back onto the bench opposite him.

Up to that moment Monroe hadn't thought about Stevie or how he felt about her. He'd ignored her, more out of shock than intent, not able to cope with a reunion with Greg and with her at the same time. Over the last few weeks he'd tried to blot her out of his mind, blaming her for much of what had happened. As he watched her settle down, he could tell she was trying her hardest to build bridges.

He was glad she'd agreed to stay.

Behind her head, he saw a waitress approaching their table. She was carrying a tray with the food and wine that they'd ordered earlier.

'OK,' he said forcibly, sitting back in his seat on the opposite bench to his wife and son.

'I think I've got it. Juliet's threat of going public about the mine disaster scares the shit out of Joe Walters. He speaks to his boss.' Monroe looked across at Greg.

'Jan de Boer or something? I think,' he added.

'That's it, dad.' Greg was sitting upright, both hands on the edge of the table.

'A playboy sort, I believe.'

Monroe leant forward a bit. He put his elbows on the table and looked first at Stevie then at Greg.

'Jan de Boer,' he said in a low, confident whisper, 'terrified what the bad publicity could do to Miax and his own lifestyle, gets somebody to murder Juliet and make it look like me.'

'How do they make it look like you?' Stevie asked, her right arm folded over her left on the table, her hand clasping her left elbow. She was bending forward; seemingly intent on Monroe's every word.

Monroe looked at her, pleased to answer her question. He picked up a chip from a big wicker basket and dipped it in a bowl of tomato ketchup.

'Come on, tuck in.' He took a chicken leg for himself, gesturing to the other two to help themselves.

'Don't you see,' he replied to Stevie, motioning with his food still in his hand.

'The break in, the strange phone calls, the gun. They were all designed to make you think I killed Juliet.'

'OK,' Stevie replied, picking at the chips and looking a little bemused. 'How did they get the police to form their opinion?'

Monroe looked at Stevie. He wondered how she'd take what he was going to say. He turned to Greg, looking for some reassurance.

'I guess they planned to keep the pressure on you until you ran to the police.' Monroe met Stevie's gaze. She seemed to have bridled somewhat at his remark.

'As it turned out, you went to them fairly quickly.'

Stevie dropped her chin into her open hands, her palms caressing her cheeks, her elbows resting on the table. Monroe had expected her to look angry, instead she seemed concerned, worried about something.

'Do you think Joe Walters was involved?' she asked.

'No,' Monroe answered quickly.

'Oh dad, come on. If Miax are involved, so is he. He couldn't get me out of his office quick enough when I started suggesting a connection between the mine disaster and mum's death.'

Monroe shook his head 'No, he's straight. Look at the way he handled your mother's death. He behaved impeccably. He's just been kept in the dark. Jan de Boer is the guilty guy.'

'Hold on, Monroe,' Stevie said, leaning forward to engage Monroe head on.

'Joe Walters's is going out with my mother. They have been ever since you introduced them at our wedding.'

Monroe was confused. Why hadn't Stevie told him this before?

'How long have you known that? he asked, sitting back.

'Not long.' Stevie paused. She rubbed her hand through her short hair.

'I went to mum's after coming back from seeing Greg in Durham. He was there. He told me to go to the police.'

'He what?' Monroe shouted in utter amazement. 'What did you tell him?'

'Look Monroe. I went to my mother's house because I had nowhere else to go. As soon as I arrived I regretted it, knowing my mother would gloat. At first I spoke to Joe, alone. He seemed pleasant and straightforward, telling me he had no doubt you didn't murder Juliet.'

'But he told you to go to the police? I don't understand.'

'He said it as I was about to leave. "Tell the police about the gun you found, it'll help Monroe's case."'

'Don't you see, dad,' Greg said, having listened to Stevie and Monroe. 'He's using Stevie's mother to find out as much as possible about you.'

'You reckon so?' Monroe replied, not entirely convinced. 'That's a bit far fetched.'

Stevie moved her glass away to the right. She tapped all her fingers down on the table, simultaneously.

'Look at it like this, Monroe.' She stopped to check she had Monroe's attention.

'Say we're agreed Miax were responsible for Juliet's death and that Joe Walters was involved. He's introduced to my mother—not your greatest fan—at our wedding. My mother, who's always on the look out for men, particularly rich ones, crawls over him like a rash. Joe, who I believe is no great womaniser, must have thought it was Christmas.' Stevie looked away for a second and then turned back to Monroe.

'Some nymphomaniac, who's got an axe to grind against Monroe Lidlington, starts to jump all over Joe. What's he going to do, ignore her?'

Monroe sat back and looked at them both. *She's got a point,* he admitted.

'So if it's true, where do we go from here?'

'I need to find mum's old computer and back up stuff. They hold the key.' Greg looked across at his dad. 'Do you know where they are?'

Monroe thought for a minute. 'If they're anywhere, they'll be in the loft.'

Greg looked up. Behind his father a determined looking woman, flanked by two uniformed policeman was striding across the pub garden to where the three of them were sitting. She approached Monroe and put her hand on his shoulder. He turned around to face her.

Inspector Symes glanced quickly at Stevie and Greg then back at Monroe.

'Mr Lidlington,' she said with authority. 'I'm arresting you for breaking your bail.'

# 24

Stevie put both her hands up to her left ear lobe and detached her earring. She did the same to her right ear, placing the two bronze pieces of jewellery down on the wooden worktop with an audible clunk. Her back to the kitchen wall, she stretched out her arms behind her and took hold of the edge of the work surface and leant back. She felt shattered. Over in the corner Greg was placing a couple of slices of bread that he'd found in the freezer into the toaster. She wondered what emotions he'd be enduring. He turned to face her, smiled weekly for a second and took a couple of paces to one of the nearby old kitchen chairs.

'Was that real?' he said as he dropped into the seat.

Stevie looked at his young pained face. She wasn't sure how to respond. Her logic and sensibilities had been invaded by feelings of guilt. After the police interrogation she'd been shocked to the core of her emotions, convinced that she was responsible for the blight that had struck deep into the souls of Monroe, Greg and herself, looking on her share of the ordeal as self-inflicted punishment.

She knew she had to reply; holding back any longer would compound Greg's hurt even more Fearful of his reaction she said,

'Greg, I'm so sorry for all of this. If I hadn't been so impulsive none of this would have happened. Your dad would be here now and that offensive woman detective wouldn't have put us through the hell we've just suffered. I don't think I've ever met someone so rude and unpleasant. She…'

'Don't,' Greg said as the toaster popped up. 'Forget it, Stevie,' he added, facing the wall while removing the slices of toast to two plates and spreading each piece with the scrapings from of an old jar of Marmite he'd found in a cupboard.

'It won't get us anywhere.' He turned to face Stevie.

'All that's important is to find mum's report on the mining disaster. Here, have this,' he said as he pushed a plate in front of her. He put his own plate down next to hers and placed one of his long arms around her shoulders.

'Don't blame yourself. It's negative, it'll get us nowhere.' He picked up his chair, placing it next to Stevie with a decisive thud

'Let's sort these fuckers out,' he said as he sat down.

Stevie looked at him. His eyes were puffy and red with large bags under them, his face was white and pallid with signs of exhaustion and strain. For the last two hours the two of them had been held at Padstow police station, questioned individually by Inspector Symes and her team about why they had helped Monroe break his bail. Symes had threatened to charge them both with aiding and abetting. Finally, after both of them had said, spontaneously and without conferring, that they'd been telling Monroe all about the mining disaster, Juliet's threat to publish the truth, and that Greg had not seen his father for four months, she decided to let them both go on a warning and a clear instruction not to leave the country.

Stevie looked at her watch—it was 1.30 a.m. *Greg must be wrecked,* she thought.

'Why don't we leave it now and try to catch some sleep,' she said.

Greg pushed his plate a few centimetres away. He straightened up in his chair and looked intently at Stevie.

'You go if you like; I'm going in the loft to get mum's laptop. I want to make a start on trying to find the file on the mining disaster.'

Stevie knew she had no alternative. Her mind and body were drained. But if Greg was willing to keep going she had to stay with him. Somehow she had to find the energy.

'OK, I'm with you. While you get the computer, I'll see if I can rustle up some food.'

Greg stood up, his hands holding the back of the chair. He frowned. 'Go ahead. I hope you're luckier than I was. I couldn't find a thing three days ago. I don't think anyone's been here since.'

Stevie walked towards the cupboards.

'Maybe some pasta, or something,' she said, pulling open the door of one of the kitchen cupboards.

At 2 a.m. they sat round the large wooden kitchen table. Greg had the laptop up and running and furiously tapped at the keyboard. Close by his left hand was a bowl of stir-fried rice with vegetables. Stevie had found some frozen mushrooms, broccoli and peas and cooked them with a sprinkling of soya sauce and a few teaspoons of sherry.

'Try gold mines,' she suggested, shuffling in her seat, as Greg stared intently at the screen, his eyes fixed, never moving away from the changing script in front of him. When he wanted to eat, he stretched out his left arm, a fork held loosely in his hand, and felt for his bowl. Like a blind man he manoeuvred some food onto his fork and slowly took it to his mouth, a few pieces of rice dropping on the way.

Stevie, meanwhile, spurred on by Greg's motivation, something warm in her stomach and a surge of adrenaline, forgot her tiredness. She told herself, however long it took, she'd stay with Greg until they had a result.

But it didn't happen. By five, too tired to keep his eyes open, often falling forward towards the keyboard, Greg gave up. Stevie standing over him put her hand on his shoulder to offer some comfort. He turned his head to look up at her and smiled.

'Beaten for now, but I'll crack it later,' he said, tapping her hand, as if to reinforce his commitment.

Stevie tried sleeping in the bed she had shared with Monroe. It was a mistake. It smelt of him. It's shape and feel so reminiscent of when times were good between them. She tossed and turned, finding the pain of missing him increasing by the minute. She wept until the pillow was so wet she had to roll over to the side he slept on, only to find she was confronted by so many more memories. Finally at 6.30 she drifted off into a sleep brought on by sheer exhaustion. At seven she was woken by her mobile phone ringing loudly and vibrating on the bedside table.

'Yes,' she said in a tired, almost incoherent tone. It was her mother.

'Dead,' she shouted down the phone as she leapt out of bed and grabbed her t-shirt.

'What do you mean, dead?' Stevie listened as her mother told her how Joe Walter's body had been found in the car park of The Miax Corporation's head office in Bishopsgate. Apparently, he'd been shot through the head two nights earlier; the day Greg went to see him. The significance of which was not lost as Stevie grappled in her mind for an appropriate response.

'How awful, mum,' she said at last. 'Do you want me to come up?'

'Who'd do such a thing?' her mother replied, sounding calm and unemotional.

Stevie believed she knew the answer, but she couldn't and didn't want to tell her mother.

'How should I know?' she replied quickly and then added, 'Do you want me to come up. I'm in Cornwall.'

'No, dear. I'm all right. It's just such a shock. I've got Sylvia here. She's staying until the funeral.'

Stevie was doubly relieved. She didn't have to go tearing up to London, and was more than happy to stay out of the way of Sylvia, one of many of her mother's friends, more interested in the perceived status and wealth of people she met than anything else. At first she found her mother's apparent lack of emotion and sangfroid disconcerting, almost abnormal, until she remembered that there was little that touched her mother's steely heart.

*This is serious*, she thought, finishing the call and rushing to tell Greg.

He was fast asleep in the spare room, so sound she thought twice about waking him. Maybe she'd shower and go to the supermarket and get stuff to make him bacon and eggs, she thought. Ten minutes later, invigorated and refreshed by soap and warm water, she stepped out of the shower cubicle, dried herself down and pulled on yesterday's navy jeans, a fresh top, wore a different pair of large dangly earrings and pushed her feet into her well-worn flip flops. She dabbed a little make up on both cheeks, made use of a touch of lipstick and brushed her hair with her hands.

Outside, she wished she'd brought her denim jacket. An early autumn chill had hit the morning air. Quickly, she ran to her car, parked a few metres up the road. The drive to the supermarket was strangely unsettling. At first she found the quiet and stillness of the morning strange compared to the bustle of London. But after a while, it was the familiarity of it all that concerned her. The parched fields from the endless summer, the grazing sheep and cows, the undulating terrain, the leafy trees and the aged old stone walls—all so beautiful and reminiscent of happier times. She hoped, sincerely, and more earnestly than anything she'd ever hoped for before, that all would turn out well and she could be united with Monroe again, and they'd live happily together, maybe with Greg.

In the supermarket she became convinced people were starring at her, muttering to themselves that she was Mrs Lidlington—the new wife of Monroe, the one he murdered his old wife for. She became so neurotic about it she selected her goods in double-quick time and rushed to the vacant till point.

'Mrs Lidlington is it?' the elderly woman at the cash point said to her with a knowing look. 'Haven't seen you around for some time. Everything all right, then?'

*God, you nosy bitch*, Stevie said to herself, struggling to keep her emotions in check. She felt like giving the woman a piece of her mind.

Instead, she replied, 'Fine thanks,' and tossed a twenty-pound note onto the checkout surface. Silently, she packed her purchases, collected her change and sped out. She drove home, often unable to see clearly the road in front for the floods of tears that flowed from her eyes.

*   *   *

'Hi,' Greg yelled as he heard the front door open. 'I'm in here, good news. I've found it.'

He was sitting barefoot in the kitchen, the laptop open in front of him, wearing a pair of khaki shorts and an old torn sleeveless vest he'd found in his room, his thick hair, tousled and unkempt, had a thatched appearance. To his left stood a large tumbler of water. He was so wrapped up in what he'd unearthed on his mother's computer that he didn't hear Stevie walking down the hall. When she dumped the shopping next to him he stopped and looked up.

'Stevie,' he said, seeing her tear stained face. 'What's up?'

Stevie walked to the kettle.

'Let me make us some coffee. I've got fresh milk, bacon, eggs and loads of stuff. I'm just wound up and upset. It'll pass.'

Greg stood up and followed. He stood next to her and looked into her eyes. 'Come on, it's more than that. You've been crying.'

Stevie flicked on the kettle and shook granules of instant coffee into the two mugs she'd placed nearby.

'I have, but that's not what's bugging me.' She poured boiling water into the mugs, added some fresh milk and took the two drinks to the table. Greg returned to his previous seat.

'Joe Walters is dead,' she said, turning to look right into Greg's bright blue eyes.

'What,' Greg exclaimed, sitting bolt upright, running a hand through his dishevelled head of hair.

'How?'

'He was shot. The same day you saw him.'

'Murdered?'

'Yep. Someone topped him in the Miax car park.'

'Bloody hell.' Greg sat back, trying to take in the shocking news. He put his right hand up to his mouth and covered it. His elbow rested on the table. He looked at Stevie, waiting for some response.

'Do you think it's connected?'

'Must be, Greg. Too much of a coincidence.' Stevie took a tissue from her bag and wiped her cheeks. 'Maybe he contacted someone after you'd been and…'

'Jan de Boer, you mean.' Greg had dropped his hand from his mouth. He was leaning forward with both hands on the table.

Stevie shifted in her seat, turned her mug around a few times. 'I guess so,' she replied. 'Maybe Joe was too much of a risk. Knew too much.'

'How do you think that leave us?' Greg said, thinking he knew.

'Not so good, I reckon.' Stevie turned to catch Greg's eyes. 'Have you found the file?'

'I have, the whole report,' he replied hastily. 'But this is a setback.'

Stevie rested her chin on her clenched hands. 'Well,' she said, with an air of reluctant acceptance. 'Suppose we are able to convince the police that Jan de Boer is behind all this.'

Greg saw Stevie's concerned expression. His earlier optimism and elation at finding his mother's report started to deflate. He knew what she was going to say.

'We've just lost our star witness,' Stevie added.

Greg put both his hands flat against his cheeks. He leant forward and frowned, nodding his head.

'You're right,' he replied, thinking about their next move. 'I'm going to try to get hold of Ayanda in Johannesburg.'

Stevie looked at him quizzically.

'Who?'

'Ayanda. He's the journalist I met in Johannesburg from the Sowetan. He's covering the case. He wants me to keep him up to date and tell him all I find out about mum's report.'

'I remember,' Stevie replied as she rose from the table with her bag of shopping.

'You do that, I'll do a fry up.' She smiled.

'Want some?'

'Do I,' Greg replied, comforted by the thought of some real food. 'I'll print mum's report. We can look at it over breakfast.'

'Do that, Greg,' Stevie said, reaching up for the large solid frying pan and the caste-iron griddle pan hanging above the cooker.

* * *

Stevie opened the top half of the stable door. The neglect and disorder before her stood as potent symbols of Monroe's dire mental state. Dead and dying plants were everywhere. Those once trailing whimsically from pots, hung in dry, waterless clumps, devoid of colour and past any possible chance of resuscitation. Early falls of brown leaves were scattered randomly across the burnt lawn and unswept patio. Roses, once magnificent and luxurious in their subtle colours, had formed buds where their petals had died on the stems, and looked tired and desperately thirsty. She turned and walked back to the hob, vividly reminded of what Greg and her had to achieve.

She chucked the two big flat mushrooms into a large pan, tore open a pack of bacon, dropping the rashers carelessly into the griddle pan, beat up four eggs with a little milk and butter in a bowl, shoved it into the microwave and called Greg. She could hear him talking in the living room next door. He sounded serious. When the toast popped up and she was ready to pull the bacon, eggs and mushrooms together she popped her head around the living room door to give Greg a final call. He had stopped talking and was sitting back, the phone resting on his lap. His face was white and expressionless, his eyes glazed and with a far away expression.

'What is it?' Stevie asked, walking towards him, wearing oven gloves.

'Ayanda's been killed,' Greg answered, looking out of the window.

'Oh no. How awful.' Stevie rushed forward to sit next to Greg.

'Poor guy. How did it happen?'

'He was killed in a car crash a few days ago.' Greg's vacant eyes remained set on some distant image in the garden.

'And the government inquiry into the mining disaster cleared Miax completely.'

'What,' Stevie shouted indignantly.

*This is wrong*, she thought. It's all some great conspiracy. She turned to look at Greg. He still seemed to be staring into space. She put a hand on each of his shoulders.

'Greg, look at me. Tell me what's going on.'

Greg turned to face her. His blue eyes had lost their sparkle, they looked dull and drained. His face had an almost anaemic look to it.

'They out to stop us, that's for sure. Another reporter from the Sowetan, the one who told me about Ayanda, said the judge heading the enquiry was nobbled.'

'How?' Stevie asked, horrified. She withdrew her hands from Greg's shoulders and sat looking at him. He wrinkled up his forehead and opened his hands in an expression of hopelessness.

'Apparently, Jan de Boer still has enormous influence among certain members of the old white elite.'

Stevie felt sick. Revolted that people were able to carry out a crime with impunity.

'What. Money?' she asked.

'That's what he said.'

'How can he get away with it? I thought the government had purged all of that out of the system.'

Greg's expression changed. He looked less resigned, more positive. His eyes met Stevie's.

'That's what everyone thinks. But there are still some of the old crowd around in a few places of influence. They play the game, never stepping out of line so as not to incur any suspicion from the government, and then when someone needs a favour done.' Greg looked away for a moment and then back at Stevie.

'People like Jan de Boer. They ring up, or whatever, and call in their request.'

'That's fucking shit. Can't it be stamped out? If the guy you talked to knows that, why can't he go to the police?'

Greg shook his head. 'Because there isn't, at present, a scrap of evidence. Ayanda died in what was a straightforward car crash. No signs of any foul play. Cause of death—an unfortunate accident.' Greg leant back and put his hands in his pockets.

'Of course, the community are up in arms. The whole thing is being called a whitewash and there is a huge clamour for yet another investigation. But until anyone has some proof nothing will happen. Jan de Boer is out of the country, Ayanda and Joe are dead and we are the only people with a shred of evidence.' Greg stopped, he looked at Stevie with a shocked expression.

'Something's burning, Stevie.'

'Oh fuck,' Stevie said tearing into the kitchen. Smoke was everywhere. Both the griddle pan and frying pan contained black charred remains, the scrambled egg was cold and dried up and the metal espresso maker, once a matt silver colour, was red hot.

\* \* \*

After they'd cleared up together, a therapeutic process that livened their joint resolve, they worked through all that Greg had found in the files of Juliet's laptop. They found a copy of a letter she'd written to Joe Walters, dated three days before she died.

*Dear Joe*

*You know I have expressed my misgivings about the incorrect press release concerning the mining disaster at our gold mine near Welkom on July 8th when 30 miners lost their* lives. Regrettably, I feel from a moral standpoint that I have to put my concerns in writing.

1: The Miax internal investigation found that a back up fan had not been fitted despite recommendations to fit that fan after a previous disaster. This was denied in the press release.

2: Had this fan been fitted, it's quite possible that the lives of many of those who died would have been saved.

3: Why, when 4000 miners were underground at the time, when our management knew of a methane gas leak, always potentially fatal, did they not stop work and evacuate all the workers to safety?

4: We've admitted that a build up of methane gas caused the explosion. The same thing happened at one of our mines last year. After that disaster it was recommended that back up fans be fitted in all mines. We didn't fit one here. Why? And why will we not admit it?

All of this brings me to believe that the true facts of this awful disaster are being deliberately withheld. I cannot be part of that.

I have to give you notice that I will not be responsible for publishing anything that is designed to hide the truth.

Further, I feel morally obliged to post the truth about this disaster on the Internet if the company (Miax) has not been completely transparent about the matter within seven days.

Yours sincerely
Juliet Lidlington


At 7.30 in the evening, Greg came across the report that Juliet finished the night she died, dated and ready to be posted on the Internet.

## THE TRUTH ABOUT MIAX
Facts concerning the explosion at the Miax Butix gold mine, near Welkom, South Africa, on Tuesday July 8

Thirty miners died on July 8th. Their deaths were due to an explosion of methane gas. Miax's officers detected a broken fan the night before, but work was still allowed to continue the next day. The broken fan would have reduced air circulation and increased the danger of a gas build up. ( See annex i ).

A similar accident occurred in one of Miax's gold mines almost exactly a year ago on July 15, last year. After that disaster Miax's internal health and safety committee recommended that back up fans be fitted in all mines.

No back up fan was fitted at this mine because the local manager was looking to save money. (See Miax's own internal investigation, annex ii ). This fact was not mentioned in the press release issued last week.

Miax, headed by Jan de Boer, grandson of the founder, deliberately misled the general public and relatives of those who died in the disaster.

*Juliet Lidlington*
*The Miax Corporation*


'That's dynamite,' Stevie said, sitting next to Greg on a stool in the room where Monroe had done his writing.

'I agree,' Greg replied, his hands covering his mouth in a sort of tent-like pose as he rocked back on the old leather seated wooden chair that Monroe used for his work. It had a broad, deep back, solid wooden arms and a swivel base with brass caster feet. The leather that stretched from the top of the back, across the seat and down the sides was held in place by small circular brass studs, no bigger than a large drawing pin and beautifully etched with shell designs. Greg liked sitting in it, it reminded him of his father. He stroked his forehead with both his hands and dragged them through his thick mop of hair.

'I'm shattered, Stevie. Can't think anymore.'

265

Stevie looked at him. She shivered a little and tightened the skin around her eyes by pulling it towards her ears.

'Me too,' she said. 'Let me have another go at getting some food together.'

After eating a couple of steaks, some salad and sauté potatoes they both felt human. Greg had drunk a large whisky and half a bottle of wine. Stevie had stuck to water. They lay on opposite sides of the living room, outstretched on each of the couches. They'd agreed a plan of action. In the morning Greg would take a print of everything he'd unearthed, plus the laptop to Inspector Symes. Greg had wanted to act immediately, posting all he'd found on the BBC message board that night, until Stevie had suggested it was probably wiser to let Symes, as much as they both hated her, have first sight of it all.

'You know,' Greg said suddenly as they both listened to Coldplay, 'I had a girlfriend in Vietnam. Her name was Kim and she was beautiful.'

Stevie turned to look at him. 'Tell me about her.'

Greg sat up. He'd been itching to tell Stevie about Kim for ages, but the time had never seemed right. He looked across to where Stevie was now sitting, facing him. She seemed genuinely interested.

'Go on,' she said.

'We had to split for me to come home and sort this out. She'd been orphaned a year back when her parents were killed in an air crash and couldn't face me raking over the past. She reckoned it would bring back too many painful memories for her.'

'Tell me more. What she was like, how she looked, how you met.' Stevie smiled at Greg. 'Only if you want to. If it helps to make you feel good about her. She sounds nice.'

Greg did feel good. He wanted to go on.

'We met in the restaurant where we both worked in Hanoi. Both of us were getting hell from the owner.'

'Which restaurant? I was in Hanoi.'

'When?' Greg asked, surprised and pleased.

'Before I met you dad.'

From then the conversation didn't stop. They'd found something in common, and like the time Stevie went to see Greg in Durham, before she blew it, they clicked. Greg told Stevie all about Kim and how, with no success, he'd tried to contact her everyday since he left Hanoi and had almost given up, suspecting that she'd changed her mobile phone number and moved on somewhere else or met someone new. Stevie sympathised, and tried to be optimistic for him. She told him all about her travels and how maybe the three of them should go back to South East Asia together one day.

'That'll be good,' Greg said, feeling relaxed and optimistic. The possibility of his father being released seemed real, at last.

A little later, the noise of a car door slamming directly outside bothered them. They ran to the front door. Through the gloom they saw the shadow of a person running away from Greg's car. He gave chase, but whoever it was had slipped out of sight and was too fast for him. Greg returned after a few minutes. Stevie was waiting by the front door.

'Some joker trying to steal my car, no doubt. Why they would want such an old banger, I don't know?' he said, closing the door behind him.

'I agree,' Stevie replied, not moving from the spot she been standing on for the last few minutes.

'Greg?' she asked with a slight tremble to her voice and looking into his eyes.

'Yes,' he answered. He screwed up his eyes, an expectant expression crossed his face.

'I don't think I could sleep in that bed alone again. Will you sleep with me? I don't mean…'

Greg's expression changed. He seemed worried.

'Just for company?' he asked.

'Yeah, of course. Nothing else.' Stevie paused for a few seconds and said, 'Will you, Greg?'

# 25

Greg woke early. He flung the duvet back, swung his legs to the floor and searched for the clothes he'd discarded the previous evening. While he dressed, he glanced at Stevie, asleep on the far side of the bed. She seemed as though she hadn't moved since he awoke. He straightened his t-shirt, adjusted his belt and made for the kitchen. While waiting for the kettle to boil he called Inspector Symes.

She'd see him at eight, she said. By 7.30, his mum's laptop, the back up stuff and the all the printouts were loaded in the back of his car. He swigged down his tea, bit on a piece of toast, called out to Stevie to say goodbye, and left.

\* \* \*

Stevie had been dreaming of walking through the streets of Hanoi; Monroe and Greg by her side. Her dream was ended by a terrible bang, immediately followed by an ear splitting, shattering sound. Dust, debris and shards of glass covered the duvet, much of it had fallen on her, smudging her naked body and pricking the surface of her skin. Small droplets of blood randomly appeared all over her.

'Oh my God, what's happening,' she shouted hysterically, her eyes taken immediately to gaping holes with jagged edges that once were windows.

'Greg, Greg, where are you?' she yelled as she pulled on a cotton nightdress, oblivious to the scratches and dirt that covered her from head to foot. Barefooted, she tiptoed through the chunks of plaster, broken glass, splintered wood and dust that covered the bedroom floor and edged her way toward the new, sinister hole in the wall.

'Oh no, no. My God, no,' she cried as she fell back onto the bed sobbing.

'Please God let him be alive,' she yelled as she pulled herself up and raced down the stairs to the front door. She tore it open and raced out to where the remains of Greg's car lay in a twisted heap of metal, some three or four metres from the side of the road where it had been parked. As she drew closer she stopped. Her hands went up to cover her mouth. She felt sick. A stream of blood was pouring from the remains of the car's offside door, forming a puddle that crept across the road to the opposite gutter. A man barred her way. It was the milkman, his face a ghastly white. Blood was splattered all over his striped uniform and across his face.

'Don't, Mrs Lidlington,' he said in a sympathetic tone and put his arms around Stevie as she collapsed into his embrace.

Stevie sobbed and sobbed, gradually sinking to the ground. For a time she wasn't aware of anything. People had gathered around her, some comforting her and bringing out mugs of hot tea from their houses. In the background sirens sounded. After a bit she looked up. A paramedic was sitting besides her, taking her pulse and massaging her arms and legs. Somebody had wrapped a warm blanket around her shoulders.

'What happened,' she said, not really aware of what was going on.

'There was an explosion, luv. A man's been taken to hospital. He was in a pretty serious condition. You'd better go back into your house. It'll be safer there.' It was a female paramedic who spoke.

Stevie looked all around her. The street was swarming with police. They'd sealed off an area and were collecting all the fragments of Greg's car, crawling all over the twisted and charred remains. A large trailer appeared and it looked as though they were about to load the car onto it. She suddenly remembered the laptop and all the prints of the information.

'No,' she shouted. 'There was important stuff in that car,' she yelled loudly as she rose to her feet and tried to walk towards it.

A large policeman barred her way.

'Nothing left in there, madam. If it's the computer you're after, it ended up half way down the street, shattered and twisted into many small pieces.'

'What about papers? There was some urgent stuff,' she asked desperately.

'You wouldn't like me to tell you the state of anything we found inside, madam. All…' the policeman looked away for a moment. 'A right mess.'

Stevie felt her head spinning. Her legs started to buckle under her. She leant forward and was violently sick. She collapsed into the arms of a policewoman and a paramedic.

* * *

She woke later in hospital. She was in a room on her own. Her eyes roamed around, up and down the soft pink walls, focusing occasionally on the one or two paintings of local scenes that had been positioned to blend in with the ambience. A large perspex jug of water sat next to a glass on a bedside table adjacent to where she lay. Gingerly she sat up, feeling mentally and physically as though she had been rung out and hung up to dry. She poured herself some water and took a sip. Her thoughts went to Greg. She wondered if he'd been brought to the same hospital as herself. And then, in waves, the awfulness of the whole terrible event started to hit her.

*Is he alive?* she asked herself. Does Monroe know? How has he taken it all? What state was the house? Where was she? Floods of questions without answers took over her mind. She took another sip from her water and swung her legs over the side. As she did, the door opened and a smiley-faced nurse entered carrying a tray of food.

'How are you, Mrs Lidlington?'

Stevie sat with her legs swinging over the side of the bed and looked at the nurse.

'I don't know,' she answered, as the nurse drew nearer and placed a tray with a ham salad and a piece of bread and butter on the trolley that sat over her bed.

'Some lunch?' the nurse asked, looking closely at Stevie.

'How is the man who was in the car?' Stevie asked, looking at the nurse for some signs of the truth.

The nurse sat next to Stevie, pushing the trolley further away.

'I don't know, Mrs Lidlington. But I can find out. I don't think he was taken here. Is he a friend of yours?'

Stevie looked at the nurse, surprised she didn't know the connection between her and Greg. She seemed bright and straightforward.

'He's my stepson. I have to know how he is.'

'Oh, I'm sorry. I didn't know.'

'Why are you sorry?' Stevie asked quickly. 'Is he dead?'

'No, Mrs Lidlington.' The nurse took hold of Stevie's hand. 'I just know he was badly hurt. I'm sorry if I upset you.' The nurse reached for a thermometer.

'Try to relax please, Mrs Lidlington. Your pulse and blood pressure are going all over the place.'

Stevie looked at the nurse. *Doesn't she understand*, she asked herself.

'Why am I here?' Where am I?' she barked, overcome by an urgent need to get out of wherever she was. She had to go to Greg and Monroe—see how they both were, find out what she could do to help.

The nurse packed up her equipment. She looked at Stevie and

smiled. 'You've had a shock. We've just bought you in for observation for 24 hours. If your pulse and blood pressure stabilises, you'll be able to go out tomorrow.'

'Tomorrow,' Stevie retorted indignantly. 'Can't I go now? Where am I?'

'You're in Bodmin Hospital. I'll ask a doctor if you can go earlier.'

'I can always discharge myself, can't I?' Stevie said hesitantly, not really sure if she was up to leaving immediately, but she had to try.

'You can, but we wouldn't advise it.' The nurse looked down at Stevie's tray. 'Try and eat something. We'll come and see you after lunch.' She turned and smiled again at Stevie, got up and walked out.

*Patronising bitch*, Stevie thought and pushed the tray of cold food away.

\* \* \*

At 3 p.m. she arrived at the main London neurological hospital in Holborn. She ran in, her car dumped hazardously around the corner on the first available space. When, earlier, while visiting Monroe in the remand centre, they'd been told that Greg's condition was critical and he might not survive the night, she agreed with Monroe that she should go immediately to be with him. She was met on the fourth floor from the lift by a tall, white coated young doctor, his hair lank and unkempt, his face strained and pale. He looked as though he hadn't slept for days. He was standing in the small lobby where the lift arrived. To his left, two wooden swing doors led to the wards. Apart from him and Stevie, the area was empty.

'Mrs Lidlington,' he said in an unemotional tone.

'Yes,' Stevie replied, trembling and looking into his expressionless face. She feared the worst.

'Your stepson is in a very serious condition.'

Stevie felt her heart beat faster and faster. The trembling she felt had turned to uncontrollable shaking. She put her hand to her mouth.

'Both his legs are broken, he'll have to have an arm amputated, he's got severe lacerations on his face and a broken jar and...'

Stevie sniffed and started to cry. Her lips trembled. She put her fingers in her mouth and started to bite on them.

'Please,' she sobbed, closing her eyes to clear some of her tears.

'Can I sit down?'

The doctor seemed perturbed. He looked around the three metre square space, one wall of which housed the lift entrance, two others were blank, the third contained the swing doors. A small upright chair stood alone to the left of the lift door. He motioned towards it with his hand. Stevie assumed he was offering it to her.

'He's also suffered multiple head injuries, which possibly have damaged his brain. That's why he's here. We have a specialist neurosurgical unit.' The doctor looked away, raising his head in the air. 'Probably the best in the world. He's in good hands.'

'Oh no,' Stevie gasped and covered her sodden face with her hands. *This is awful. Poor Greg.* She looked up at the doctor, standing impassively above her.

'Will he live?'

'I can't say. We're operating now to remove all the metal fragments from his head. If he survives that, we have to carry out several scans to determine if there is any brain damage and to what extent. If that's OK, we'll set his broken legs, amputate his mutilated arm and set his jaw.'

Stevie didn't speak. Her head was in her hands. She felt as if someone was slugging her time and again with a great fist. As one blow finished, another came pounding in. She wondered if all it was real, could it all be some sort of awful dream. She opened her eyes to see the doctor still standing in front of her.

'What do you think?' she asked, focusing intently on the doctor's face. Hoping he might give her a little hope.

'As I said. It's touch and go. He's undergoing major surgery. Anything can happen.'

'Thanks, doctor,' Stevie said, looking away vacantly. She wasn't going to get anything positive out of this guy. All she wanted to do was to go somewhere and cry.

'Do you have a room I can wait in?' she asked without looking at him.

They gave her a cell like room, just big enough for a small collapsible bed and a table with a scratched laminate top. The walls were grey, dirty and covered in marks and splodges. Stevie didn't notice. She closed the door behind her, took off her trainers and flopped onto the bed. After she'd been in the room for a couple of minutes, a male nurse knocked on the door and brought her a jug of water and a glass.

For two hours she lay on the bed. Sometimes she was rational, convincing herself that Greg would pull through, planning what she would do to help him with his rehabilitation, and thinking that worrying would do no good. *I must be strong. Try to sleep*, she kept telling herself.

But whenever she closed her eyes she'd start descending into a bottomless pit of uneasiness, worrying about Greg, tormenting herself over how her actions had caused so much grief, thinking about Monroe. She'd cry a lot, feel sick and often think she was about to pass out. Nobody came to see her. At seven a lady doctor, who smiled when she entered the room, came to tell her the operation was over and had gone well. Greg was in the intensive care unit, on a ventilator and heavily sedated. The doctor told Stevie they'd set his broken legs and amputated his arm at the same time. She threw up.

She walked gingerly towards his bed. Two nurses stood over him. One on either side of the bed, checking the readings on the various pieces of equipment attached to him, ensuring that each tube or dressing was doing its job. His head was covered in a huge gauze bandage, wrapped around like a turban. He was propped up, his eyes flicking open for seconds and then closing. She looked nervously towards the remains of his left arm. A large gauze wad, tightly wrapped around the poignant stump, was supported by a sling that supported the awful symbol of the living hell he was enduring, high in the air and above his head. Both his legs were encased in plaster up to his waist. Wires, plastic tubes and bandages seemed to be attached or stuck to whatever space was left on his wrecked body. She thought she'd collapse, wondering if she had the strength to keep going.

'Greg, it's me, Stevie' she said as she placed a hand gently on his one remaining arm.

His eyes didn't move, he showed no sign of recognition, only the dials on the ventilator, moving up and down with the rhythm of his breathing, confirmed he was alive. Stevie wept. It wasn't until that moment that she'd given any thought to the intimacies she'd shared with Greg the previous night. Deliberately she had banished it from her mind. She cried for him, she cried for Monroe and she cried for what she had done.

'Please God, let him live.'

\* \* \*

Amongst the archipelago of coral atolls in the Southern Indian Ocean, known as the Maldives, can be found the tiny island that is Jan de Boer's most secret and secluded retreat. The atoll was uninhabited until Jan made it one of his many homes. He called it Van Island, after his father, and built a luxurious villa on stilts that reached into the clear aquamarine sea. At night, occupants of the villa could sit on the sea veranda and, if quiet enough, could watch turtles walk up the soft yellow sands to lay their eggs.

Jan de Boer, wearing only a pair of knee length bathing shorts and a yellow sleeveless vest watched as the helicopter descended slowly onto the landing pad at the back of his villa. He was sitting with a beautiful Sri Lankan girl, dressed only in a sarong around her waist, her upper body naked. The two of them were eating breakfast.

Jan felt slightly anxious. He'd received a telephone call two days earlier to confirm that his instructions had been carried out, but he wanted confirmation. He'd told his agent and fixer he needed proof and that proof, he hoped, would be on this helicopter.

'Excuse me, dear. I just have to go and pick something up from the plane,' he said to the girl.

'Be quick, Jan,' she replied with seductive eyes.

'Yes, I will,' he replied without looking at her and striding towards the parked helicopter. The pilot greeted Jan and handed him a pile of mail. Jan thanked him, walked clear of the large rotor blades and sat down on a sand dune. He went immediately to the jiffy bag and tore it open. A copy of The Times, The Telegraph and The Mail fell out. On the front of each paper was a large picture of Greg's distorted car after the explosion. Each had similar headlines.

## SON OF MURDER SUSPECT BLOWN UP IN CAR BOMB ATTEMPTED MURDER OF MURDERER'S SON MURDER SUSPECT'S SON CLOSE TO DEATH

Jan scanned through each article. At first he was a little worried and slowly read each piece over and over again, becoming less and less concerned. Finally he put the papers back in the jiffy bag, sealed it up and dumped it in a rubbish bin close to the back of his villa. All the papers pronounced Greg Lidlington close to death, he told himself as he climbed the wooden stairs, walked to his bedroom and slipped off his shorts and top and joined his latest girlfriend, naked on the large bed.

# 26

Monroe sat on a rickety straight-backed chair, its thin foam padded seat stained and faded from the numerous people who'd used it before him. His left hand rested on Greg's only arm. He was unaware of Stevie standing behind him, her hand on his shoulder. She'd been sitting next to him for a while, but as the dreadful moment seemed to be close she had risen and stood besides him, hoping, no doubt, to be of some comfort. On the other side of the bed a caring nurse mopped Greg's feverish brow. Monroe's eyes were firmly focused on his son's chest, watching every erratic and faltering up and down movement that indicated the ebbing of Greg's life. Monroe's face was grey, his eyes red and sore, his normal three or four-day stubble—untouched for a week—looked straggly and unkempt. His short grey hair had a dull, lifeless hue to it. He hoped and prayed for a miracle, unwilling to give up hope until the inevitable would signify that further hope was useless.

Greg had slipped into a coma a few hours after his lengthy and complicated operation a week earlier to remove the fragments from his brain and to reset his damaged limbs. Monroe had been allowed to visit him once, accompanied by two prison officers. When the prison authorities told him a few days later that his son had succumbed to an infection, causing dangerously high temperatures and wild, irregular heart beats, and that he was likely to die within three to four days, Monroe was allowed to be by his side, again accompanied by two prison officers. He hadn't asked Stevie to be with him. She'd taken it upon herself to be there. Both of them had mounted a non-stop vigil for two days.

Greg's face shook, his mouth twitched, his eyes flicked open and closed. Monroe's heart missed several beats. He gripped Greg's arm, leant forward to within a few centimetres of his face and said, 'Greg, Greg, its dad. I love you.' Greg's face jerked and twisted. His eyes opened, stared unnaturally at Monroe, and remained open. Monroe thought he saw a weak smile.

'Hi, son,' he said, touching Greg's cheek.' Stevie looked at Monroe and then to the nurse, whose eyes moved quickly between all the monitors and then down to Greg. His eyes seemed to be glazing over, the flicker of light had gone, and he had a strange, distant look on his face. The nurse reached over to his right arm and felt his purse.

She looked up at Monroe. The earlier glimmer of hope in his eyes replaced by moisture, filling up each corner and beginning to trickle down his face. His cheeks were wet, his bottom lip started to tremble.

'Is this it,' he mumbled weekly, looking at the nurse.

She gently nodded, holding her lips tightly together.

'I'm sorry, Mr Lidlington,' she said softly. With the slightest, unobtrusive hand movement she reached to Greg's eyelids and gently closed each one.

Monroe shut his eyes and leant forward so his face was close to Greg's. His lips touched Greg's cheek. He remained still for several minutes, Stevie and the nurse watching respectfully.

'Goodbye, son,' he sobbed and gave Greg a last kiss.

Stevie put her hands on each of Monroe's shoulders. Gradually he stood up, his whole body heaving, his sobs loud and irregular. He turned to face her, his face ashen, soaked in his own tears. Inside him a deep, dull ache had reached every part of his body. His heart was leaden, his life seemed over. Unconsciously he reached for her open arms and wept on her shoulder. She cried too, but he wasn't aware of anything. Nothing had any meaning anymore. No purpose, no reason for going on.

# Snowdrops

On February 1ˢᵗ Monroe walked away from Risley remand centre a free man. All charges against him had been dropped. Stevie, who had found a floppy disk left by Greg containing a copy of all the information he had planned to give Inspector Symes, had he not been blown up, had worked tirelessly with Monroe's lawyer to expose the truth. After the explosion the police had been ready to listen and quickly discovered a link between the death of Joe Walters and Greg. Subsequently, time and continual pressure from Stevie brought about the abandonment by the crown prosecution of its case against Monroe.

Monroe had gone through a rough time. He'd been overcome with uncontrollable grief, suffered bouts of suicidal depression and endured weeks of self inflicted starvation. Stevie had pressed the prison authorities to help him. By luck, he seemed to respond to the psychiatrist who took on his case. He walked away from the prison gates to Stevie's car with hope; the pain of Greg's death remaining, but an emotion he was prepared to try to live with.

He was the first to enter the house. In the hall a large bowl of daffodils, in bloom with big yellow trumpets, stood magnificently in a tall white vase.

'That's nice,' he remarked as he dumped his bag on the wooden floor. He walked to the kitchen.

'Fancy a tea,' he asked, reaching up to the cupboard where the mugs and cups where stored.

*The house, it feels good,* he thought, looking around. Nothing had changed, no walls had been painted but it seemed right. It wasn't unnaturally tidy or looking like it had been recently spring cleaned, but just as it had been when he and Stevie had lived there.

'Thanks,' Stevie replied. 'I'll have a tea.' She watched Monroe closely. His eyes were roaming the room.

They took their drinks into the living room. Stevie went first. Monroe made for the big leather chair he'd always sat in. He lowered his drink onto the small oblong wooden table that sat next to the chair. Stevie kept her eye on him. After he'd let go of his mug he stayed stooped, his hand on a 24 by 15 centimetre picture in a light wooden frame. He picked it up and stood holding it at a distance.

Stevie, still standing, walked towards him and put a hand on his shoulder. 'Like it?' she asked, looking into his face.

Monroe smiled a little. He wiped a small tear away from the bottom of his left eye and sighed. He turned to look at Stevie.

'Thanks,' he said.

'Where did you find it?' He looked down again at the picture of Greg and himself. They were sitting, chatting at a restaurant somewhere. Both had big happy smiles on their faces. Monroe put it down on the table, looked at it one more time and grinned. He was pleased that Stevie had done it. Something he wouldn't have done himself. He'd be too afraid of the hurt and sadness he'd feel while sifting through the photos. He wondered if she doubted what she'd done, worried that it might have triggered painful emotions.

'That was taken just before he went to Vietnam,' he said, still staring at the image of Greg.

'Juliet took it. It was in the restaurant we went to for his goodbye meal.' He turned to Stevie again.

'I'm grateful,' he said, nodding his head. 'Thanks. I really like it.' He sat down, his back to the picture and took a sip from his tea.

He pushed against the chair's deep back, his arms resting on the smooth, solid arms. He was surprised at how at ease he felt. In the car, coming home, he worried about entering the house, how a memory, an action or a word would plunge him into a pit of grief. He looked across to Stevie. She'd been watching him, quietly sipping her tea, and seemingly allowing him to find his level. Next to where she was sitting, on an old ship's chart chest, which he used for an occasional table, stood a large antique glass vase full of red roses. The house seemed to have a warm, peaceful atmosphere, he thought, smiling at Stevie.

He stood up and strolled to the french windows, gazing into the garden. He didn't remember the neglected, uncared state he'd left things. Instead he warmed at the sight of his prize collection of pots, their summer blooms cut back or emptied, ready for next spring. The patio was tidy, swept, devoid of any traces of autumn. The small lawn, its green blades of grass beginning to lengthen, looked lush and healthy. He caught sight of the long patio table, the chairs in which he'd sat so many times with Greg and Juliet, now so quiet and empty, the slate of the table top catching the weak winter sun as it dipped in the corner of the garden before disappearing for the night. There was poignancy to it all that didn't scare him. Greg has gone, he thought, but he's here, in this garden, the house, forever. He turned to find Stevie standing behind.

'Thanks again, bun,' he said, putting his arm around her shoulder. He knew he was going to cry. He turned, with her by his side, and stared again down the garden, both of them focusing on the large bunch of snowdrops that stood so proudly around the bottom of old birdbath.

Printed in the United States
51527LVS00003B/253-300